I0674944

Dani's Decision
by
p.m.terrell

DANI'S DECISION
By p.m.terrell

Published by
Drake Valley Press, a Division of P.I.S.C.E.S. Books, LTD.
USA

This novel is a work of fiction. Any resemblance to actual persons, living or dead, is entirely coincidental except as noted under "A Note from the Author." The characters, names, plots, and incidents are the product of the author's imagination. References to actual events, public figures, locales, or businesses are included to give this work a sense of reality.

ISBN 978-1-935970-52-1 (Trade Paperback)
ISBN 978-1-935970-51-4 (eBook)
        Smashwords Edition, License Notes
        This Ebook is licensed for your personal enjoyment only. This Ebook may not be re-sold or given away to others. If you would like to share this book with others, please purchase an additional copy. Thank you for respecting the hard work of the author.

Author's website: www.pmterrell.com

1

Friday, February 21, 1971

The bolt of lightning illuminated the far reaches of the bedroom as it entered through a corner window. In the next instant, it had retreated as quickly as it had appeared. Seventeen-year-old Dani Evans began to count as she meticulously painted her lips, but she'd barely whispered "One" before the thunder roared. It clapped and rolled as if it was not early evening in mid-February but a hot summer night, the kind she'd become accustomed to in the Mississippi antebellum home. Still, it was unusual for winter, but they'd also suffered through a stifling week that had been sorely in need of a breeze. It was as if the weather had lost track of the season.

She hesitated as she listened to the wind whipping around the corner of the house. It was powerful, and it had an ominous feel to it. She'd left her internship at the newspaper less than an hour ago. It had been a hubbub of activity as word spread regarding a family of tornadoes making their way across northwestern Mississippi. The facsimile had continuously run. It had been Dani's job to tear off the pages and rush them to the appropriate newsdesk, but it wasn't long before the entire newsroom gathered around it. The tornadoes had lined up for over 300 miles, a distance she could hardly imagine, reportedly leveling entire neighborhoods. At least one tornado had purportedly reached F5 status in neighboring Louisiana, something the newspaper was reluctant to report until they verified it. No one had ever remembered a tornado reeking such devastation.

At one point, the editor, Jimmy Bob Carole, had turned to her as if seeing her for the first time. "What are you doing here?" he demanded.

"I'm working," she'd replied incredulously.

"Get out of here," he'd roared. "Go home!" Then he began pointing. "You, you, and you stay here. Everybody else, go home!"

It wasn't until they'd gathered their umbrellas and rain jackets and lined up at the front door that she realized Jimmy Bob was terrified. The building had begun to shake, the lights to flicker. Even the facsimile had abruptly quieted. She'd taken one last glance at his face, pale and stunned, before rushing through the howling winds and rain to her car. She'd fought against the mounting storm in her tiny Triumph Spitfire, struggling to keep it from skirting sideways into the adjacent cottonfields as she made her way the few miles to her parents' home.

Once she arrived, she'd discovered her mother trying to choose the perfect dress for a celebratory evening, as though she was living in a completely different universe. Moreover, she wanted her daughter to drive her into town, and no amount of reason managed to penetrate.

Dani finished and replaced the lipstick cap with a resounding click. The lamp on the dressing table flickered, causing her reflection in the mirror to appear ghostly, her long, light blond hair and pale skin like an image on a hazy black-and-white television screen. A moment later, the bulb shone true once more, revealing large, celestial blue eyes. They stared back at her as she analyzed them; even with the muted purple eyeshadow, she could not make the irises appear violet, as her idol's eyes were. But then, there was no similarity between herself and screen legend Elizabeth Taylor. None at all.

She rose and ironed her dress with her hands, though no wrinkles were present. As she left her bedroom, another lightning flash appeared, and with the next roll of thunder, the lights went out, casting the hallway into darkness. The crackle of the radio abruptly ceased, leaving in its place the sound of the wind moaning around the corner of the house, the wail increasing to a high-pitched shriek. It was a stark contrast to the easy melody of BJ Thomas's "Raindrops Keep Falling on my Head." In a wicked twist of humor, the station had played songs about rain and wind all afternoon. The AM frequency had ebbed and flowed, becoming more crackle and hiss than music, but the few notes had served to quiet her, broken only by the top of the hour news. Lasting only five minutes, it still had the power to instill images of discourse as Vietnam War protests, Civil Rights marches, and the Cold War intermingled to form a troubled nation.

Now she stepped to her nightstand and turned off the dial.

"Really?" she said aloud as she groped for the wall to find her way. She'd hoped the sound of her voice would provide her with levity and comfort, but it had the opposite effect. She sounded like a frightened little girl.

To be sure, the loss of electricity was not unusual. If ever there was a storm without cutting the power, now that would be worthy news indeed, as the utility poles carried the lines past swaying trees and open fields. She'd been born in this house, not by design, but simply because her mother's labor was so short, there was no hope of getting her to Clarksdale, a good twenty minutes' drive away. By the time her father had returned home from his office to transport his wife, Dani was already halfway out and ready to get her life started. And it had been that way for the seventeen years that followed. Her spirit was always years ahead of her body, ready to get on with things.

She groped her way to the broad, curving staircase in the center of the house. The worn wood appeared mottled with shadows that filtered in through the screen door. When she was young, she was convinced demons that lived in the cypress swamps came out after dark. The shadows cast by the tree branches that surrounded the house were, in her mind, the ghouls' fingers, waiting for an opportune moment in which to snatch her.

Now they appeared particularly active, the branches curving nearly to the ground, some scraping against the side of the house.

She took the stairs quickly, nearly gliding upon them as her toes barely touched each step, eager to reach the foyer. As her feet found the rug between the staircase and the door, the lights flickered back on, the dim bulbs in the hall appearing more like muted gaslights. With the sudden glow came the muffled sound of women talking.

She raced to the doorway and grappled with the heavy front door as the storm struggled to enter. When at last she thought she'd heard the latch click, she realized the rain had pelted her clothing and the foyer floor as it had swirled across the deep front porch. She turned toward the back of the house, futilely wiping her damp hands against her skirt.

The back door, like the front, was open, allowing the storm another entry point. Now Dani wrangled the door shut as the screen door swung open like ghostly hands were determined to claim the century-old house. Forward-thinking architects had designed it to take advantage of the summer breezes, the area between the front and back doors uninterrupted. Now that she'd closed both doors, the corridor felt dark and humid. For the umpteenth time, she wished her father would agree to the installation of air conditioning. All her friends had it, but he insisted it would be a costly and involved endeavor, and for the little time he spent here, it wasn't worth the trouble.

The voices grew louder as she reached the back of the house and pushed open the swinging door into the kitchen.

"Thank God," her mother said when she spotted her. "You're going to make me late."

"We're crazy to go out in this weather, Mama," she answered.

"Well, how do I look, Dani?" her mother asked, taking a slow swirl in the middle of the kitchen. Jilly Anne Woodson Evans might have been Dani twenty years into the future. Her light blond hair was past her shoulders, but tonight she had it swept into a French twist and secured with a pearl comb. She had the same innocent blue eyes, which were all the more disarming when her earthy humor emerged. Her figure hadn't changed in twenty years but remained svelte. Tonight she was wearing a pastel pink dress with gentle pleats that ballooned outward as she twirled, a sure sign she intended to dance the night away.

"Beautiful," Dani said dutifully.

"Is that all?"

"Stunning. Gorgeous. The pearls are a nice touch."

"Classy, aren't they? Have you noticed how my necklace and bracelet match the pearls in my hair?"

"They match perfectly," she replied. Out of the corner of her eye, she thought she caught the servant's eyes roll, but it happened so quickly that she might have imagined it. Mae Booker's role defied description. She was equal parts cook, housekeeper, nanny, nursemaid, and the glue that kept the family together. In years past, Mae would have spent half the night with Dani, telling her stories in the rocking chair on the front porch and allowing her to eat supper wherever she wished, usually the bed. Those days were gone now, ended when Dani turned fifteen. She supposed it was just as well; Mae's back was bent and crooked now, her hair fringed in silver.

"Now, Miz Dottie," Mae said, turning her attention to the refrigerator, "you know all you got to do is ask, and I'll get you whatever you're looking for."

Dani's grandmother kept her head inside the frig as she answered. "Well, I don't know what I'm looking for, Mae. I might get hungry later, and I don't know what I'll be hungry for. I think I want pickles. Or maybe Cool Whip."

"Mother," Jilly Anne said, exasperated. "Didn't we fill your kitchen with food just yesterday?"

Dottie hesitated. "Did you? But you might have something I don't have."

"Fix her a platter, Mae."

"I don't want no platter," Dottie answered petulantly. "I want peanut butter and jelly."

"Really, Mother." Jilly Anne's voice became shrill, sounding increasingly more rankled.

"Now, Miz Dottie," Mae said patiently, "last we counted, you had a hundred and twenty jars of peanut butter and near 'bout as many jellies."

"Well, I'm out of potato chips."

"You won't find them in the icebox. No, ma'am." Mae stepped to the pantry door and opened it, revealing shelves overflowing with potato chip bags. "I'll get you a grocery bag of fixin's."

"No, you won't," the older woman answered.

"You'll miss your bus if you don't leave right this minute. And you'll be late for your party, Jelly Jam."

"You know I hate it when you call me that," Jilly Anne said, pouting.

"Get outta here," Dottie said, waving her hands as if shooing them out the door.

"Well, stay here until the rain stops."

Dottie guffawed. "You call this rain?"

"It isn't just rain, Mama," Dani said, turning toward the window. "Look out there. We have tornado warnings."

"When do we not have them?" Jilly Anne said as she waltzed through the kitchen door into the hallway.

"Miz Dani," Mae called after them, "I made you plenty to eat now when you get back from driving your mama."

"Thank you, Mae," she answered before disappearing behind her mother. "You're a doll. I know it'll be delicious." She hesitated and turned back. "Do you need me to drive you home, Mae?"

"No, ma'am," Mae answered. "I enjoy the walk."

"But not in a tornado!"

"The Lord takes care of me, yes, He does."

"Okay, then," Dani answered, but her voice faded with the next roll of thunder as the lights flickered again.

"Oh. I almost forgot," Jilly Anne said as she turned into her husband's study. "Your daddy told me to bring a file to him." She knelt on the other side of a massive mahogany desk. "Oh," she whined. "What is that combination? Mae!" She called out. "Mae, what is the combination to Cole's safe?"

Mae appeared in the doorway. "Now, Miz Evans, you know Mister Cole don't give me the combinations to safes around here," she chuckled. "All I can tell you is he says he's had the same number for near eighteen years."

"Oh." Jilly Anne reached under the desk to a safe that was nearly hidden from view. "That's it! Thank you, Mae!"

"Hurry, Mama, if we're going," Dani said, watching through the window as the trees swayed in the rising storm.

"I've got it, I've got it," Jilly Anne said as she rose onto her feet. In one hand, she had a red file folder. "How am I supposed to keep this from getting wet?" she mused to no one in particular.

It was difficult to believe it was only half-past four; the skies were as pitch black as though it was midnight. They both donned summerweight raincoats before they made a mad dash off the porch for the carriage house, her mother squealing as if the raindrops were penetrating her broad yellow umbrella held above her matching slicker. Once inside the carriage house, Jilly

Anne shook it out with a flourish while Dani started her car. Then she shoved her umbrella into the back floorboard and climbed in with the eagerness of a debutante. The file was soaked through.

"Are you sure about this?" Dani asked.

"What are you suggesting? I can't miss the celebration!"

"Why does Daddy even keep files like that here?" Dani asked. "I'm sure there's plenty of space at his office."

"I know, but he keeps things here that he doesn't want anybody else to see, even those that work in his office. Especially those," she added.

With a sigh, Dani backed the Spitfire out of the carriage house and into the storm. They didn't bother closing the carriage doors, which would have required one of them to get out in the driving rain. Instead, Dani took off down the winding drive, glancing into the rearview mirror to catch a glimpse of the old structure, the open doors swinging on their hinges. Above them, the oversized lantern cast a wide arc of light across Dottie's silhouette as she made her way from the big house to her smaller in-law cottage set in the woods by the creek. From the way she rocked as she walked, it appeared she carried an armful of food.

"Don't hit her!" Jilly Anne exclaimed.

Dani jerked her eyes back to the road just as Mae's figure loomed in front of her. The woman jumped off the gravel drive and into the sodden grass as the car rolled past.

As the car began to slow, Jilly Anne asked, "What are you doing?"

"I'm going to offer her a ride. It's storming!"

"You are not. She's soaking wet, and she'll ruin the car. Besides, there's nowhere for her to sit."

Dani hesitated. There wasn't sufficient seating; that much was true. The Triumph Spitfire was a two-seater. The poor woman wouldn't be able to straddle the tiny area between the bucket seats. Dani sped back up, but her eyes continued to stray toward the rearview mirror. Maybe it was her imagination, but it appeared that Mae's thin clothing had soaked through to her skin. The older woman trudged along in the gloom and rain, each step appearing more tentative than the one before.

They reached the rural road, and Dani turned onto the asphalt. As she steered the car toward Clarksdale, she was aware of her mother chatting nonstop, but she was no longer paying attention. In her mind's eye, Dani envisioned Mae's six-mile hike to the bus station, where she'd board the evening bus that would take her within a mile or two of her home on the outskirts of Shelby. They were going in the opposite direction, and there would not have been time to drive Mae to the station, she told herself. Still, as they sped into the darkness, she couldn't help the pang of guilt that swept over her.

2

Every window of the Evans Law Firm glowed. The radiance was a pleasant contrast to the raging storm. Dani pulled in front of the three-story office building and waited patiently for Jilly Anne to decide on just the right moment to dash through the rain to the overhang. Then she sought out a parking spot, not a small feat as the courthouse employees had not yet left for the day. She fumbled in the back for her mother's umbrella, finally wrapping her fingers around it as she opened her door.

She was a block away. The wind brushed the rain sideways across the sidewalk. She passed a café, closed now that the breakfast and lunch crowds had long departed. Long shadows crept across the path in front of her, the dim lights from the occasional storefront no match for the storm. What had seemed like a short walk now felt as though it would never end. She tried to speed her steps, but she slipped on the glassy concrete, catching herself just in time. Her heart began to pound, but it made no sense. She'd traveled this area countless times; there was no need to be nervous, she admonished herself.

When she reached the front doors to the Evans Law Firm Building, she was breathing a sigh of relief as she stepped under the overhang—and nearly ran right into a man.

He'd been leaning against the building in the gloom of the nook. His dark pants, shirt, and leather jacket blended into the shadows, casting his face into darkness. At the sight of Dani, his eyes widened, the whites visible against the gloaming. He did not move, though he was nearly blocking the door. Instead, his eyes raked over her very slowly, as though he was undressing her.

She pursed her lips. "Excuse me," Dani said curtly. Her voice sounded more confident than she felt, and she wondered if he could hear the pounding of her heart. He did not attempt to move, so Dani reached past him to grab the door handle. At that moment, she felt him brush against her, and she gasped as her head spun around to stare at him. Then she gasped again as a passing car's headlights illuminated them for the briefest moment.

His eyes were inky, the depths appearing soulless. A jagged scar sliced one eyebrow in half while another cut through his lips. He stared insolently at Dani as if daring her to speak to him.

She grabbed the door handle with both hands and yanked it open.

Dani found her mother in the outer office on the second floor. Her father's secretary was clearing off her desk for the day. Jilly Anne chatted while she adjusted a radio dial, settling on the same crackling station Dani had listened to in her room. They were playing Brook Benton's "Rainy Night in Georgia." Dani glimpsed her father through the doorway to his office.

Cole Evans was a lanky man. His shoulders were narrow, but he cut an imposing presence through his height and his charismatic demeanor. His light brown hair was short, revealing a prematurely receding hairline. He caught sight of Dani, and as he strode across the expansive office toward her, his blue eyes twinkled. "There's my girl!" His voice sounded as though it should belong to a much larger man, the baritone oddly out of place in his slim physique.

"Daddy," Dani said, kissing him on the cheek.

He took a step back and studied her clothing. "You're not going to celebrate with us?"

She shook her head. "I have studying to do."

"Always with her head in a book," Jilly Anne chimed in. "She can't even take the time to celebrate her father's big win!"

"Big win?" Dani smiled uncertainly.

"Pour a glass of champagne for my girl," Cole directed to no one in particular. Yet, two junior attorneys and the secretary bolted into action, competing for the table where champagne rested in a bucket of ice.

"Yes, his big win," Jilly Anne said. "Only the biggest win of his entire career. He could end up with offices in Jackson now!"

Cole chuckled as Dani declined the offer of champagne. "I defended Dele Mason," he said, "and I won!"

"Dele—?"

"Never mind the name. It's unimportant. Trumped-up charges anyway—kidnapping, rape—"

"Trumped-up charges?" Dani asked, incredulous. "How do you exaggerate that?"

"No doubt he was guilty as sin," Cole said, his smile broadening. "But that doesn't matter. What matters is I turned the tables. I planted the seed of doubt in the jury's minds. And by the end of the trial, half of them must have thought the girl brought it on."

"Oh."

"It's been on the front pages of all the newspapers," Jilly Anne chimed in. "The girl is ruined. Absolutely ruined." Her tone was gay, as if she was declaring a happy occasion.

"I need to go," Dani said.

"What's the hurry? You just got here."

"Daddy, I need to study. I have a big exam coming up."

"What do you care?" Cole pressed. "You'll graduate in a few months and marry Richard. You'll have little need for math and science at home."

"It's English literature, Daddy. And I'm trying to get into Ole Miss—"

"Why? Because Richard went there?" Cole laughed, and the others joined in.

"Because I'm studying journalism. I want to work for a newspaper. You know this, Daddy."

He waved away her words. "Journalists don't make good money."

"It isn't about the money."

"And they don't need women. That's a man's job. Your husband is following in my footsteps, Dani, dear. You need to follow in your mother's."

She felt the heat burning in her cheeks. She grabbed the glass of champagne that a junior attorney still held for her and made her way to the window. The crisp chill of the glass cooled her embarrassment as she concentrated on the street below. The courthouse employees were leaving in droves now, crowding the sidewalks. She set her glass on a nearby credenza. "See you at home," she said on her way to the door.

"Don't wait up for us," Jilly Anne's voice carried behind her. "We're going to party the night away!"

She felt cold now, though the air was thick as a summer's heat. She took the stairs to the first floor and nearly raced out the doorway onto the sidewalk. Thankfully, the man she'd seen earlier was gone. She blended into the crowd of courthouse employees, allowing them to sweep her toward her car and safety.

3

The lights of the Mississippi State Penitentiary, known in these parts as Parchman or Parchman Farm, twinkled like giant stars through the driving rain as Dani made her turn. She drove not toward her home but in the direction of Shelby. Shortly after, she spotted Mae's figure stepping out of the roadway and onto the tall grass by the roadside ditch to make room for her vehicle to pass. She pulled alongside her, reaching across the petite car to open the passenger door.

"Get in!" she called, her voice drowned out by the storm.

Mae shook her head, and Dani insisted twice more before the woman, soaked to the bone, finally relented. As she climbed into the passenger seat, she said, "You know this ain't right, Miz Dani."

"God will decide that," Dani answered. Still, she glanced in the rearview mirror as if the Ku Klux Klan was on her bumper before shaking the thoughts from her mind. It had been several years since three bodies had been found nearly three hours away in Philadelphia, Mississippi. But the violence hadn't stopped there; it had only intensified with lynchings and cross burnings a regular occurrence.

Only one set of headlights beamed through the darkness. They were still a distance away, the lights appearing like a Monet melting in the storm. The door was barely closed before Dani was pulling away again.

It was Reconstruction interrupted, her history teacher had said. The Black population had begun to rise in the decade after General Lee surrendered. But any gains were stripped away by the 1876 Presidential election between Samuel J. Tilden and Rutherford B. Hayes, which ended in a dead heat with no clear winner. In the bitter aftermath that threatened to plunge the country back into civil war, the Dixie Democrats conceded. But there was one condition. Washington agreed to keep their hands off the Deep South. Mr. Lindbergh, her history teacher, spent a good deal of time outlining how the South descended into hatred, eventually leading to the Jim Crow Era, the rise of blatant discrimination, and a Deep South that appeared intent on burning out the Black population.

That was before Mr. Lindbergh was unceremoniously removed from his position and sent packing. Word had it that he landed at the University of Chicago. Some said he was expelled from Mississippi because he was a Jew, but Dani believed his Reconstruction views were to blame. It was a pity he was gone. She'd enjoyed his classes. She found them to be illuminating.

They rode without conversation as she became lost in her thoughts. The only sounds were the windshield wipers and the steady drips from Mae's clothing onto the seat and floorboard. Nervous, Dani turned on the radio. A different station came in more strongly now, and Mae appeared to relax a good bit as they listened to Marvin Gaye sing "What's Going On."

Shelby seemed little more than a crossroads, the sign heralding the town the "City of Justice" nearly obscured by the rain. She slowed the car as she drove through the middle, a short series of squat brick buildings with requisite awnings to keep the scorching sun off the heads of pedestrians. The sun had long since disappeared, and not even the moon was visible in the night sky.

At the opposite edge of town, perhaps a mile from the entrance to it, Dani pulled in front of Mae's tiny home. It was a shotgun house, so named because a man could sit in the back of the house with his shotgun trained on the front door, presumably to scare off the revenuer come to collect taxes. Gossip had it that the houses consisted of two rooms, a third if one was lucky enough to have a kitchen. Their bathroom was an old bucket out back that they squatted over, sometimes filled with old cotton bolls to soak up the urine. Again, if they were fortunate, they had an outhouse, but a glance told Dani that Mae's home was likely two rooms only with no frills. Though lights had flickered in town, only candlelight struggled to lighten the interior from the single front windowsill.

As her wipers cleared the sheets of water from the windshield, she spotted three faces at the window, now more fully illuminated by her headlights. She recognized Mae's husband Petey, who worked as a laborer in the fields, and their two grandchildren. Petey had done twenty years at Parchman Prison for stealing a potato and green pepper at the farmer's market. He'd aged fifty.

His face disappeared as Mae opened the car door. She'd barely said, "Thank you kindly, Miz Dani," before Petey's figure was crossing the open doorway, a broken umbrella in his hands. He sloshed through the puddles that had formed in the Mississippi clay, holding the umbrella high to cover his wife.

"Thank y', thank y'," he repeated to Dani. "Lordy, we was worried." He wrapped an arm around his wife, hurrying her back to the house as the wind made the broken umbrella only a useless stick held above them.

She'd wanted to ask about Mae's family. She'd wanted to ask how Petey was, about their daughter Dionne, and about the two grandchildren they raised. She never asked about her son, who was serving a life sentence at Parchman for smoking marijuana. Mae's face always sank when she mentioned Dooley; he'd been barely 18 when deputies caught him and his friend Doodle behind the liquor store. Now they both were rented out to farmers for nine dollars a month. Modern slavery, Mr. Lindbergh had called it.

Five people, she thought, in an area the size of Dani's bedroom. But the time had come and gone, and now Mae was inside. The door remained open, perhaps for ventilation.

The deejay's insistent voice replaced Marvin Gay's hypnotic one. There were tornadoes in the area, and he warned residents to take immediate cover. There were no sirens here, though Dani heard big cities had them. If one wasn't listening to the radio or watching television, she supposed they had no way of knowing what wrath was heading their way.

She trembled as though a chill from the storm had finally penetrated her, and she placed the car in reverse and backed up over water-filled potholes and loose gravel. She turned around on the vacant road and headed back through Shelby. At the single stoplight, she noticed the frontend of a vehicle protruding from an alley. She didn't know why it should cause her heart to beat faster. The headlights were off, and for some reason, it felt like a spider waiting to pounce. The light turned yellow as she approached, and she accelerated to get through the deserted intersection.

A tiny structure down a side street illuminated a brief swath of road. Dani cracked her window to dissipate the condensation that clung to her windshield. The faint but unmistakable cords of Delta blues reached her ears and faded into the night as she sped away.

~~~~~

The doors to the carriage house were partially closed, the wind banging them against the frame. Dani stopped the car and hopped out, racing to the doors to swing them open. By the time she returned to drive the Spitfire inside, she was every bit as drenched as Mae had been, her teeth beginning to chatter.

Dani closed and secured the doors before sprinting across the lawn to the wide front porch. Four massive columns graced the front of the house like antebellum sentinels. She stopped at the porch swing to remove her soaked heels. Dani found the front door had swung open again by the same strong winds that had blown the carriage doors, though she could have sworn when she'd closed it earlier, she'd heard it latch. The screen door was banging against the side of the house. She wrestled it closed, placing the hook into the eye. Then she pushed the heavy door until it latched before locking it with the stubborn deadbolt. Sighing heavily, she dropped her shoes onto the mat by the coat tree.

The house was dark, the shadows long, as she

groped her way to the wall switch. She flicked it twice, mumbling under her breath as she realized the power was out. It was anyone's guess when it might return. Sometimes, it mysteriously hummed back into service as if a wayward branch pulled back on its own. Other times the county had to dispatch a woodcutter to remove a tree across a downed cable before the lineman could restore service.

She felt the strength of the storm as she made her way down the hall to the back door. She opened it and paused briefly to peer outside. The back, like the front, had a wide porch with columns, so, in times past, visitors could approach the house from either direction and view an identical impressive entrance. Nowadays, the road leading to the back was private. It wound through fields of cotton broken up by the occasional cornfield, the efforts of the farmers that had leased her family's land for decades. It was black as pitch now under the roiling, angry clouds. She placed her hand on the door and had begun to close it when she stopped once more, her eyes drawn to a light in the woods.

The giant oaks and sycamore trees would obscure Grandma Dottie's house when their leaves emerged in the spring. When Dani was a child, she'd hurried along the garden path with images of the big bad wolf pushing her feet ever faster. She was always relieved to see her grandmother at the door to the cottage, beckoning her inside. The path had grown shorter as Dani's legs had grown taller, and what once seemed like miles was now barely a hundred feet.

Spanish moss graced the naked trees, hanging in long folds from their branches and partially blocking the cottage. But Dani could still make out a glow from the front window; Grandma Dottie had started up the fireplace. Despite the warm, humid weather, it would provide her with muted light until power returned. She pictured her inside, bent over a quilt or a piece of embroidery, creating her art one thread at a time.

A flash of lightning lit up the night sky, and Dani closed the back door and secured it with the deadbolt.

She pushed through the swinging door to the kitchen, narrowing her eyes to see past its length to the laundry room. The servants' entrance, used these days exclusively by Mae, appeared closed. She recalled her words about supper and had taken a few steps toward the refrigerator when another burst of lightning illuminated the room. In that instant, a large, dark shape appeared beside the house and was gone the next.

Dani stepped to the window, pulling back the curtain sheers so she could see more clearly. Now, nightfall bathed the landscape in blackness once more, the shape partially concealed by massive tree trunks.

She'd been alone in this house countless times over the past three years, but she still longed for the comfort of Mae's presence. As a child, her imagination had turned simple objects into malevolent beings bent on sucking her soul from her. Mae had always managed to calm her fears.

It was only a woodpile, she told herself. She pushed the niggling doubt from her.

A sound behind her caused her to jump. She whirled around to find the door swinging as if someone had just passed through. "Mama?" she called. "Daddy?" Even as she called out for them, she knew they were in town, celebrating her father's recent legal win. They would not return until the wee hours of the morning.

She considered exiting through the servants' door and racing down the path to Grandma Dottie before chastising herself. This was her home, as it always had been. There was no one there, just as there had never been.

Dani pushed through the kitchen door with an elaborate jolt, causing it to bang against the wall before it swung back into place. She moved down the hall, her footsteps growing more rapid as she neared the staircase. Then she felt her way up the stairs, her hand gripping the banister as she tried to calm her nerves. Her imagination insisted the shifting shadows upon the stairs were warnings of intruders, while her more logical mind scolded herself for her childish fears.

She reached the upper hallway and glanced behind her. No one had followed her up the broad, curved staircase. No one was standing in the foyer below, staring back at her. Of course, they weren't.

She came to her bedroom door and hesitated as she stared down the hall toward her parents' room. Once the power came back on, it would all appear normal again, she told herself. But now, the skeletal branches of the giant oak outside their window cast wavering shadows on the open doorway and stretched like fingers across the floor.

She pivoted, stepping into the bathroom across the hall. Her clothes were saturated through to her skin, and she was trembling. She closed the door by habit before quickly reopening it; even the muted light in the hall was preferable to the gloom of the windowless bath. She stripped down, allowing her clothes to pile at her feet. Then she grabbed a towel on the rack.

Another bolt of lightning emblazoned the skies simultaneously with a wicked roll of thunder. A sound like a tree cracking split the night air, and she instinctively whirled toward her bedroom door. But rather than face the shadows of a tree cleaved by lightning, a hulking figure stood in the doorway.

In a split second, her mind registered the silhouette. It might have been a man or a ghost or a trick of the imagination in the darkness. Then she realized she could smell him. It was a mixture of stale liquor, a laborer's unwashed body drenched in sweat and rain, and something else—something both unfamiliar and terrifying.

She tried to scream, but her throat constricted to a croak as her body burst into action, her feet ready to race her down the hall to safety. But as she took that first step, the silhouette grew in front of her until she was able to pick out the outline of a man's arm holding an object high above her. Then it was a silhouette no longer but a muscular arm and a beefy hand. Her forehead exploded, and her legs collapsed beneath her. As she fell, she was struck once more beneath her chin, causing the back of her head to ricochet off the wall. The taste of blood filled her mouth. Somewhere in the back of her mind, she felt she was drowning in her own blood, but as Dani sank to the floor, she realized she could do nothing to save herself.

4

As she began to awaken, the sound of moaning grew persistent. One eye popped open, and she realized it was her voice she'd heard. She could not open her other eye. Confused, she attempted to move her hand to her face, but her wrist was caught somewhere above her. As the memory of the man in the doorway assailed her senses, her heart began to pound. Despite the pain, she forced her head to turn toward one hand and then the other. They were bound above her head, each wrist tied to opposite corner bedposts. She tugged and grappled, but the knots were tight, her movements only serving to cut the rope into her skin.

Her ankles were similarly bound, splaying her legs apart to opposite bedposts. She tried to scream, but her mouth was stuffed. She used her tongue to push at the fabric, her breathing labored. Her mouth and throat were parched. It felt as though every muscle in her body was crying out in pain. She tried to see her body, but the limited movement prevented it. She felt rather than saw herself naked upon her parents' bed, a sticky substance against her back. Blood, she thought in rising panic. She was going to die here in a pool of her own blood.

She heard the footsteps before the man came into view. He leaned over her, revealing a shadowy face marred with scars. One split an eyebrow while another crossed his lip. Certain features became emblazoned upon her mind, the wide nostrils and open pores, soulless eyes concealed in shadows, a pointed chin sprinkled with the coarseness of an evening shadow.

He laughed, the cackle menacing and maniacal, as he climbed atop her. She realized only then that he was naked, his body lean and muscular. Instinctively, she tried to close her legs, but the ties prevented her from moving. With only her torso able to rotate, she tried wiggling her body away from him.

To her rising horror, he climbed closer to her face. She shook her head vehemently as she realized his intent while tears poured down her face. Her distress only appeared to motivate him. As he straddled above her, he removed the gag from her mouth.

"I'll bite you!" she managed to croak.

"No, you won't." From seemingly out of nowhere, the butt of a pistol slammed against her jaw, and she seemed powerless to close it. Then a second strike landed on her temple, and she no longer cared.

5

The next time Dani began to regain consciousness, there was a ringing in her ears. She thought she heard footsteps upon hardwood floors, but the ear-piercing noise interfered until she wasn't sure of anything. Her soul seemed to be pushing her to awaken, the voice so deep inside her that she wasn't even sure she existed anymore.

Then the sound of her mother's laughter grew near, and she forced herself to open one eye. The pain of brightly lit lamps assaulted her, creating a searing pain that shot through her head, sickening her. She groaned, her thickened tongue somehow wrapped around the gag that was once more inside her mouth.

"What on earth—?" Her mother's voice cut through the cloud around her.

In an instant, her parents were upon her. She opened one eye and struggled to open the other. Her parents' faces filled her vision. The expression on her mother's face was one of drunken disbelief. Her father seemed to realize his daughter was naked before him, and he instinctively covered his eyes and made his way out of her line of vision.

She moaned again. The man was there in the house; she knew he was. They were all in danger.

Her mother wrestled with the knot that bound her wrist to the corner post, finally freeing it. Another jolt of pain shot through her hand and arm as sensation came back into her limbs. Dani could not bring her hand to her mouth quickly enough. She removed the gag—her panties—as her mother worked to free her other wrist.

Cole returned to the room with long, purposeful strides. Jilly Anne tossed the bedspread over her daughter's torso to cover her as she moved to the ties around her ankles. He stood over them, holding a shotgun with both hands.

"He's here," Dani managed to croak. "He's in the house."

"How many?"

"Just one—I think."

"Stay here. Both of you."

As Dani's senses struggled to return, she realized there was only one telephone in the large house. It was mounted downstairs on the kitchen wall, at the opposite corner of the house. Cole first searched the bedroom and attached bath, the closets, and under the bed. Satisfied the assailant was not there, he ordered the door closed and locked as he exited.

As soon as her feet were free, Dani swung her legs over the side of the bed. Fighting dizziness, she reached for the water decanter on the nightstand. Not bothering to pour the water into a glass, she instead began to guzzle it, swishing it around her mouth and spitting it back out.

"My word, Danielle." Her mother's voice was one of disgust. Jilly Anne reeked of alcohol and cigarettes. Though she backed away from her daughter, the odor permeated Dani's consciousness, adding to the confusion and pain.

Dani fell to her knees on the floor and vomited.

"My rug!" Jilly Anne's words were slurred. "Couldn't you at least have gotten to the bathroom?"

Naked and crouched on the rug, she lost control of her body. Everything happened at once, emptying the contents of her bowels, her kidneys, and her stomach.

"Oh, Good God!" Jilly Anne exclaimed, covering her mouth and nose.

Dani felt rather than saw the windows open, the coolness of the night breeze finding its way to her hot and perspiring skin. It was still raining. Jilly Anne was ripping the covers off the bed, wadding them into a loose ball, and pitching them into a pile near the door. She swayed back into Dani's line of sight as she tossed her two towels.

"Clean yourself up," Jilly Anne ordered. "Then you're getting into the bath."

Dani was unsteady, her hands uncoordinated. She couldn't see her body. She felt her face. It was bulging and bloody, and one eye was completely closed. Her other one was not much better. Swelling had ballooned her jaw to twice its size. Everything swam before her, and everything hurt.

She struggled to rise onto her feet. Unable to stand, her mother lifted her as best she could, causing her to cry out with the pain. She wanted to sit on the bed, but

Jilly Anne stopped her. "Not as filthy as you are," she admonished.

Her knees began to buckle, and Jilly Anne grabbed her by her waist, holding her up nearly an arm's length away from her chiffon dress.

There was an urgent knock at the door. "It's me," came Cole's deep voice, now rushed with adrenaline.

Jilly Anne lugged Dani with her to the door and opened it.

Cole stood in the doorway. "The house is empty," he said. "I've searched every room." He stepped toward them but stopped himself, glancing away from them. "There are fresh tire marks by the side of the house. Looked like he parked in the woods. He's gone now."

"He—it was—" Dani tried to form the words.

"Not now," Cole said. "Later. We'll talk."

"Get in the bath," Jilly Anne said.

As Dani made an effort toward the master bathroom, Jilly Anne pointed her in the direction of the hall. "Not my bath. Yours."

"I'll call Dr. Nash," Cole said.

"His office won't open for hours," Jilly Anne said, the words stumbling over one another as though she was struggling for clarity.

"He'll open for us."

"Don't touch the walls," Jilly Anne said. As Dani faltered, she once again came to her aid, placing her hands around her waist and managing to hold her up as they made their way into the hall bathroom. She helped Dani step over the rim of the tub and sink inside it, both women resting a palm on the wall to steady themselves. Jilly Anne shakily turned on the taps. "I'll be back to rinse your hair out. You can't be seen looking like that. What would the neighbors think?"

Dani's body acted on its own, sinking back against the tub as the water rose around her. As it turned pink with her blood, she heard her mother's voice calling from the master bedroom.

"It's all ruined, Danielle! My beautiful spread, my Oriental rug. I'll have to throw it all out. And we were having such a wonderful evening. You ruined it all!"

~~~~~

Cole and Dani rode in silence to Dr. Nash's clinic. The storm had turned to a steady downpour that flooded the shoulders of the rural road. Cole's lips were tight; his bloodshot eyes focused on driving as he straddled the faint middle line to avoid the rising waters. Dani slumped in the passenger seat, the occasional bump in the road jolting her to semi-consciousness, each time soliciting a choked scream. She wore a cleaning rag over one side of her head, held in place with duct tape. More rags were taped to her torso, strategically placed to prevent her from bleeding all over Cole's plush Lincoln Continental.

It barely registered when they'd pulled into the parking lot. Only Dr. Nash's distinctive cherry red Chevrolet Chevelle rested underneath a floodlight; the color oddly cheerful under the circumstances. She hardly heard her father's voice as Dr. Nash approached. As they opened her door, the ringing in her ears overrode all other sounds. Their faces swam before her, their voices droning somewhere in the distance as their faces turned into impressionist paintings made even vaguer by the heavy rain and wind.

As they helped her exit the car, her legs gave out beneath her, and she nearly collapsed on the wet asphalt. She was faintly aware of their strong hands beneath her arms as they caught her and lifted her back to her feet. They remained on either side of her, half-carrying her to the clinic doors. She tried to raise her head and rally her legs into supporting her, but her head was too heavy and the effort too great.

When a shadowy form of consciousness struggled to return, bright overhead lights in a tiny exam room accosted her senses. Dani closed her eye, but the light stubbornly penetrated through the thin eyelid. Her other eye was covered by a bandage neatly taped into place.

"Ah, there you are," Dr. Nash said. His voice was calm and soothing, as though he treated similar injuries on a routine basis. She felt rather than saw him, with his full head of white hair, kind eyes, and cherubic face. "You've been out for nearly an hour."

She was aware of a cuff on her arm. She cried out as Dr. Nash began to take her blood pressure, the pain returning to her limbs as she regained full consciousness.

He patted her hand reassuringly. "I've given you something for the pain, dear," he said. "It'll take effect in a minute or two. Just try to hang in there."

"Is my face broken?" she managed to ask through cracked, swollen lips.

He placed an ice cube against her mouth. "Hold this against your face there," he directed softly. "Don't worry your pretty little head about your face. You'll be as gorgeous as ever."

But that wasn't what I asked, Dani thought as agitation began to build in her throbbing head. She wanted to ask more—needed to ask more—but Dr. Nash was gone, closing the door softly behind him.

A moment later, she heard his voice in the room adjacent to hers. The wall was thin, most likely no more than two sheets of dark paneling stapled to studs. "She appeared to have been pistol-whipped," Dr. Nash was saying. "I'll have to redo the facial x-rays; there's just too much swelling."

"Good God." She recognized her father's baritone.

"She's suffering from a concussion. I've stitched up her head..."

Dani reached for her face, feeling her nose, her chin, and her cheekbones. It did not feel like her face at all. A thick bandage protruded from one temple. Through a separate dressing, she could feel one eye was swollen shut, and the other didn't seem too far behind. She struggled to concentrate on the discussion taking place next door.

"... ribs broken," Dr. Nash was saying. "...wrapped up..."

She heard her father's voice murmuring, but she failed to make out his words.

"There's more," the doctor continued, his voice rising with indignation. She strained to hear him, but she could only make out a word here or there. "...sexually assaulted...vaginal tears, rectum, too...hospital..."

She felt tears escape down her cheeks, though she felt too numb inside to register her emotional pain.

"No hospital," Cole's voice rose as he spoke the words. "We can't have rumors..."

"Home then," Dr. Nash said. "I can supply a nurse..."

She barely heard the rest. There was something about instructions, but the overhead lights were too searing, the metal table too hard, and the dizziness too great.

6

She dreamed she was working. She'd wanted to be a journalist from an early age. She saw herself in her mind's eye at the age of nine, wearing a makeshift newspaperman's cap and traveling with a pencil and pad everywhere she went. She'd published her "newspaper" for months, painstakingly copying the articles from page to page and selling them for a penny apiece before giving them away just to get rid of them. She wrote about the alligator found in a ditch beside the mall and about the mysterious owl that took up residence in the post office attic. She even wrote how Priscilla Whiting's skiing accident had derailed her Olympic dreams, a real coup given that she was able to interview Priscilla herself.

Dani saw each of these self-administered assignments as if from above. She watched the young girl riding her bicycle for several miles a day to track down stories. She swallowed the pain of begging people to accept her newspaper and saw the man that tossed his unread in the street trash can as though it was currently happening.

Then she saw herself at the age of seventeen. Her part-time job had begun only a few months earlier, though now it seemed like a distant lifetime ago. When the school bell sounded each afternoon precisely at 2:30, she was off like a dart to the local paper offices, where she labored for two to three hours a day.

She came prepared with her pad filled with ideas of current events. The new grocery store announced they would carry milk, which could lead to the milkmen door-to-door industry's decimation. She could interview the Evans family's milkman, who had worked his beat for over fifty years.

Then there was Mabelle Morrissey's mama, who was learning to get her driver's license, and she'd run over every trash can set out for pickup last week. On a particularly windy day, she'd strewn the refuse for miles, including the Walsh family's old tax returns, which detailed monumental losses at the Walsh Marine Repair Corporation at a time they'd publicly reported profits.

On a national scale, anti-war sentiment had led to protests around the country, and the FBI had just arrested Hank Hennessey for desertion. Turned out, when he told his family he was on leave from the Vietnam War, he'd forged a few signatures. Rumor had it, he was on his way to Fort Leavenworth.

The editor, Jimmy Bob Carole, was a burly man with a barrel chest and a bald head. His office reeked of yesterday's lunch and last week's breakfast. She'd never seen him behind his desk. He was forever striding off in this direction or that with a fistful of paper and a rosy red face like a heart attack ready to happen. He struck fear into everyone—everyone except Dani. She saw him as a challenge.

By now, she knew the routine. After school, she would rush in with her newest scoops and tidbits, and Jimmy Bob would bark at her to fetch his coffee. It had to be black, it had to be strong, and if it poured out of the battered metal percolator like tar, it was just right. So she'd fetch it and try again with her pitch as she ran along behind him. She was the only female in the office other than the front desk receptionist, Mary Jane, who alternated between typing and doing her nails.

Now she worried fitfully in her dreams that she'd been unable to show up for school and work. At times, she imagined Jimmy Bob had fired her. At other times, she fretted that she'd be held back another year in school. She had the sensation of time passing and time sitting still, and of no time at all but her linear life packed into one concurrent event.

The next time she awakened, she was in her bed, the sheets tucked neatly around her. Daylight streamed in through the window, illuminating the buttery wallpaper with its tiny purple clematis. It had always been a soothing sight as she awakened, but now it assaulted her senses. She rolled her one fairly decent eye away until it came to rest on the opposite side of the bed.

Mae sat in a simple chair, her head bowed. Both hands covered her heart as her lips moved with silent words. She finished, wiping tears from her eyes with the hem of her apron. Then her eyes widened as she noticed that Dani had awakened.

"Oh, Lordy," she exclaimed. She reached for a wet rag laid across Dani's forehead, adjusting it as she looked down at her. "Oh, Lordy, you gave us quite a scare."

Dani tried to speak, but her lips were parched and cracked. They were not the too-thin lips she always tried to plump, but someone else's thick, swollen lips that could not be compelled to move.

"Let's sit you up, if'n you can," Mae said, her voice a mixture of gentleness and excitement. "I've got you some nice sweet tea." She slipped one capable hand behind her back, pulling her into a seated position while she adjusted the pillows behind her. "Now," she said as she grabbed a glass on the nightstand, "let's get this down you."

"The police?" Dani managed to croak as the tea lubricated her parched and dilated throat.

"What about the police?" Mae hesitated as she helped hold the glass.

It hurt to swallow, and the words came haltingly. "Daddy—did he call—?"

"Why on earth would he call the police? Weren't the Klan that run you off the road, was they?"

"What?" Her head throbbed, and the room began to spin. There was so much she wanted to say, but her body was unwilling to cooperate.

"Lordy, Miz Dani, you gave us the scare. Those tornadoes lasted thirty-three hours! I've blamed myself for you runnin' off the road. You shouldn't have gone after me to drive me home."

"Tornadoes?" she managed to croak.

"You're a lucky one. One hundred and twenty-three folks done met their maker, their souls done carried to heaven on a tornado." She pressed one hand against her heart. "They say nearly 1,600 folks injured, you included."

"I don't remember a tornado," she said. Her head throbbed.

"Why, it lasted from one day right on into another."

"How long have I been asleep?"

"Lord, young'un, you've been out nigh on three days!"

She didn't know which statement shocked her the most. As she closed her eyes against the glaring sunlight, she tried to remember the storm. There had been thunder and lightning and, she supposed, a tornado.

"I ran off the road?" she managed to say. "My car—?"

"You don't remember? Your Mama, she filled me in. It was that night you drove me home. Lord, I have blamed myself." She shook her head. "Anyways, child, the water, why, it swept you right on off the road."

"Mama said I ran off the road?"

Mae nodded. "And you got mighty messed up, young'un. Mighty messed up."

"And I've been out for three days," she said woodenly.

"Three days. "

"And where is Mama now? Why isn't she sitting here with me?"

"She's at her book club meeting. You know she go every Tuesday." She chuckled. "But you don't know it's Tuesday, do you? She'll be home in a few hours, just like always. Yes, ma'am. Life goes on, don't it?" Mae watched her drink the rest of the tea. "I've got a pitcher here for you. You must be mighty thirsty."

Dani leaned back against the pillows. The bedding smelled stale and medicinal. "Will you open a window?" she asked.

"Yes, ma'am. I sure will." Despite her age and size, Mae was spry as she opened both corner windows.

"I told your mama fresh air was good for you, but she said…"

Her words faded in and out as Dani felt her head splitting in two. She reached up to touch her eye. A patch covered it. She vaguely remembered lying in the exam room and feeling the bandage for the first time. The swelling might have gone down a bit, but it was difficult to tell under the layers.

"Tell you what I'm gonna do," Mae said, crossing her hands in front of her apron. "I made some homemade chicken soup for you. It'll go down nice and easy. And I've got peach ice cream. Made it myself from those peaches I canned last summer. You just sit right there, and I'll be back in just a minute or two."

Dani tried to nod but was overcome with a wave of dizziness. "Where is Daddy?"

"At work, child, of course. He'll be home for dinner, same as always. Tuesday night is pot roast, if'n you feel up to it. But I'll tote it up here to you; you ain't in no shape to take them stairs…"

"And nothing else has happened?"

"Well, Delta City done been destroyed, they say. And Inverness mostly gone, too. They say it's done been litter ated."

"Obliterated?"

"Railway cars tipped on they sides. Inverness courthouse just gone. *Poof!* Evanna plantation, it done been wiped off the face of this earth. Oxford done hit bad, too."

"Rich—?"

"Rich is fine, child. The Lord watched o'er him. They say it was a family of tornadoes, like a mama and daddy, and a whole passel of children. They sayin' Oxford has half a million dollars in damage." She shook her head. "Can't even imagine that much money.

Anyways, your Rich, he just fine. The 'family' done joined up and cut a road ten miles long into Holly Springs Forest. Ain't no path there no more. It's a road now."

Mae picked at her apron as if to wipe away nonexistent crumbs. "Other than that, Miz Dani, every day just like the last. Only you slept through it." She shook her head and made her way toward the door. "Sure is nice to hear your voice and see you sitting up for a change. Yes, ma'am, sure is..."

~~~~~

Dani couldn't be roused to full wakefulness when Mae returned with the soup and ice cream. In the days that followed, she continued to drift in and out of consciousness, suspended somewhere between the life she had and events she remembered or envisioned. Dani relived nights as a child sitting in her daddy's lap watching television long after her bedtime had come and gone—the show was always Dean Martin scooting across the piano like an endless loop. She recalled Mae watching over her when mumps and then measles ravaged her thin body, her mama too afraid of catching her illnesses to venture near her. She dreamed of awakening to get to school on time, of faithfully doing her homework, of visiting her best friend Janie, whose parents were always so much more attentive than her own.

She dreamed she was a deer with a hunter on her trail, and she felt paralyzed, unable to flee. Then she dreamed she did escape, all the way to New York City. The skyscrapers morphed from steel structures to glimmering buildings that reminded her of the Emerald City in *The Wizard of Oz*.

Sometimes, she awakened to find Mae sitting dutifully at her side. Other times, Mae's daughter, Dionne, lured her awake as she read aloud to fill the hours. Dionne was beautiful with flawless skin and large doe eyes. She had two children who lived with Mae, and Dani had never known whether Dionne had married their father. Dionne worked as a library aid during the day and cleaned office buildings in the evenings. Her diction was clear and precise as she read Daphne du Maurier's *Jamaica Inn* until Dani imagined it was she in the moors, running from an assailant. Then the assailant morphed into her attacker until they were one and the same, and she fitfully drifted off yet again.

Grandma Dottie was often there as well, reading from a markedly different book. She seemed to select Bible passages that focused on fire and brimstone, hell, and damnation. It did nothing to rally Dani's spirits but had the opposite effect of pulling her down further to an abyss that often appeared to have no exit. She then dreamed of hell and demons, and her attacker was always among them, taunting her.

Dani's best friend, Janie, arrived in the late afternoons or evenings. Sometimes as Dani lay with her eyes closed, she listened while her friend filled her in on all the gossip from their high school. Later, she'd awaken to wonder whether she'd dreamt the latest story or if it had all been real.

Mabelle was home after a year's recuperation in Alabama, and wouldn't you know it, during that same time, her mama got pregnant and had another child? Janie snickered as she told the story because everyone knew it was Huck Bobby Woods' child, having been conceived under the bleachers during the homecoming game. Anyway, Mabelle's mama was fifty years old with a bone disease; she didn't fool anybody. And

Mabelle's illness was intentionally vague, which nobody bought, either.

Once, Dani managed to open an eye while her friend chatted away. Janie hadn't noticed; she was standing in front of the dressing table, primping her bleached locks, which was all the rage. She was a few inches taller than Dani, with billowing hair that nearly reached her hips. Janie was studying to become a beautician, attending classes every weekend. Once school ended, she'd switch to summer classes to obtain her license by autumn. Her mama had arranged a job for her at a local salon, where she'd already started washing clients' hair a few times a week.

Once or twice as the days turned to weeks, she awakened to discover Rich there by her side, his forehead lined with worry. Unlike Dionne and Janie, he remained silent, an air of aloofness surrounding him. He had no book in his hands but sat staring out the window beyond Dani's bed as though he was deep in thought. For some reason, she always seemed to struggle during those times, and later when she awakened again to find him gone, she could not remember if they'd spoken.

Then, of course, there were her parents. Her mother was fidgety as she sat, flipping through *Glamour's* latest editions or the racier, scandalous *Cosmopolitan*. She often paced from one window to another like a caged animal longing to be free. She tried on Dani's lipstick and brushed her hair with Dani's coveted soft-bristled brush. When she spoke to her daughter, she was likely to share fashion trends; wide belts and bellbottoms were all the rage.

Her father read the newspaper, and on those occasions when Dani stirred, he informed her of world events. Gasoline had soared to nearly forty cents a gallon, and if inflation continued as it had, a letter would soon cost almost a dime to mail. There was mounting pressure on President Richard Nixon to lower the voting age to eighteen because boys were being drafted at that age and sent to fight in Vietnam. Anti-war protests were continuing across the country. The demonstrations had worked to the extent that both Australia and New Zealand, both American allies, were pulling out. But on a positive note, Americans were still talking about Alan Shepard playing golf on the moon.

Cole was particularly interested in *Swann v. Charlotte-Mecklenburg Board of Education*, a North Carolina case heading to the Supreme Court. Depending on which way the court leaned, the verdict could enforce school busing—and desegregation—in Mississippi.

The days turned to weeks, and the weeks passed into a month. Dani's body began to heal, but her mind became stuck in an endless loop as if every night was the night of the attack. She regularly awakened with a scream or a cry. Nearly delirious, she tried to climb out of bed to warn everyone that the assailant was in the house.

If Mae happened to be in the room, she'd attempt to convince her that she'd only had a bad dream. On Dionne's watch, the younger woman would get spooked and rushed to fetch Mae.

Janie asked questions, her brows knit together as though she genuinely did not understand her friend's hysteria, but she wanted to know more like she was listening to a good piece of gossip.

In turn, each person tried to reassure her that no one was coming to finish her off. But as she regained consciousness for longer stretches, she slowly put the pieces together. The realization that her parents had never reported the assault to the police became painfully more apparent.

Her brain shouted the obvious within her: it meant they were doing nothing to protect her.

It was Rich by her side when the fever finally broke, and her mind sliced through the intense fog that had enveloped her. She opened both eyes and marveled at the fact that she had sight in both. She raised a hand to the one that had once been swollen shut. To her surprise, she pulled an intravenous tube along that was connected to the back of her hand. "What is this?" she whispered.

Rich stood from the bedside chair and leaned over her. "What did you say, Dani?" His voice was soft and patient. As he stood over her, she was struck by the compassion in his eyes. They were nearly sapphire in their intensity and slightly hooded, which gave him a bit of a hound dog appearance as he peered down at her.

She touched the line with her other hand. "What is this?"

"It's been pumping fluids into you. Medicine, too." He sat on the side of the bed and held her hands. "You've been in and out for a month, Dani."

"A month," she repeated incredulously.

He nodded. "You looked pretty beat up the first time I saw you." He gently smoothed her hair. "You're looking a lot better. Doctor says you're healing up real good."

"I've gone to his office again?" she asked, puzzled.

"He's been coming here every week. Don't you remember?"

She shook her head, the slight movement causing vertigo.

"Your folks didn't want you in a hospital. Who knows what kind of care you'd get there?"

"Where are they?"

"Your folks?"

She nodded.

"Your mama's at a ladies' luncheon. Your daddy is at work."

"Why aren't you at school?"

He grinned sheepishly. "When my classes end early, I've been coming here to check on you. It gives Mae a break, and she always feeds me before I go. I've been right worried about you. We all have been."

She tried to return his smile, but the happy gesture fell short as the room began to spin. "Thank you." She closed her eyes and tried to push down a bit of nausea.

"Do you want anything to drink? Are you hungry?" He squeezed her hand.

"You know what? I'm actually starving."

"Doc Nash said you could have soft foods. Mae's been cooking up a storm. I'll run downstairs to let her know you're awake."

"Before you go…"

"Oh, what's wrong with me? You have a pitcher of lemonade right here." He poured a glass and helped her sit up.

She sipped the cold liquid. The ice cubes were barely melted, which meant the pitcher had just recently been changed out. "Rich?"

"Yes?" He looked at her expectantly. It seemed scandalous to see him standing there in her bedroom. His smooth, sandy hair appeared as if he'd just brushed it. He had an angular face with a strong jaw, his skin appearing so soft that she instinctively ran her fingers along his jawline. Despite the room's warmth, he wore a striped, cable-knit sweater that made him seem more like a Harvard graduate than one from Ole Miss. "What is it, sweetheart?"

Dani turned her attention to her own shocking appearance. She pulled the sheet over her breasts, though she wore a gown, and she ran a hand through her hair, which felt a bit greasy. She hated for Rich to see her this way. She must smell something fierce.

"What happened to me?" Dani asked. She tried to place the lemonade glass on the nightstand.

He gently took it from her and placed it on the tray beside the pitcher. "You don't remember?"

She didn't respond but waited for him to continue. He took a breath. "Well, it was a dark and stormy night." He chuckled shyly. "To quote *A Wrinkle in Time*. Actually," he grew serious, "the newspaper says it was the worst tornado outbreak since the 1800s. You wouldn't believe the damage, Dani."

"I drove Mama to Daddy's office that night."

"What were you thinking? What were *they* thinking, letting you do that?" He shook his head. "You don't remember your drive home?" Without waiting for her answer, he continued, "The winds were awful that night, just awful. I was in my dorm, and the windows shook like they were going to come out from the casing. At the storm's height, they had us huddled in the hallway with our knees up and our heads down. You remember how we used to practice hiding under our desks in a storm?"

She nodded.

"I swear to God. It sounded like a freight train barreling over our heads. The tornado skipped the dorm but did a lot of damage to the campus. A lot of damage," he repeated for emphasis.

"But you weren't hurt?"

"Just shook up, is all."

"I was home by that time," she mused.

"You were probably in the ditch by that time," Rich corrected. He squeezed her hand. "Even if you'd been in a heavier car, you didn't stand a chance against those winds. That little Spitfire must have been picked right up. Your daddy said they found it floating in a cottonfield."

"What?"

"You were knocked unconscious. You weren't even in the car; they found you lying up by the road. You weren't wearing your seat belt, Dani? You could've died."

"Rich," she said. Her voice sounded stronger than she felt. She struggled to sit up straighter. As he helped her, she continued, "That isn't what happened."

"Oh?" He looked puzzled. "You've been in and out, Dani. I'll get you some food, and you can tell me everything. Then I'll tell you everything you don't recall."

"No," she said. Her voice was firmer as she squeezed his hand. "I might not be awake when you get back. And you need to know. Someone needs to know."

"Okay." He took both her hands in his. "I'm listening, sweetie."

"I didn't run off the road, Rich. I didn't. I came straight home that night, and someone was in the house. I was attacked." She nodded toward the doorway. "Right outside the bathroom—and in my parents' bedroom."

Rich appeared doubtful. "Then how did your folks find you in the road with the car in the cottonfield?"

"They didn't. That's what I'm trying to tell you. They made it up."

Rich cocked his head and narrowed his eyes. "Why would they do that?"

Dani shook her head. "Embarrassment? Shame?"

"Because you were attacked? That doesn't make any sense, Dani. You don't know what you're saying."

"I know exactly what I'm saying. I was attacked right here, in this house."

"So... That's why you've cried out each time you started to regain consciousness?" He said it as a murmuring as if more to himself than to her. "That's why you kept saying he was here?"

"He's coming back," she said with conviction. "He's going to find out that I'm still alive, and he's coming back to kill me."

"Nothing's going to happen to you, sweetie."

"How can you say that?"

"I won't let anything happen to you."

"You'll quit the university?"

"What?"

"I didn't think so. You can't protect me, Rich," she said, her voice softening. "I know you want to. But you have classes. You have a future to prepare for—"

"You're my future, Dani."

"Then get me out of here." She struggled to sit up higher.

"Why? This is your home."

"That's why I have to leave. He knows I live here, don't you see that? He'll come back for me. He's not finished."

Rich patted her hand. "Let me get some food in you. You'll feel better once you've eaten." He stood and stepped toward the door.

"You don't believe me, do you?"

He hesitated as if trying to form his words. "I'll get you something to eat."

7

It was another week before Dani was firmly on her feet. Her legs had become unaccustomed to bearing weight, but she was determined to become independent as quickly as humanly possible. The fear of her attacker returning while she was incapacitated spurred her on. Now she finished stripping the bed, and she opened a window to allow the room to air. The fragrance of boxwood and honeysuckle was faint on the wind, but it was there nonetheless, heralding the coming of spring.

She caught a glimpse of her reflection in a mirror. She stepped toward her dressing table and studied her wan face, the dark circles under her eyes, and her underweight frame. The weeks had taken a toll on her, but she resolved to turn a corner.

She packed her bags with clothing and toiletries. She'd spoken to Janie the night before as she'd sat by her bed. Janie believed her; she was sure of it. And now she had only to tell her parents that she planned to remain with her best friend as they finished the school year together.

It wasn't the first time she'd moved into Janie's house. Her mother's drinking problem had reached a crescendo when Dani was fourteen. Jilly Anne had been a social butterfly for as long as Dani could remember. Alcohol buoyed her mother's party persona until it was impossible to determine where the liquor left off, and Jilly Anne's personality began. She was always concerned about others' opinions, so she hid her secret behind laughter and smiles and a wit quickened by alcohol. Mint juleps were her favorite. Though it had a reputation as a genteel Southern drink, especially for the ladies, it was surprisingly potent, especially when Jilly Anne supplemented the two ounces of bourbon for four.

Behind closed doors, alcohol was the only thing about which Jilly Anne seemed to care. Mae stepped in, as she always did, but she had her own heartbreaks and family drama.

Grandpa Matthias was still alive the first time Dani moved out; he and Grandma Dottie lived over three hours away in Natchez. It wasn't until the past year that Grandpa passed away from a sudden massive stroke. Shortly after, it became apparent to just about everybody that her grandmother's mental faculties had deteriorated into a state they all referred to as a bit touched in the head. It was clear that she could not continue living alone, so she came to live in the cottage beyond the house, further complicating a tricky situation.

So Dani had moved out at the age of fourteen. She did not doubt that Janie's parents had provided daily updates to Cole and Jilly Anne. But at least there,

Dani had been surrounded by relative normalcy. Ken Branson, Janie's father, was a scholar who taught at the University of Mississippi and had written numerous books. Her mother, Shirley, was a public school librarian. They'd moved to the south from someplace up north, and they carried with them radical ideas such as working women and civil rights.

It had only been after Cole convinced Dani that her mother's drinking was under control that she moved home again. She soon discovered the problem was still there, just more deeply hidden. Jilly Anne had replaced her mint juleps with a concoction of vodka, lemonade, and club soda served in a traditional sweet tea glass with plenty of ice and a mint garnish. To anyone willing to be fooled, it looked as though she now had a penchant for lemonade.

The thought of her parents now brought a stab of pain. They'd always been self-absorbed, so they'd never been ones to hover, but since the attack, they had been emotionally absent. When they checked on her, they avoided looking her in the face, their eyes flitting around the room as though they wished to be somewhere else. Meaningful conversation was nonexistent.

Well, that was about to change.

It was early, the sun barely rising above the distant horizon. She left her bags on the bed and made her way downstairs. She found Mae in the kitchen, but Dani backed out before Mae could spot her. She was on a mission, and she did not want even a brief conversation to derail her. She discovered her parents in the adjacent dining room. Her father was reading the newspaper, a cup of coffee in hand, while her mother spread jam on a biscuit. They both glanced up as she entered.

Dani stood at the opposite end of the table from her father, grasping the chair back with both hands.

"Join us for breakfast, dear—" her mother began.

"Why did you lie?" Dani demanded.

Cole neatly folded the newspaper before setting it down beside his plate. "You need to forget about what happened."

"Forget about it?" It felt as if a rock had become lodged in her gut.

"We've told everyone it was the storm," Jilly Anne said. "You can hold your head high—"

"I was raped," Dani spat. "Do you even understand that? I've been nearly comatose—"

Cole snickered. "Dani, don't get theatrical."

"Apparently, I have to because you don't understand. The police—"

"No, you don't understand," her mother said calmly. "We're leaving the police out of this."

Dani felt her jaw drop. "Why would you do that to me?"

Jilly Anne sighed. "Your father is one of the biggest defense lawyers in the state—"

"What does that have to do with anything?"

"I'm in the newspaper," Cole said. "Every week. Sometimes every day." He held up the newspaper as if offering proof.

Dani spotted his grainy, black-and-white picture above the fold but averted her attention back to her mother. "But I—"

"A story like this," Jilly Anne interjected, "would be picked up by every newspaper in the state. It would become a circus." She spread her hand in front of her face as if capturing a headline. "'Defense attorney's daughter assaulted'—how do you think that would play? There would be people who'd say he had it coming; the hens have come home to roost—"

"This isn't about Daddy. This isn't about either one of you. This is about me. I was the victim of a crime, not either of you."

"And I'll play this out for you," Cole said. His jaw was rigid as he spoke. As he set down the paper, the air grew tense. "You file a police report. Local reporters sift through them every day. This one's a juicy one. Maybe the man that attacked you is never identified— that would be the easy way out."

"But don't you—"

"Or," he continued, his voice rising, "he is identified. He's charged with the crime. Then someone like me defends him. His attorney will rip you to shreds on the witness stand."

"I didn't do anything!"

"Now, Dani," Jilly Anne said, tapping her red manicured nails on the table, "you must have done something to entice him."

"What?"

"I told you those short skirts of yours—"

"I don't care if I paraded myself naked through the streets—which I didn't. Nothing—*nothing*— justifies a man attacking me!"

"That's not what the newspapers will say," Jilly Anne answered coldly, one perfect brow rising. "You'll forever be known as a slut and a whore. This is a rural county filled with small towns—and small-town gossip. We have to live here, Dani. You have to live here. And you don't want to spend the rest of your life as 'that woman who claimed she was raped'—"

"Who are you people?" Before they could respond, she spun toward the door. She'd taken two angry steps away from them as her mother's voice rang in her ears.

"You'll understand someday, dear, and you'll thank us—"

Dani pushed the swinging door with a vengeance. She was across the threshold before she realized Mae had been standing just beyond the doorway. One look at the woman's face told her she'd heard everything. Dani brushed past her, taking the steps two at a time. Her hands were shaking as she zippered her luggage. When she turned around, Mae was at the door.

"Where do you intend on going, child?"

"Janie's house."

Mae stepped into the bedroom. "Give me those bags. I'll bring 'em down for you."

"Mae—"

"It ain't right, what they said to you. Just ain't right."

Dani only nodded her head. With nothing more to say, she grabbed her pocketbook and keys and started for the stairs. With any luck, she'd be out of there before her parents had left the table.

8

The tile floor was dingy and chipped. The baseboard was missing behind the toilet, revealing thick strokes of glue now black with grime. A cockroach lay in the corner, its legs up and paddling the air as it struggled to get off its back. The muddy Mississippi water that filled up the bowl looked like swamp water and stained the porcelain.

Dani leaned her forehead against her hands as she grasped the toilet seat, now propped against the sweating tank. Just outside the door, Jimmy Bob Carole shouted, "Where is that girl? Where the hell is my coffee?" She pictured his face ruddy and swollen as his blood pressure soared.

She painstakingly rose to her feet and stared back at the toilet as if it held answers for her. As the shouting increased, she moved to the sink and washed her hands and face. She caught a glimpse of her face in the mottled mirror. She looked wan and sickly.

She dried her hands on the material that swung from the towel dispenser, a grimy piece of coarse linen that appeared to be a permanent fixture as it dangled from the pitted metal. Then she took a deep breath, grabbed her notepad from the corner of the sink, and turned toward the door.

It was three o'clock in the afternoon, and she was still vomiting. It might have been a touch of the flu, she told herself, though she knew on an innate level that it was not. As she opened the door, the hot Mississippi sunlight blasted through the tall windows to catch her full in the face.

"Do I pay you to take bathroom breaks?" Jimmy Bob screamed, his voice rising in octaves. "Do I pay you to sit on your throne? Where's my coffee?"

Dani made her way to the metal table about six feet from the editor's elbow. The inside of the metal percolator was stained nearly black, its contents like oil. She poured it into a chipped mug and handed it to Jimmy Bob. "I have a news tip," she said, trying to force enthusiasm into her voice. "Out at Parchman Prison—"

"I don't give a rat's ass. You can't tell me anything I don't know. Besides, Parchman's been front-page news if you cared to read your own employer's paper."

She glanced at her notepad. "The spring azalea festival—"

"Tom is already on it."

"Mrs. Buckshire has nearly a hundred azaleas in her front yard, the pictures—"

"I said Tom is already on it." He drained the cup and handed it back to Dani. "More."

As she poured another cup, she tried to tamp down rising nausea. "The Magnolia Book Club is reading *Love Story* by Eric Wolf Segal—"

"Is he coming to Mississippi?"

"Who?"

"Segal," he barked.

"No, sir. But—"

"Then it isn't news." He pointed to the table. "Clean that up."

She turned back to the table. Tracks of sugar and powdered cream lay across the dark brown tabletop. A plastic spoon was draining coffee onto a balled-up napkin. "Yes, sir, but—"

"Cleaning rags are in the mop room, same as always. Then clean those windows. They're filthy."

Dani tucked her notepad into her dress belt as she headed toward the mop room. It was beside the bathroom, and she hesitated briefly, her eyes moving instinctively to the toilet. She'd forgotten to put the seat down. She stepped inside and gingerly closed it before peering at her reflection in the mirror again. It took every bit of effort she could muster to keep her from slamming the door behind her and going back down on her knees.

"And make more coffee!" Jimmy Bob yelled. "Somebody get me the dailies!"

"Yes, sir!" Tom's voice rang out.

She quietly exited the bathroom and ducked into the mop room. She found the rags bunched up on the metal storage rack. Grabbing one along with a bottle of cleaner, she hastily bolted out the door and almost collided with Tom.

Tom let out a surprised gasp and clutched his fistful of papers more tightly lest they sail through the newsroom. "Whoa there, Dani. Slow down."

She took a step back. As he moved past her, she followed. "Mrs. Buckshire has added the season's newest azaleas—"

"All azaleas are the same," he retorted as he strode toward the editor's office.

"Not these. They're hot pink—"

"Besides, her azaleas are a hundred years old."

"Yes, most of them are, but she added these—"

Tom stopped so suddenly, Dani almost ran into him. When he turned around, his face was close to hers. He was just short of gaunt, his cheekbones and jawline prominent as if there was insufficient flesh to cover them. Freckles sprinkled his aquiline nose. His hair was cut short and was nearly the color of a ripe carrot. His family consisted of proud Irish but for some strange reason, a saying popped into Dani's head: *Red on the head where the Viking tread.*

His voice was a hoarse whisper. "You really want to do something journalistic?"

She nodded.

"I need the point of view of a defense attorney. Your father could have practiced any type of law he wanted. Why did he choose to defend some of the state's most vicious offenders? Get me an interview, Dani." He smiled then, his lips tight together. "Get me the interview, and I'll show you how journalism works."

Before she could respond, he turned on his heels and continued to Jimmy Bob's office. As he stepped inside, Dani came up behind him. "This isn't for your ears," he whispered before closing the door in her face.

Dani turned around to face the newsroom. It seemed as if all eyes were upon her. There was a deadly silence as she took in the desks stacked with newspapers and notepads, Remington typewriters, and bulky black phones. Then the clacking of the keys began once more as everyone returned to their work.

Dani made her way to the table against the far wall. She began to clean it of the debris left by the others.

Her eyes wandered to the windows. They started about three feet from the floor and reached six feet up. Each was open in a vain attempt to let in the fresh air, but the room was still stifling, and the air was stubbornly stale. Above the tall windows were open transoms. The screens were aged with dubious pockmarks, the mesh torn, so they no longer protected the office against the myriad of flying insects searching for shade.

She'd need to pull the ladder out of the mop room, she thought. She pictured the bucket she'd need, the cleaning cloths, and the elbow grease required to make the glass halfway presentable.

Someday, she thought, she would not be getting coffee and cleaning windows in a newspaper office; she'd be writing the stories instead. She took a deep breath. But for now, her pay of a dollar and sixty cents an hour would help her get to college and get the journalism degree she craved. Then they would take her seriously.

As she moved toward the mop room, she wondered why Tom wanted to interview her father. It certainly wasn't a fluff piece; Tom didn't do those. She thought of the type of journalism she wanted to do. It could be painstakingly slow, with no one's story taken without question. Facts were checked, double-checked, and triple-checked with corroborating evidence. Though a story always had a slant, the true journalist sought out the opposing side's argument for a well-balanced, factual accounting.

Ah, she thought as she struggled with the ladder, that was it. Tom was writing about a crime victim.

~~~~~

A week later, Dani stood in the doorway to Janie's bedroom. Her best friend lay prone on her bed, one hand twiddling a pencil while the other turned the pages of a textbook. The window was open, and the sheers ballooned in the warm breeze. It was barely April; the early warmth appeared to herald a hot and humid summer. Yet, Dani felt disconnected from the scene of normalcy, as if her body had become suspended in a purgatory she did not deserve.

Janie glanced up and smiled as she noticed her friend, but her lips quickly turned downward. "What's wrong?"

Dani trudged across Janie's bedroom. She pulled a chair closer to the bed before she responded. Her eyes locked onto her friend's as she took a ragged breath. Her lips trembled, and her eyes filled with tears. "I'm pregnant."

The words hung in the air. Janie's expression morphed from one of astonishment to happiness to mortification. "I didn't know you and Rich—you've been holding out on me—" She added teasingly.

"We haven't."

"But, how—oh, no." She exhaled the last words as though she had just been notified of a death.

Dani began to sob. "What am I going to do?"

Janie sat up on the bed and tucked her legs under her. She reached for her friend's hands. Cupping them in her own, she asked, "Is it from the rape?"

Dani nodded. As the tears flowed, her head began to pound, and she felt dizzy and sick.

"I wondered where you were this afternoon; you skipped out of school."

"I saw Dr. Nash."

"He's not a gyno, is he?"

"No. I thought I still had effects from the assault. It never occurred to me..."

"And he said you're pregnant? For real?"

"Six weeks, he thinks."

"Oh, my God." She climbed off the bed and grabbed the calendar from the wall. "Your wedding is at the end of June. You'll have a baby bump."

Dani moaned.

"Have you told Rich?"

"Not yet. I told you first."

Janie carried the calendar back to the bed. "You'll be about four months pregnant when you get married. Then the baby should be due in November, right?"

"I guess. Dr. Nash didn't give me a due date." She emptied her bag until a wadded piece of paper fell out. "He gave me the name of an obstetrician."

"Have you made an appointment?"

"The receptionist at Dr. Nash's office made one for me." She groaned. "What am I going to do?"

"You can do what Mabelle did."

"Move away for a year? There are so many holes in that plan—"

"Name one."

"My wedding is halfway through the year."

"Okay—"

"And my mom would never go for it."

"That's two holes."

"She wouldn't dare leave her social clubs," Dani lamented. "I can't imagine her being gone until November—and then, for her to return with a child? No way. She'd never pass it off as her own. Plus—Janie, plus—I'm getting married in June!" She began to pace.

"Okay. Don't panic. Let's think this through. You're getting married. The baby will have a father. What if you move up the wedding?"

"It's always been June—everybody knows that."

"And who is 'everybody,' huh?" Without waiting for an answer, Janie continued, "See. Not everybody knows. Just your inner circle."

The door slid open a couple of inches, and Janie's brother Brandon popped his head inside. Dani quickly turned toward the window so he wouldn't see her tears, but not before she got a glimpse of his tousled dark brown hair and infectious smile. He was seventeen and Janie's twin, and because the three had been born on the same day, they used to joke that they were triples. As time had gone by, he grew taller and more muscular with broad shoulders, so he now appeared older. Brandon was on the football team. It was a running joke that more girls tried to get onto the cheerleading team since he started playing.

"We're busy, Bran," Janie said.

Undaunted, he asked, "Want to go shooting?"

"What are you shooting at?" Dani asked from the window.

"Clay pigeons. Going up on the ridge."

"Some other time, okay?" Janie said.

"Dani?" he asked.

"Some other time." She half-turned and forced a smile.

He hesitated as if unsure. "Everything okay?"

"Just dandy," Janie said.

"Just dandy," Dani repeated.

"If you're sure," he said, sounding unconvinced. "Close the door behind you, okay?"

After a moment, the door clicked shut, and Dani turned back around. She rubbed her stomach. It was still as flat as a pancake, but she poofed it out as though she could feel a baby bump. "It isn't Rich's child."

"He's a good guy, Dani. You know that. He'll raise it as his own."

"It's not the same… I was a virgin, Janie. I was saving myself for Rich." The tears welled up again. "Getting pregnant wasn't supposed to happen like this. We had our whole lives planned out." She sat back down and then abruptly stood and walked to the window again. She stared outside for a moment without really seeing the landscape before her. "Rich is going to work at my dad's law firm as soon as he graduates next month. He'll pass the bar exam, and then they'll add his name to the firm's name."

"He can still do that. A baby won't change those plans."

"I was going to Oxford. I've always wanted a degree in journalism. Jimmy Bob and Tom helped set up interviews with papers closer to the university. I was going to work at a newspaper while I worked on my degree."

"Your folks are on board with that?"

Dani smiled sardonically. "Of course not. They think I'm silly for considering a college degree. Rich is supposed to take care of me." She said the last part sarcastically, but the truth in her statement jarred her.

"But you're doing it anyway?"

"Of course, I am."

"So, you get a sitter."

"I hadn't planned on getting pregnant," she continued as though she hadn't heard her. She paced to the bed and then back to the window, finally ending up beside Janie again. "I wanted to start my career — Rich wanted to start his. If we had a child — and that was a big *If*—it wouldn't be for several years."

"So, you start a bit sooner than you expected."

Dani shook her head and returned to the window. "I don't know how I'm going to do it."

"Get a sitter," Janie repeated.

"With what money? We'll just be starting out."

"Your folks will help you."

"I bet they won't."

"Of course, they will. Their first grandchild? Of course, they will."

"You're talking about my parents, not yours; you realize that?"

Janie's face fell. "Of course they will," she said, though her voice lacked her earlier conviction.

"And what if they do? I can see it now. I'll get up early every morning, get a baby ready, then take her to the sitter and go to school myself. Then how do I study every evening, with a baby on my lap and a bottle in one hand?"

"You'll manage. You won't be the first woman to get pregnant before you've planned it, and you sure won't be the last."

Dani wiped her forehead with the back of her hand. Her skin was sticky. "My whole life was planned out. I wanted a child when I felt prepared to be a mother. I wanted to be better than my own."

"I know. But you know the adage about the best-laid plans…"

She turned around to face her friend. "What if the baby looks just like him?"

"Like — oh. No, it won't."

"How do you know?"

Janie shook her head. "Surely, God wouldn't —"

"Don't even talk of God to me," Dani lashed out. "Where was God when I was being raped?"

"The baby will be half yours. It will look like you. Or maybe it won't look like anybody. Maybe he — or she—will be a completely unique little human."

"And what if it isn't? What if it's a boy, and he's the spittin' image of his daddy?"

Janie sat on the edge of the bed and looked down at the calendar she still held. "You never told me what your assailant looked like."

Dani shrugged unconvincingly. "I don't remember much about him. I tried to block the memories, I guess." She sighed. "His eyes were in shadow. I remember that. They looked like they had no soul. And he had scars on his brow and lip like his face got in the way of a machete."

"When are you going to tell Rich?" Janie asked.

Dani turned back around. "I can't put it off," she groaned.

"Maybe you can. Maybe you can wait until you know for sure—"

"I know now. Besides, we'll have to move up the wedding date—way up. I can't say I had a baby four months early, and out he pops looking full term."

Janie returned the calendar to the corkboard.

"I'm going to Oxford to tell Rich."

"Now?"

"Now. I have to get this over with."

"Do you want me to go with you?"

Dani shook her head. "Best if I go alone."

Janie wrapped her arms around her friend. As she pulled her close, Dani felt a myriad of emotions. She felt even more damaged now than she had before, physically, emotionally, and spiritually. It took her a long time to claw her way back to life after the beating she'd taken. Now she would have a reminder of that night every time she looked at her child. She wanted to feel love for it, to feel happiness. But all she felt was sickness and dread.

"Okay," she said, pulling away from Janie, "I'll be back late."

"Are you sure you don't want me to ride with you?"

"Any other time, I'd say yes. You know that. But I need time alone. I need to think this through." With that, she grabbed her pocketbook and started toward the door. She caught a glimpse of her image in the dresser mirror. Her nose was red, her eyes watery, and her cheeks flushed. The disheveled appearance reflected how she felt inside—raw, miserable, and humiliated.

9

Oxford felt like the center of a wheel sometimes, as no less than eight highways converged upon it from all directions. Antebellum buildings filled the historic area, known as The Square, with some reminiscent of New Orleans' famed French Quarter with elaborate second-story wrought-iron balconies. Only the crowds were missing; even with the University of Mississippi resting on its doorstep, it was a sleepy town. The population was just under nine thousand, and tonight it appeared they were all indoors, the shops shuttered, and restaurants closed.

Once on the University of Mississippi's campus, she passed by a twenty-nine-foot Confederate soldier statue. It was no one in particular, unlike many Southern cities, that honored specific Civil War generals. It had been just over a hundred years since the war ended. The Centennial a few years back had been a big deal in the South. Dani remembered sitting on her father's shoulders to get an enviable view of the parade. Of course, the participants had long ago passed away. Still, there had been no shortage of reenactors in various uniforms, all flying the Mississippi state flag with its Confederate flag in the corner or the Confederate flag itself. She supposed she was out of step with most Mississippians; they'd lost the war and paid a heavy price for their insurrection. She'd never understood why they continued to honor the rebellion's leaders with near-worship fanaticism.

Ole Miss' Confederate statue depicted the average soldier—a smartly uniformed man with a thick mustache that appeared to be looking over a nonexistent battlefield. It had been erected in 1906 by the United Daughters of the Confederacy during the Jim Crow era. The height of the physical statue was one thing, but its long shadow something entirely different. It served as a reminder to the Negro population that the South had fought long and hard to maintain the status quo. The Civil War battles might have ended, but the war had not.

It had been nearly ten years since the race riot erupted over the first Negro student's admission, known by the locals as the Battle of Oxford. It had begun on the night of September 30, 1962, when a Black Air Force veteran named James Meredith had enrolled in the all-White school. When it was over, more than three hundred people were injured. Two died, including a French journalist covering the story. One-third of the 500-plus federal officers dispatched to accompany Meredith were injured. The standoff and animosity between the Mississippi Governor, Ross Barnett, and President John F. Kennedy and his brother, Attorney General Robert F. Kennedy, were legendary.

Of course, they had lost, despite scores of Mississippians that had driven through Black neighborhoods with speakers blasting "Dixie" and sporting bumper stickers that read "The South Shall Rise Again." Two years later, the Civil Rights Act of 1964 was signed into law by none other than a Southerner, Texan Lyndon B. Johnson. Scores of Dixiecrats fled to the Republican Party. The local newspapers reported President Johnson admitted losing the Democrats for a generation over the law's signing.

The Jim Crow era was officially over, but the undercurrent remained. Times could be challenging in the Deep South, and jobs scarce. The hierarchy ensured that Whites would get better-paying jobs, such as there were, and Blacks would be kept in their place at the bottom of the heap. Even now, in 1971, violence was apt to erupt in the space of a heartbeat, ending lives and changing others.

Tonight, the campus was deceptively calm and quiet, and Dani imagined a time in the distant future when people paid no more attention to the color of one's skin as to the color of their eyes. After all, she thought, having a particular eyeshade didn't make one more intelligent or wiser or more entitled to succeed. Neither did porcelain skin versus tanned or freckled. Then, wouldn't it stand to reason that skin color didn't, either? Race was always foremost in her thoughts when the South's history was on display, as it was now as she drove slowly down Rebel Drive, eventually stopping in front of one of the residence halls, a stately red brick and concrete structure.

The last time she had been there was at Rich's invitation. She took a ragged breath and shook the thoughts that had so far enabled her to escape from her predicament. Rich did not know she was coming this evening. She was tempted to turn around and head straight back to Janie's house, but the presence inside her belly felt overwhelming. She found a place to park and headed up the imposing front steps.

Before she'd reached the top step, she heard Rich calling her name. She turned to discover him coming up behind her.

"What are you doing here?" he asked as he drew near. He placed an arm around her shoulder. "Is everything alright?"

"Yes," Dani answered, the word escaping her before she'd had time to think. "Can we grab a fountain drink somewhere?"

~~~~~

The five and dime was nearly empty, despite being the only store open. Only a short, repurposed school bus sat out front, rainbow letters along the side proclaiming it was from The Little Acorn Orphanage. In contrast, another car sat along the side with a rusted undercarriage and a nearly flat front tire. Everything from BC Powder to CoverGirl foundation filled the musty aisles. In one corner, the cheeps of chicks filled the air. A woman with a severe bun perched at her nape made her way to the register, her veined hands clutching a polyester slip in one hand and a bunch of bananas in the other. Several children, perhaps four or five years old, lollygagged behind her with a caged guinea pig.

Dani found a table for two in the secluded front corner and settled into a red vinyl chair. There were bar stools at the counter and no other dining customers, but she wanted the wall to her back and plenty of privacy. She watched as Rich ordered two root beer floats. He smiled at her while he waited for the soda jerk to make them.

"You want anything else?" Rich called to her. "Burger or anything?"

The woman with the children whipped her head around, her brows furrowing as if he'd shouted in a library.

Dani shook her head. It was the third time he'd asked her. "No, but you go ahead if you're hungry," she said in defiance of the woman. She eyed the hushed children, their eyes like saucers as they stared at her.

"I ate already," Rich said.

The soda jerk handed him the floats in tall, curved glasses with red and white straws and shiny spoon handles sticking out of the top. Rich carried them to the table and settled in beside her, the tiny round surface now feeling dwarfed by the two drinks.

The bell tinkled as the group left the store, and Dani watched it dangle for a moment until both the door and the bell stilled once more. One of the children spoke, though Dani couldn't hear him, and the woman slapped him across his mouth. The smallest child, a little girl, hid her face behind her hands, her shoulders slumping.

"So, what's up?" Rich asked. His back was to the scene she'd been watching, and now he took a long drag on the straw.

Dani opened her mouth but then closed it.

"Something's not right," Rich said. "I can tell by the look on your face."

Her mouth dry, she took a few sips of her drink. The tartness of the root beer mingled with the sweet vanilla ice cream. She wished she could relax and forget all about her situation and simply enjoy Rich's company.

"Out with it," he said.

"It's been six weeks..." she began tentatively.

"Six weeks," he repeated. His brow creased. "Oh, since... You should try to forget that, Dani. Don't count the weeks."

"I haven't been." She leaned forward and concentrated on her drink. "The doctor reminded me this morning."

"Dr. Nash?"

She nodded.

"Everything okay? You're healing up?"

"Not for another seven months or so." He was silent, and Dani glanced up to find him watching her curiously. "I'm pregnant, Rich."

Stunned, he leaned back in his seat and placed his hands in his lap. "You're what?"

"We can move up the wedding; the sooner, the better. That way, when the baby is born, everyone will simply assume it's yours. And there's no need for anybody to think any different. I'll just—"

"You're what?" he repeated. His voice was louder, and the soda jerk glanced in their direction.

She swallowed. She waited for Rich to say something else, but he only stared at her. His face was pale, and his blue eyes had darkened. "I'm pregnant," she said in a voice that was barely more than a hoarse whisper.

"How is that even possible?" He looked away from her, his eyes roaming until he found a spot on the floor that seemed to hold his attention.

"I've never cheated on you, Rich," she said quietly.

After a long moment, he half-nodded.

"You do believe me, don't you? I swear I was saving myself for you..."

He closed his eyes momentarily. When they reopened, he resumed staring at the floor.

The silence was deafening. Dani wanted to fill it, to keep the noiselessness at bay. "If we wait until the end of June like we'd planned, I'm likely to be showing, and then folks would think you and me, before we were married..."

He slowly rolled his eyes from the floor to her face.

"So, I was thinking; we could speed everything up and have a ceremony in the next couple of weeks. Mama might be upset that it's not all glitz and glamour, but—"

"I'll be in class, Dani." His voice was flat.

"Well, we'll just choose a time when you aren't in class. It can't be that difficult, can it?" She tried to chuckle, but it came out sounding like a strained cough.

"We weren't going to get married until I'd graduated. Until I'd started my new job."

Dani tried to take another sip of her drink just to wet her throat, but she was so nervous that she stopped drawing on the straw before the liquid reached her lips. "I know, but—"

"We planned everything out, Dani."

"I know, but—" She took a deep breath. "Sometimes, things don't go as planned."

"You just assumed I'd want another man's baby?" He was staring at her now, his expression incredulous.

"It's—it's not like I—I cheated on you. I was attacked—"

"And this guy that attacked you, he looked just like me?"

"Of course not. What does that have to do with anything?"

"Look at us, Dani. Look at us."

She stared back at him, but her brain was beginning to feel as if a fog had rolled in. Rich looked at her as though she should have understood his meaning, but he may as well have been speaking a different language.

He leaned in. "Blond hair, blue eyes—the both of us. Do you remember describing this guy to me?"

"I don't remember what he looked like," Dani said haltingly. "All I clearly remember are the scars."

"My words aren't registering with you." He paused before continuing, "Brown eyes trump blue. Brown hair trumps blond."

She felt the blood drain from her face. "So, you're afraid the baby won't look like either of us."

"I'm saying there's every possibility it won't. It isn't rocket science."

"But, you're assuming my attacker had brown eyes, brown hair. He might not have. I don't remember."

"Figure the odds he looked just like me."

The store felt deathly silent. Dani could feel the soda jerk's eyes on her, but when she turned around, he was nowhere in sight. The register clerk was watching them, her arms crossed as she leaned her back against the counter.

"It isn't like I want to have it," she said finally. "I'm a victim in this."

"Well, so am I, Dani. So am I."

She stared at him.

"My life is planned out, Dani. I'm going to be a defense attorney—"

"You can still—"

"And my reputation as it stands today is spotless."

"It's—"

"And I intend to keep it that way."

He leaned back in his chair, and she leaned back in hers. This wasn't how she'd planned for the conversation to go, and she wished she could start over.

His eyes moved from her to the store as if he was taking it all in. Another employee, an older boy perhaps close to high school age, began sweeping the aisles.

"What are you saying?" Dani asked when the silence between them had grown too oppressive.

Rich sighed. He looked around the store once more before turning his attention back to Dani. "I'm saying that if you have this child, I can't marry you."

His words fell on her like a ton of bricks. Her chest constricted, and she struggled to breathe.

He wrapped one hand around the base of his float but did not attempt to drink it. After a moment, his hand dropped back into his lap as he looked away from her.

When she spoke, her voice was barely more than a strained whisper. "What are you suggesting I do?"

He shook his head. "I don't know what a woman does in these circumstances."

"But—I don't understand."

"It isn't my baby, Dani. It's yours."

"It isn't—"

"It *is*. It's yours and—*his*."

"But—but, you know the circumstances. You know I didn't willingly—"

"I don't know what happened, Dani. I wasn't there."

Her jaw dropped. "Are you insinuating—?"

"No. I'm not. Look, I know you were badly beaten. I know you might've died. And I know you want to put this behind you. But, damn it, don't you understand this baby is part you and part him? And I want nothing to do with it."

"Rich." Her lower lip trembled. "We've been together since I was thirteen."

"I know." His finger brushed his eye in a sudden movement, but he kept his eyes downcast, so she wasn't sure if it had been a tear.

"I thought I would always be with you," she said lamely.

"Well, you have a decision to make then, don't you? You can have this—" his hand waved in her direction "—this baby, his baby. Or you can marry me."

"But, you're saying that I can't have both."

"We can put this thing behind us, and we can move on. We'll keep our wedding in June, just like we planned it. I've already got an apartment rental lined up; you know that. I'll be at my new job, and you can pursue your hobby in journalism…" His voice faded, or maybe he'd continued speaking, and she simply couldn't hear him any longer. After a moment, he stood. "Listen. I've got to get back."

She stood, too. "I'll drive you."

"I'll walk."

"It's a couple of miles—"

"I want to walk." He scooted the chair toward the table. The chrome legs made a screeching sound against the black and white tile. Both their drinks were nearly untouched. She didn't know why, but the scene felt emblazoned upon her psyche. She knew she would remember this dingy five and dime with the vinyl seats and chrome tables, the mingling scents of fried burgers and live chicks, and every word Rich had spoken to her there.

Dani followed him through the store. He held the door for her as the bell tinkled, but he didn't look at her. They strolled toward her car. He opened the door. She hesitated as she began to get in, but he did not attempt to kiss her. He was staring in the direction of the university.

"Listen, Dani. Let me know what you decide, okay?" His voice sounded strained and distant.

She nodded.

"Be careful going home," he began, and then he stopped himself. Without another word, he began to walk.

Dani watched him until the gloom of the evening had surrounded him, and he became no more than a shadow dancing among all the other shadows.

10

The sun bathed Vicksburg National Cemetery in an orange glow as it rose above the distant horizon. Dani sat near the top of the hill, her chin resting on her knees. It had been a long night, and as the day broke, she knew a long and challenging day awaited her.

After she'd left Oxford, she'd driven aimlessly through rural Mississippi, eventually heading south to Vicksburg. Several times along her route, the moon was visible through thinning clouds. Full and pale, it was so large, she could see the variations in its landscape as though she was looking at continents and mountain ranges. Eventually, she'd arrived at the Vicksburg National Military Park, where she'd made her way around its dizzying hills dotted with Civil War monuments and plaques until she'd stopped at the cemetery nestled above the Mississippi River.

She'd spent a good portion of the night staring at the moon and then the rows of grave markers that stretched between her perch and the river. The white stones shone eerily in the moonlight while the shadows of ancient trees danced among them.

Each one of the men that fought and died on this vast battlefield had plans, she thought. They had been boys once; they'd gone to school or worked on a family farm or performed chores around their home. Each might have fallen in love and possibly married or had plans to; many of them might have fathered children that were waiting for them to return from the war. All had mothers and fathers, maybe sisters or brothers, and certainly a friend or acquaintance or two.

Owls occasionally hooted through the night as Dani bundled herself against the chill. In the shadows that formed and pirouetted among the stones, she saw a young man teaching in a one-room schoolhouse or stocking shelves in a general store. She saw them readying for university, as she should have been doing, or preparing to graduate as Rich was.

Some of the men that died on these heights had traveled mere hours from home, while others had traveled hundreds of miles from places she would never see. With each forced march, they journeyed further from their hopes and plans. Each footstep carried them closer to destinies that would cut short many of their dreams for the future.

She could not imagine that any of them had planned to fight a war. Sure, there were career soldiers among them, but the percentage of those compared to the number involved was very low. In any event, those that had made the military their career had most likely envisioned protecting their country from foreign invasion. They certainly could not have imagined fighting their fellow man. Yet, she supposed, those who joined the Confederacy ranks probably did believe they were fighting a foreign invasion.

And here they'd fought, and here they'd fallen. Some battles would pit brother against brother and friend against friend. And here, they found their dreams shattered, their lives derailed—if they were lucky enough to have survived.

The experiences must have forever altered those that managed to survive Vicksburg and the Civil War. To this day, those four years still haunted the South. Often, the ghosts of those that fought seemed alive once more. Yet, at other times, the war served as the inspiration to fight again. Some that fought on these hallowed grounds would carry physical reminders; perhaps they'd suffered the loss of a leg or arm and became a burden to the families they'd vowed to protect and support. Others would have appeared normal, their scars hidden deep within their psyches. She wondered how they'd managed to move forward in life after the horrors of war formed the most unforgettable memories they would ever have encountered.

Perhaps, she thought, there wasn't a person that existed then or now whose life had unfolded according to plan. How naïve she and Rich had been just two months ago. One night had altered her psyche, perhaps in the way a soldier meets battle that very first time. Up close and personal, seeing the whites of their eyes and their facial expressions, absorbing the stench of unwashed bodies or gunpowder, could leave an imprint that altered their souls.

The river was turning orange now as the sun rose higher. An intricate mosaic of spider webs in the manicured grass was made more visible by the morning dew. The air felt still and calm, broken only by chickadees' morning songs and warblers stirred from sleep.

Dani placed a hand on her belly. How innocent and gullible she'd been, thinking she could marry Rich, have a rapist's child, and move on to live the perfect little life.

The child was innocent, of course. Even if he or she was born blond-haired and blue-eyed, Dani might still remember the most horrific night of her existence every time she looked their way. But if Rich was right and dark hair and eyes were predominant, the child might look just like the father. What would she feel then, looking into those soulless eyes and seeing not the child she'd birthed but her attacker instead?

She shook her head as if to rid it of evil thoughts. The child was innocent, Dani reminded herself. Their outward appearance didn't matter.

Only it did. It did matter in a way that only the Deep South understood. It mattered when an individual's skin didn't reflect British or Scottish roots or when their eye color wasn't the traditional hazel, green, or blue. It even mattered when the last name was Italian, Irish, or German. There was plenty of hatred to go around. It had never stopped with non-Christians, Asians, or Blacks but gained an ever-widening circle.

As the sun burned away the mists of night, she struggled through her mind's fog. She tried to imagine how she would move forward in the coming year. Rich could not have been more clear; if she had the child, he would not marry her. That would leave her a single mother.

Mississippi was a network of small towns. As one moved from one to another, their reputation often seemed to precede them. There was always someone that knew someone else from the place left behind. Imagining her life without Rich caused her throat and chest to constrict. Dani was angry with him for not standing by her and heartbroken that he'd given up on her so readily. The emotions warred within herself until she felt sickened by it all. Rich had been her future, *their* future. Without him, it was as if a tornado had picked up all she'd known and destroyed it. Without Rich, she would have to start from the beginning and build a different life. Right now, she couldn't imagine being happy or content. She had difficulty imagining anything at all.

Dani sighed. She considered returning home. The big house held unspeakable memories of that night, memories that eclipsed any positive ones. But perhaps her parents could build a cottage similar to Grandma Dottie's house. She could raise her child there.

It wasn't what she wanted, her mind argued. She wanted to be a journalist. She wanted to write newspaper and magazine articles. She wanted to write books like Truman Capote's *In Cold Blood*. She didn't want to live her life on a farm that was miles from anywhere.

They'd talked of going north, she and Rich. He had planned to work for her father first, building his reputation throughout the state. Then they might move to a big city. There were many to choose from, like Memphis, Nashville, St Louis, and Chicago. She could envision her career in any of those places or even further away—maybe even New York City. She sucked in her breath. New York would be the perfect place for her to pursue journalism. She might, if she worked hard and established a stellar reputation, even someday work for

The New York Times. Wow. That would be the pinnacle of success.

But, her mind argued, those plans had all been made long before her attack. What could she accomplish now? If she imagined, painful as it might be, a future without Rich, she couldn't fathom how she would manage to have a career and raise a child by herself. Moving would be out of the question. Her life would be spent in the Mississippi Delta, and doing what? If she was truly fortunate, she would get through college and find a job as a reporter at one of the small papers that dotted the state. *The Delta Democrat Times* was the big paper in the region; maybe, if she was lucky…

She groaned as she reluctantly rose. Her muscles ached from driving and then sitting on the ground in a hunched position. She hadn't slept, but strangely, she wasn't sleepy. She was only tired. Bone tired. Her head was pounding.

She watched a tugboat pushing a barge up the Mississippi. That's what she needed in her life: normalcy. But right now, that appeared to be out of the question.

How would she explain her child? It wouldn't be the product of a loving, committed relationship. As Rich had pointed out, there might be no doubt it wasn't his. She'd yearn to explain to everyone that she hadn't cheated on Rich, but that would mean reliving the rape time and time again. Would everyone she'd known her whole life suddenly turn on her, accusing her of being a whore and a slut, as her mother had claimed?

Her stomach constricted as she realized she hadn't yet told her parents. If they had been so opposed to publicity after her rape, what would they possibly think of their daughter's growing belly?

And what of the child? He—or she—would grow up with a cloud over their head. Schoolchildren could be monsters; they would call him a bastard and worse. There would be rumors following him throughout his life.

Maybe she should move. She could concoct a story about the child's father; perhaps they were married, and he was killed in a tragic accident. But could she give the child a normal life? What if the child was a boy, and he grew up looking exactly like his father?

She burst into tears. She thought she had been placing the attack behind her. Now she realized it was growing inside her.

11

Dani found her parents in the kitchen shortly after she'd arrived home. The aroma of cooking led her to the rear of the house, where she discovered Mae at the stove. Grandma Dottie was there as well. She wore a thin pink shift and thick, furry slippers as she poked her head into the refrigerator. Dottie's hair was cut short and permed, but now as Dani spotted her, she saw a lone pink foam curler randomly clinging to the back of her head.

Dani took one glance at her father as he poured a glass of sweet tea. He wore brown and blue plaid slacks and a lightweight blue argyle sweater over a casual shirt. "What are you doing home?" she asked.

"It's Saturday," Cole replied. "I just played possibly the best game of golf ever."

"He's been telling me all about it," Jilly Anne said with a roll of the eyes.

"You wanting some lunch?" Mae asked, slightly turning to reveal a spatula in her hand. "I'm cooking up your favorite—fried banana and peanut butter sandwich."

Any other time, Dani would have jumped at the offer, but her stomach was turning somersaults inside her. She shook her head. "Just tea." She retrieved a glass from the cabinet and handed it to her father, who poured the glass nearly full.

"There's some fresh mint I brought over," Grandma Dottie said, gesturing to a pile of unwashed crabgrass on the kitchen counter.

"Thanks, Grandma," Dani said, casting a sideways glance at her father. "I think I'll pass on the mint this time."

"Janie's mama called," Jilly Anne said. "Said you weren't at their place last night; she was checking to see if you were here."

Dani added a few more ice cubes to her tea and swished it around.

"Well, where were you?" Jilly Anne demanded, her voice growing shrill.

"I need to talk to you and Daddy," Dani said, taking a sip. It was cold and refreshing as it traveled down her parched throat.

"Well, talk," Cole said.

"Make it fast. I'm getting my hair done this afternoon." Jilly Anne patted her blond hair, which appeared precisely in place. A rumor once circulated that a tornado uprooted trees and tossed cars like toys, but every hair on Jilly Anne Evans' head had remained in place.

"This'll be up in a jiffy," Mae said. "Y'all go on into the dining room, and I'll bring it to you."

"Well, hurry it up," Jilly Anne said. "Don't make me late for my appointment."

"No, ma'am."

~~~~~

They settled into the tall, cane-backed chairs. It felt odd sitting there; the energy had changed somehow for Dani. The heavy drapes with their golden pineapple pattern were pulled back and tied neatly, allowing the sunshine to find its way into the room. The distinctive scent of old furniture and worn hardwood floors mingled with the fading aroma of breakfast sausage and bacon.

Their places were set as they always were, the padded vinyl placemats arranged for four, though she couldn't remember the last time she'd eaten there. She put her iced tea glass at the edge of the mat and slid her chair back. She watched as Grandma Dottie came down the hall, entering the room across the foyer, only to cry out that someone had moved the dining table before Jilly Anne took her by the elbow and led her to the correct room.

Grandma Dottie hadn't quite settled in before Jilly Anne spoke.

"Well, where were you?"

"I was with Rich," Dani said. She looked from her mother to her father and back again.

Jilly Anne shook the packet of sugar before adding it to her already-sweetened tea. "All night?"

"Part of the night. Then I went on a long drive."

"You shouldn't be gone like that, Dani. People are going to talk, and then you'll get a reputation."

"Mama, nobody cares where I was."

"Don't talk to your mother like that," Cole said, but his voice was weary, and he checked his watch as though he had someplace to go.

"I have something to tell you," Dani said.

"You're repeating yourself," Jilly Anne said, examining her manicure.

"Mama, you're not making this easy for me." She looked from one to the other. "Mama, Daddy. I'm pregnant."

Cole's head jerked up, and his eyes widened.

"Lord have mercy," Jilly Anne said. "And both you and Rich promised."

Dani vaguely remembered her mother urging them both to promise not to have sex until they were married. She seemed to recall making the promise simply to stop her from continually bringing it up. "It isn't Rich's."

Grandma Dottie huffed and puffed as she wiggled in her chair. "My butt hurts."

"Lord have mercy," Jilly Anne repeated. "I never took you for a slut—"

"It's the rapist's." The words hung in the air. Dani placed her hands in her lap in a vain attempt to keep them from trembling. After a long moment of stunned silence, she looked at her father. He was staring at her. His face was flushed and his eyes wide, but she could not read more into his expression, so she was left wondering if he blamed her for this predicament. She didn't want to look at her mother, but as the seconds ticked by on the noisy grandfather clock in the hallway, she forced herself to meet her mother's eyes. Her expression was one of sheer horror, her hand on her heart as if Dracula had just appeared at their table.

"It's God's way," Grandma Dottie said, wiggling herself into a proper position.

"God's way of *what?*" Jilly Anne asked.

"Punishing you," Dottie said, her eyes locking onto Dani's.

"*For what?*" It was Dani's turn to ask incredulously.

"You must have done something to lead him on," Dottie said.

"To lead on a rapist?"

"Ain't no such thing as rape," Dottie retorted.

Mae entered the room with a large tray of sandwiches, her eyes widening before she averted her gaze.

"A woman entices a man, and he's got no control but to follow through," Dottie continued, her voice taking on the tenor of an old-time gospel minister. "He wouldn't have done the act if you hadn't encouraged it."

Mae met Dani's eyes from across the table. A moment later, she slipped a plate in front of Dani. Despite declining lunch, Mae had made it anyway. She opened her mouth slightly as if to say something but clamped her teeth down on her lip instead.

"I did nothing to encourage him," Dani said. "I'd never seen him before that night."

"Only takes one night..." Dottie said. She waggled her finger. "It's up to the woman to keep her legs together."

"Apparently," Cole said.

"How do you know it's his?" Jilly Anne asked.

"Because it's the only time I've ever had intercourse."

"No need to curse, young lady."

"I wasn't cursing."

Jilly Anne took a deep breath. She stared at her plate for a moment, as they all appeared to be doing.

The ice in the tea pitcher tinkled as Mae worked silently at the buffet table. "Well," Jilly Anne said. "We'll just move up the wedding."

"Rich won't marry me if I'm pregnant."

Cole unfurled his cloth napkin with a flourish. "Don't you worry about that. I'll have a word with him."

"I don't want you to, Daddy. We talked last night, and…"

"You talked. But he hasn't talked to me yet."

"And what would you say, Daddy? That if he doesn't marry me, his future at your law firm is toast?"

"It's a package deal."

"What kind of deal is that?" Dani asked. "He gets a meteoric career if he marries me? Where is love in that?"

"If he truly loved you, he'd marry you," Jilly Anne said.

"Love ain't got nothing to do with marriage," Dottie sniffed. "It's survival, pure and simple. You think I loved my husband? Not for one day—"

"He'll learn to love you," Cole interjected, his voice strained, "if he doesn't love you now."

"I don't want somebody to marry me if they don't love me."

"Love ain't got nothing to do—" Dottie said louder.

"Everybody, listen to me," Dani said, her voice edgy. Mae was cutting slices of cake at the buffet and seemed to take forever doing it. "Listen, and don't you dare interrupt." She glared at Grandma Dottie. "Rich had some good points."

Jilly Anne chuckled wryly.

"He did," Dani insisted. "He pointed out that this baby might not look like either one of us. It could be obvious it isn't his."

"You don't know that," Cole said.

"He knows it isn't his. And he doesn't want to raise another man's child—regardless of how it came to be."

"You should never have told him," Jilly Anne said. "You should have come to us first. We could have found some reason to move up the wedding—"

"And pretend the baby is his?"

Jilly Anne chewed on the inside of her mouth.

"He has a right to know," Dani continued. "I thought he would marry me anyway, knowing—" she stared at Dottie "—that it was not consensual." She took a breath. "I thought the same as you, Mama. I wanted to move up the wedding date and pretend the baby was premature. He didn't want to do it." She turned to her father. "He said he's planned out his life, and raising a baby—another man's child—just isn't in the equation."

Jilly Anne's jaw dropped. "What's the alternative?"

Dani shrugged. "Have the baby without him."

"Our lives will be ruined!" Jilly Anne exclaimed, pushing her chair further from the table.

Dani took a moment to look around the table. Only Dottie had begun to eat; everyone else's plates were untouched. "*Your* life won't be ruined, Mama."

"It most certainly will be. Why, your daddy has spent decades working on his career, on his reputation. You'll destroy it with one—" she waved her hand toward Dani's body "—baby bump! And what of me? All my friends have been invited—"

"We haven't sent out the invitations yet, Mama."

"Well, they know they're coming to a wedding. Everybody knows. And now, there won't be a wedding, and it will be because Rich called it off, and he called it off because you're pregnant with somebody else's baby—"

"It's not just 'somebody else's' baby! It's a rapist's child!"

"Stop." Cole's voice rang out authoritatively as though he was in a noisy courtroom. All eyes turned to him. "There is another alternative." He paused as everyone exhaled except Dottie, who was busy eating her sandwich. "Abortion is legal in Mississippi if you can prove it's rape."

"Ain't no abortion happening in this family," Dottie said, spitting out some of her food.

"Just hear me out. If you have the baby, Dani, your life will never be the same. Maybe Rich won't marry you, and you'd be left to raise a child on your own. God help you because no decent man will have you if you've had a child outside of wedlock." As the table began to buzz, he held up his hand for silence. "Or maybe he will reconsider and marry you, and perhaps you can pass the child off as a proper mother and father. Or maybe Rich is right, and it won't look like either one of you. You can claim the child is adopted, or… The point is, having a baby you didn't want and didn't plan for is going to change your life in ways you can't even imagine. Not to mention the hardship on that child. Life is tough enough."

"Nobody has mentioned loving it," Dani said, her voice soft. She placed her hand on her belly, silently apologizing to it if it heard or understood their words.

"If you think you have love in your heart for it, then have it," Cole said. He looked pointedly at Jilly Anne. "And we'll find a way through this." Before anyone could respond, he continued. "But if you don't want the child—and it's clear that Rich does not—end the pregnancy."

Jilly Anne sucked in her breath. "She should have it—and put it up for adoption!"

"Do you know how many children are waiting to be adopted?" Cole asked. "Do you know how many move through revolving doors, waiting for somebody to accept them, to love them? Foster homes and institutions are not the gay, loving places right out of The Wonderful World of Disney. They're harsh. They can be cruel."

"I saw a foster child slapped across his mouth just for trying to talk," Dani said. Her voice was sad as she recalled the children in Oxford. "I can't in good conscience send a child into an abusive environment."

Cole's eyes became dejected as he turned to Dani. He waited a long moment before he spoke. "You can decide to continue your life just as you and Rich planned. This can be nothing more than a bump in the road."

"But how—?"

"You would need to go before a judge. You'd need to explain the situation to him and prove you were raped."

"Wait. What?" Dani felt the heat rising into her cheeks. "You want me to go to a stranger—someone I have never seen before and will most likely never see again—and ask his permission to have an abortion?"

"That's the way it works."

"I'd explain to a strange man the most intimate details of how I got pregnant? And he would decide whether or not he believed me?"

Cole nodded.

"You're kidding, right?"

"It's the only way if you want an abortion."

"But, Cole—," Jilly Anne interrupted.

"And what is this proof you talked about?" Dani continued, her voice rising. She barely noticed Mae placing dessert plates on each placemat. "How do I prove it was rape?"

Cole shook his head.

"You didn't call the police, Daddy. Nobody did."

"But, Cole," Jilly Anne interjected again. "If she goes to court, isn't it public record?"

"It is."

"And haven't you told me that's how the newspapers get some of their stories?"

Cole looked away from them as if something outside the window had grasped his attention. "It wasn't a good idea," he said. "Forget I said anything."

"Forget it because your daughter would have to beg a stranger to grant permission for one of the most personal decisions she'll ever make? Or forget it because it might bring shame down on you and Mama?" Without waiting for an answer, Dani stood.

"So, here's what my choices sound like to me," she continued. "Behind Door Number One, you can try to talk Rich into marrying me, even if he doesn't love me. We can all lie to ourselves and the community for this child's entire life. With Door Number Two, I could have an abortion instead, which might sully your precious reputations if it became public—not to mention if the judge decided he *didn't* believe me. And with Door Number Three, I could give birth and put the child into the foster system—"

"Not here, you won't," Jilly Anne interrupted. "You have that child out of wedlock, and you're going out of state to do it."

"And how am I going to do that?"

"We'll get you an apartment somewhere, someplace you'll never go again. Give the child to an adoption agency there, and then come back home."

"And tell your friends what?" Dani demanded sarcastically.

"You wanted to go away to college anyway—"

"—Something you never wanted me to do!"

"Well, you won't be going." Jilly Anne stirred her iced tea, the spoon banging noisily against the glass.

"I want to go to Ole Miss," Dani retorted. "That's not exactly out of state. And what would your friends think if it took me five years instead of four to graduate?"

Jilly Anne tossed down her table napkin. "You have ruined my day again," she said. "I am late for my hair appointment, and you've put me in a foul mood. Take care of this—" she waved her hand in the direction of Dani's stomach "—problem." With that, she stormed out of the room.

Mae quietly removed the plates from Jilly Anne's setting and placed them on the buffet.

"That will be all," Cole said as if realizing for the first time that Mae had joined them in the room.

"Yes, sir."

As Mae's footsteps faded down the hallway, Dani fought back the tears. "I trusted you," she said to her father. "I trusted you to take care of me." Without waiting for his reply, she left the room and hurried out the front door. As she crossed the front lawn, Jilly Anne's Mercedes was throwing up gravel as she departed down the country road. Dani climbed into her Spitfire and sped off in the opposite direction.

12

Janie pulled into a business' empty parking lot near the edge of town. She kept the car running while she and Dani surveyed their surroundings. The tape player was playing Three Dog Night's "One is the Loneliest Number," making Dani want to cry. She turned it off with an abrupt flourish.

The business belonged to a bail bondsman; the bullet-ridden sign mounted on a post swaying in a humid breeze. It had long since closed for the day as the cloak of nightfall settled upon them. Darkening clouds partially obscured the moon, heralding the possibility of a storm.

The business faced the main road, but it was the side street that captured their attention. It consisted of a row of dilapidated bungalows that each appeared no more extensive than the Evans' living room. Despite the murky light, Dani could make out tiny porches that held up ramshackle roofs. The houses faced a railroad track, and on the other side were identical houses facing back. Behind them was an alley barely illuminated at the far end by a dim yellow streetlight.

"This is it," Janie said, nervously looking at a piece of paper filled with penciled scribbles. "The third house. Use the alley."

"Are you sure?" Dani asked. She leaned forward to peer out the windshield.

Janie swallowed. "I'm pretty sure. Loretta said she was here just last week. Said it takes five minutes flat, and then you're out. You're to ask for Marabelle. Do you want me to come with you?"

Dani swallowed. "No."

"I can hold your hand."

"No. I don't want you to have that memory of me." She glanced around. "Are you sure you'll be safe here?"

"I'll lock the doors."

"Promise you'll wait for me?"

"I won't leave you. I promise."

Dani placed her hand on the door latch. "Okay. Hopefully, this is as quick as Loretta says."

"I'll be here no matter how long you are."

Her mouth was dry as she opened the door. She'd no sooner climbed out and heard the door click shut behind her when the loud pop of the locks engaged. The sound reverberated in the quiet neighborhood, making her feel more vulnerable and exposed now that she was on her own.

The parking lot was paved and even, but once she reached the end of it, she felt she was stepping into another world. The pockmarked ground was unkempt. Weeds and cockleburs fought for dominance, the prickly branches reaching for her ankles, cutting into her as she made her way to the alley.

Once there, she realized the shadows had grown long and heavy. A glance upward told her the reason for the darkness; all the street lights were out except the one at the far end, the broken bulbs littering the alley. She picked her way along despite the fact she could no longer see where she was going. She repeatedly stumbled as the Mississippi clay gave way beneath her, sometimes threatening to swallow a shoe before she managed to recover and pull her foot to slightly higher ground.

Noxious odors assaulted her, the gleam of battered white porcelain bowls hiding bathroom contents within them, tucked against back steps or decaying clapboard. The houses sat close together with barely enough room for two people to walk between them. Somewhere in the distance, a dog barked, and another answered.

She reached the third bungalow. She hesitated as she surveyed it. From the safety of Janie's car, it had appeared that each was one story, but now she realized each house had a second floor, perhaps no more significant than an attic space. There was a minuscule window near the eaves, a weak yellow light flickering inside as if fighting to remain alive. Obscure shadows hugged the lower level, even though a door at the top of uneven steps was open, a screen door with the screen ripped away from one corner banging as it swayed in the night air. As she remained there, a shadow crossed in front of the door.

"Don't just stand there," a woman's reedy voice called out. "We're wasting time. You want to get this over with, don't you?"

Dani stumbled up the steps and opened the door. "Are you—?"

"Two hundred dollars. Did you bring it?"

Her hand shaking, she dipped into her pocket and pulled out the money. It had taken months to save it from her job at the newspaper, and she had always intended it to go toward her college education.

As the woman counted it, Dani took in the tiny room. She was standing in a kitchen, but it was unlike any she'd ever seen. A derelict counter was against one wall, stubbornly pulling away from the drywall. The only light came from a tiny fireplace. On the hearth sat a cast iron pot containing a soupy mixture of beans, potato, and fat. Her stomach had been delicate over these past few days, and she fought back a wave of nausea.

Turning back to the rest of the room, she realized there was no sink but a washbasin filled with water, alongside a few linen cloths of questionable cleanliness. Beside those was a jumble of half-opened food containers amid buzzing flies and insects.

The woman motioned toward a kitchen table. "Take off them panties, pull up that shirt higher than your ass, and lay yourself down there."

"On the table?"

"On the table," the woman answered rudely, shaking her head at Dani's ignorance.

Dani stepped toward the furniture. It was barely large enough for two dinner plates, and she wondered how it could possibly support her weight. A ragged towel hid the surface from view.

As if reading her mind, the woman said, "Sit up there. Then scooch your tail to the edge. I'll be sitting in that chair there, and you can rest your feet on the chair back, either side of my head."

As Dani began to pull off her slacks and panties, she watched the woman approach the fireplace. Beside the fire rested half a dozen charred coat hangers, the spiral fastening pulled apart, so the hangers appeared haphazardly straightened. She took one and held it over the fire until it began to glow.

"How are you going to do this?" Dani asked nervously, holding her clothing in front of her.

"You don't want to know."

She swallowed, although her throat felt parched. It was sweltering in the tiny room. The night was dank and hot, too hot for a fire. She wiped the perspiration from her forehead. "But I do want to know."

"Climb up there. I ain't got all night. Gots me another one after you."

Dani dutifully climbed onto the rickety table. "I do want to know. It's my body, and I want to know what's going to happen with it."

The woman retrieved a metal funnel, much like one Mae used in the kitchen. She placed her hand on her hip. "It's your first time, ain't it?"

"Yes."

"Alright." She stood in front of the fire, a mere two feet from the table. "This here is gonna open that thing up," she said, holding up the funnel in one hand and the coat hanger in the other. "Then I'm gonna poke this here into it. You'll feel a tiny sting, not as much as a bee sting. You'll feel your water gush, and it'll be over."

Dani stared at the funnel and coat hanger. "But how—?"

"You'll miscarry, most likely sometime tonight. The baby ain't gonna grow without the water."

Her eyes traveled upward to the woman. She was thin as a rail, her cheeks prominent under a head rag. Her eyes were sunken, her lips chapped.

"Ain't nothing more than a blood clot," the woman said. "I reckon you've had worse monthlies."

Dani slid off the table. Her knees gave way beneath her, but before the woman could react, she'd caught herself with the edge of the table, nearly toppling it. "I can't do this."

"You ain't getting no money back!"

"Keep it." She hastily pulled on her slacks. They were up to her waist before she realized she still held her panties in her hand.

"You change your mind and want to come back, and it'll be another two hundred," the woman hissed.

"Fine."

As she hurled herself toward the door and stumbled down the steps, the woman's voice filled her ears. "You'll be back!" she called. "They always come back. Ain't no other place for you to go!"

~~~~~

Janie was waiting in the car, but she'd pulled it closer to the edge of the parking lot. She reminded Dani of the bobble-headed dog that rested next to the rear window, as her head wobbled this way and that. Dani heard the music blaring from her tape deck before she'd reached the car. Ironically, it was Three Dog Night's "Mama Told Me Not to Come." Janie appeared relieved when she saw her. She had the car in gear before her friend reached it.

"We're not alone," Janie said as Dani slipped inside.

"What?"

"Look behind us. I've been keeping an eye on them. I thought they were gonna block me from getting out of here."

Dani turned around to stare at a green Pontiac GTO with a black roof. There were two people in the front seat. "I think it's a guy and a girl."

"I'm not hanging around to find out."

As Janie whirled the car around and raced right off the curb that separated the lot from the street, Dani got a glimpse of both doors opening. The driver appeared to be barely old enough for a driver's license. He was short and scrawny, and as he watched them drive past, he ran his fingers through shoulder-length brown hair. The girl was even tinier, her figure so thin that had it not been for her attire, she might have mistaken her for a boy.

"Oh my God," Dani breathed.

"Are they coming after us?"

"No. No, slow down. They're going to the same place I just left."

"You're kidding."

"That woman wasn't lying. She did have another right after me." For a moment, an image flashed through Dani's mind of laying on the table, her legs spread, as the boy and girl entered the kitchen. "Jesus."

"They'd been sitting there ever since I lost sight of you. I thought for sure they were going to rob me."

"Jesus," Dani said again. She couldn't get their images out of her mind. They were two kids who had possibly played around in a car's back seat or on their parents' couch. Now they were walking into a grubby kitchen to stop a baby. "Jesus."

"You okay?" Janie asked nervously. "You find the Lord back there?" she joked.

Dani wiped her forehead of perspiration and then rolled down the window for some fresh air.

Janie turned off the music. "That didn't take long."

"I couldn't do it."

"What?"

"I couldn't do it."

Janie spun the car around a corner. A vehicle was traveling in the opposite direction, and she swerved to avoid hitting it. "That came out of nowhere!"

For an instant, Dani caught sight of the driver. She would have known him anywhere. There was something about the way he held his head, the arrogance dripping off him. Her face felt frigid as though a bucket of ice had just been dumped on her. "Oh my God," she breathed, the words barely managing to escape.

Then in the next instant, he was gone.

"What?" Janie said. She glanced at Dani. "It's okay. I didn't hit him."

Dani glanced behind them, but the car was nowhere in sight. As she turned around, the neon lights of a drive-in burger stand beckoned.

"I need something to drink," Janie said as she slowed long enough to whip into the parking lot. She screeched to a stop beside a menu. Without waiting to turn off the engine, she punched the button and called out, "Two Coke floats and a bag of boiled peanuts." Then she turned to Dani. "I want all the details."

13

Dani sat on the park bench, her eyes closed as she tilted her face upward toward the sun. The warmth felt reassuring as if something in this universe was still functioning with normalcy. It hadn't been a coincidence that she'd listened to George Harrison's "My Sweet Lord" on the drive over. She needed to soothe her soul, and for a few brief moments, the song had worked. Now that she was without the melody, she began to feel decades older than she had just two months prior. While part of it could be attributed to her physical condition and the morning sickness that lasted nearly all day, she knew most of the weight was due to heaviness in her soul. She had looked at her situation from every possible light, and it all appeared to point in one direction.

The bells atop the First Baptist Church rang out, announcing the noon hour. Reluctantly, she opened her eyes. The courthouse stood before her, a single-story, red brick structure with four white columns at the wide front doors. She knew that courthouse like she knew her own home; she'd witnessed many trials there over the years, watching her father argue for defendants. From the time she was barely able to attend school, she'd wandered the vast halls. There was an air of desperation inside its structure as if she could smell the fear, hatred, bigotry, and helplessness. Her father once told her that people rarely came to the courthouse on their best days. She supposed what she sensed all those years were the worst days and those times and situations that people never wanted to confront.

The doors opened, and a flood of white folks tumbled out. At almost the same time, a side door opened, and the minorities in the community did the same. Each group was careful not to come in contact with the other. About five minutes later, the crowds had cleared out. Most had gone to the diners across the way, where they'd have sweet potato casserole, speckled butterbeans, and barbeque before heading back to the courthouse. Once there, the women would fan themselves as they sat on the hard benches and tried to remain awake during the afternoon's docket. Others strode to the parking lots, where they wasted no time in leaving.

Another side door opened, and Judge Crawford stepped onto the sidewalk. His judicial robe left behind, he looked like just another businessman. His silver hair appeared like fine silk as it caught the sun's rays. He stepped out swiftly, his cane swinging outward, barely touching the ground, as though he never needed it at all.

Dani hurried toward him as he turned away and began a trek toward a side street. "Judge Crawford!" she called out as she drew near.

He turned, a scowl on his broad face. As he saw Dani, his expression softened, and he held his hand out to her. "Why, Dani, how good to see you. Is school closed today?"

She took his hand, and he squeezed it before letting it go. "No, sir. I finished my testing for the day," she said. "I was wondering if I could ask you a question?"

"Certainly, child. Will you accompany me to lunch then? It isn't every day I have a pretty lady at my table."

Dani smiled but didn't respond. As they continued walking together, she peered up ahead. She knew the judge was headed to his favorite diner, but unlike the defendants, plaintiffs, and attorneys that filled his courtroom, he would enter through a separate door and sit at a corner table in the shadows. "I have a situation," she began, her voice a bit breathless.

"Oh?" He stopped to peer at her. His eyes were green; when she was just a tyke, he told her they were the colors of Scotland's green hills as if he'd been given the memories of his home country when his ancestors immigrated to America. Now he looked at her curiously, the way a grandfather might look at his granddaughter.

"Judge Crawford, I need your judicial opinion."

"Sounds rather serious."

"It is, sir."

"Do you wish to tell me over lunch?"

"If it's all the same to you, sir, here is just fine." His eyes widened in surprise, and she added, "There are fewer ears to hear."

"Ah."

"You see, I'm expecting a baby."

"Ah." His eyes widened further. "You and Rich-"

"It isn't Rich's."

"Ah." His eyes narrowed.

"I was raped, Judge Crawford. It happened about six weeks ago."

"I'm sorry to hear that," he said, his voice softening.

"Well, anyway, I got pregnant that night—by the rapist."

"I see."

"And I understand that, for a woman to have an abortion in this state, well, I have to see a judge."

"I see." He took a deep breath. "This is highly irregular, coming to me outside the courtroom—"

"I know. I wanted your opinion."

"As a family friend or as a judge?"

"Both sir."

He beckoned to a park bench that took them slightly away from the sidewalk. As they settled in, he asked, "You have a police report of the assault?"

She shook her head.

"Why not?"

"I was unconscious. I was beaten pretty badly."

"Ah. Well, then, you were sent to the hospital."

"No, sir."

His face became ruddy. "You're saying you were sexually assaulted and beaten so badly that you were unconscious, and you didn't go to the hospital? There was no police report filed?"

"I was kept at home. Dr. Nash attended to me."

"Dr. Nash. I know the man."

"My parents—they didn't want this to become public."

"I see."

"Do you?"

His eyes narrowed further. "You know your family's stature in this county—in this state. Your father was right to keep it out of the papers."

"But, that leads me to your opinion, Judge. How do I go to court, ask for an abortion, and keep it out of the public eye?"

He leaned back and placed one hand on his knee. He smelled strongly of Old Spice aftershave. His other hand remained firmly wrapped around his cane, a highly shellacked walnut. "Your case would be on the docket. There's no way around that. It would be public. Your attorney could request the case itself be sealed, the details kept from public view." His eyes narrowed again. She felt as though she was standing in front of him in the courtroom, his sharp eyes assessing her honesty. "But your father would know that."

Nonetheless, Dani breathed a sigh of relief.

"Don't celebrate yet," Judge Crawford admonished, his thick brows furrowing. "Your father has some powerful enemies in Mississippi. He's defended some hardened criminals. There are a lot of victims that want revenge."

"But what does that have to do—"

"You're the weak link, I'm afraid."

"I don't understand—"

"They would get to him through you."

"Then, how do I do this?"

"Aside from your family's position, there's the matter of convincing a judge that it was a rape."

"But—you believe me, don't you?"

He lifted his chin, so he was peering down at her, a stance he'd no doubt perfected on the bench. "First, and perhaps most importantly, you're telling me there was no police report filed."

She shook her head. "No."

"The police have not been involved at all?"

"They haven't."

"And you're telling me you were unconscious, which was why you didn't file the report yourself."

"That's right."

"And when you regained consciousness, you still did not go to the police."

"By that time, weeks had passed, and my parents—"

"And you want me to believe your parents, upstanding citizens, did not report an assault on their only child to the authorities?"

She gulped. Heat began to rise in her cheeks.

"Furthermore, you were unconscious, and yet your parents did not call an ambulance. Where did this happen?"

"At home."

"At your parents' home? And what did they do, leave you to awaken on your own?"

"They got me to Dr. Nash. He was checking on me."

"And I suppose Dr. Nash would testify to that?"

"I guess so."

"You guess so." He slapped his knee. "I don't believe your story."

"What?"

"There are too many holes in it. It sounds to me, young lady, that you got yourself pregnant, and now you're regretting it."

"How would I 'get myself pregnant'?"

"There is no police report. There is no evidence of rape. There isn't even a hospital record. And if Dr. Nash testified on your behalf, he'd be putting his medical license on the line."

"But—why?"

"He's a doctor. He's called to tend to an unconscious woman that was apparently so brutalized that she was unconscious and a rape victim to boot, and he didn't get you to the hospital? That sounds like malfeasance to me."

"I don't understand."

"Your story doesn't pan out." He stood.

"So, if I came before you in your courtroom—"

He held up his hand. "You can't come before me. You've approached me outside the court. If the case was assigned to me, I would have to recuse myself."

"So, another judge, would they be more inclined—?"

"I can't speak for the other judges. But based on what you've told me and the total lack of evidence, I would have turned you down had you been brought before me in my courtroom."

"You wouldn't have granted it?"

"No. I would not."

"You would have forced me into having the rapist's baby, then?" Her voice grew quiet as she tried to wrap her brain around his words.

"Look," he said, his voice softening, "you said you came to me as both a judge and a friend?"

"Yes."

"Then go on an extended vacation."

"A vacation? I don't—"

"Have the baby in a place where nobody knows you, where nobody cares about you. Put it up for adoption. Come home and resume your life."

"Put a newborn baby up for adoption?" She thought of The Little Acorn Orphanage and the children without parents.

"It is white, isn't it? There are people who would adopt a white baby." He stepped toward the sidewalk.

"Now, if you'll excuse me, I have limited time before I must get back to my courtroom."

"But, Judge," she called after him. "What if I was your daughter? Would you advise me the same?"

He stopped, but he did not turn around to face her. "You'd best be getting away from here, Dani. When court resumes, I'm hearing a case about an alleged lynching. Emotions can get out of hand."

"A lynching?"

"Your daddy's the defense attorney. The defendants are claiming it was suicide." With that, he stepped out quickly. She watched him traverse the courthouse grounds and disappear down the side street. Then she returned to the park bench and sat heavily. She felt odd; on the one hand, she sensed the weight of the world settling once again upon her shoulders. On the other hand, she struggled within a daze, a nightmare so overwhelming that she could not escape it.

~~~~~

Dani was still sitting on the park bench when a few sprinkles fell. The first hit the back of her hand as it rested in her lap. A few moments later, another drop fell upon her knee, followed by several on her head. She didn't know how long she'd been sitting there. She had a vague memory of people filing past her on their way to the courthouse. She felt as though she was wrapped inside a cocoon as a beehive came to life around her. Then the hive hushed, and she was left alone again with her thoughts and emotions.

By the time the droplets became a shower, she'd come no closer to rousing herself from the shock that permeated her soul. When the storm intensified, she stood as if in a stupor and began the stroll to her car.

She didn't hear Rich calling her until she had walked a couple of blocks. He pulled just ahead of her, reached over, and opened the passenger door. The faint sounds of "Bridge Over Troubled Waters" slipped from the radio. She felt oddly comforted by the melodic sound of Simon and Garfunkel's soothing voices. "I'm soaked," she protested.

"I don't care. Get in." As she climbed in, he continued, "I've been calling your name."

"Sorry. My mind was elsewhere."

"I'd say so."

"What are you doing here?" she asked. "Why aren't you at the university?"

He pulled off the main road. Dani caught a glimpse of the Sunflower River as he drove them further from town; some said it had initially been a Mississippi River channel, but now it leisurely wound its way to the Yazoo River. The Yazoo, in turn, emptied into the Muddy Mississippi. With the sudden storm, the waters appeared black, the surface churned by relentless raindrops. She'd paddled this stretch numerous times. It could be a comfortable, relaxing ride or one strife with alligators and cottonmouth moccasins. Funny, she thought. She now felt the same about Rich.

"I was looking for you," Rich said.

"Why?"

He paused before answering. "Mind if we stop someplace and talk?"

She felt a shortness of breath, and a feeling of dread bubbled up inside her. Her heart quickened, and her skin grew prickly, much as it did when she spotted an alligator's head rising from the water. "Sure."

Rich pulled onto the drive leading to Soldier's Field. They passed a large field where the grass, brown during the winter months, was beginning to turn green with the warmer weather and spring rains. He pulled into a parking lot with a view of a picnic area and trail.

They sat silently for a long moment. Dani watched the wipers clearing the windshield, only to be covered again in a second or two. Beyond the car, the park appeared like an impressionist painting as the green grasses and abundant flowers poured into one another. Inside the vehicle, it was beginning to steam up. Rich rolled down his window an inch or so, and Dani did as well. A few drops found their way to the seat, but as wet as she'd been even before entering the car, she knew a few sprinkles wouldn't make a difference. It felt too oppressive inside the vehicle without the fresh air.

Rich drove a Chevy Nova, blue on the outside and black inside. A cartridge poked out of the 8-track tape player, and Dani absent-mindedly pulled it out to look at it. The cover was sepia, the band a trio of men with extraordinarily long beards. She smiled and put it back in the player, but not far enough to begin playing. She turned down the radio, so it was barely audible. Brook Benton's "Rainy Night in Georgia" had replaced Simon and Garfunkel. Someone at the station was having fun with the storm.

"ZZ Top," Rich said, halfway pointing to the tape.

"Yeah."

Rich turned in his seat, so his back leaned against the door. "So, I was looking for you."

"Yeah. You told me."

"I drove by the school and the newspaper, but I didn't see your car. I thought maybe you were downtown…"

"Yeah."

"So, listen, Dani. You kind of caught me off guard, you know, when you came by the campus. I wasn't expecting to hear—the news. I guess I was in a bit of a shock."

"Welcome to the club."

"I've been thinking about it, and I have a suggestion."

"Good." She slipped one leg beneath her and half-turned toward him. "I'm all ears."

"Let's—" he swallowed. "Let's delay our wedding—"

"Why?"

"Only temporarily." He fumbled with his class ring as he spoke. "Maybe we could have a Christmas wedding."

"A Christmas wedding."

"Yeah."

"So," Dani said slowly, "by delaying our wedding by—say, six months—I would no longer be pregnant."

He nodded.

"And what, maybe my mother could hold the baby during the ceremony?"

He blanched. "Dani," he said, reaching for her hand, "I know you don't want this baby. Why should you? It isn't ours."

"And delaying our wedding would do what, precisely?"

"There are places you can go. Maybe a relative's house, maybe, I don't know—places."

Her eyes narrowed. A myriad of emotions began to well up inside her. "Okay. So I leave Mississippi so nobody would have to be embarrassed by the sight of me—"

"It isn't that."

"Isn't it, though?"

"Look. You've always said you wanted to go to college."

"To Ole Miss, same as you."

"Well, maybe there's someplace better."

"Better for me, or for you?"

"You're not making this easy on me, are you?" He let go of her hand. "Look. I'm just starting out. I need to get settled in my job. We can tell people that you went to a different university. Have the baby, and come back home."

"And why would I have the baby any place other than here?" When he didn't reply, she continued, "Oh, I see. So I could give birth away from prying eyes. And then what? Bring the baby home with me after being gone for months? What would that accomplish?"

"Dani." He reached for her hand again. "There are people better able to care for a baby right now."

"Oh? And who would they be?"

He chewed his lip.

"Let's play this out, okay? This little fantasy of yours. Everybody knows we've been together forever. Everybody knows our wedding is planned for this summer. Everybody knows I want to attend Ole Miss—"

"Who is 'everybody,' Dani?"

"But you want me to pack a bag and move to— I don't know, Memphis? Attend a university there? And oh, by the way, get bigger and rounder while I'm going to school, and—oh, I forgot—start school in the summer instead of next fall—"

"We'll figure out the details."

"Yeah. It kinda looks like you've been working on that."

"Dani. When you get back, we'll start over."

"Start over. I'm guessing we'll start over with just you and me."

He nodded.

"Yeah." She turned her attention to the scene outside the car. The rain was steady now, the kind of shower that increased the humidity and made everything feel sticky. "Let's guess about your life this summer, shall we?" Before he could respond, she went on, "You're graduating in a few weeks. You'll go to work for my father. No entry-level position for you, huh? Not like me cleaning floors at the newspaper. Nope. You'll waltz in as a partner, won't you?"

"You know I have to pass—"

"The bar exam. Yeah. Got it. But that's a piece of cake for you. And then your career is nothing but up."

"We'll buy a house, Dani. I've got my eye on one—"

"I bet you do, with the cushy income you'll have."

"Dani—"

"You went to see my father, didn't you? Did he summon you to his office?"

He averted his eyes and picked at a non-existent piece of lint on his trousers.

"You weren't looking for me at all, were you? You drove to my dad's office because he called you and said he needed you there. You two had quite the meeting, didn't you?"

"He loves you, Dani. I love you—"

"Yeah. Right. But let's not invite little Dani to the meeting. Let's decide her fate for her."

"It's the best thing to do. Let me take care of you—"

"Take care of me? Where were you—and my father—the night this happened to me?" She poked at her belly. "Where have you been since then?"

"You know I stayed at your side every chance I got—"

She pushed the door open.

"Where are you going?"

She stepped out and slammed the door shut.

He opened his door and called to her over the hood. "Dani, at least let me drive you back."

"I can walk."

"It's—"

"I know how far it is."

"You're being unreasonable."

"Yeah. Right." She turned her back on him and purposefully cut a path across the park where he couldn't ride alongside her. As if in answer to her tumultuous emotions, a roll of thunder broke through the monotony of the rain. The clay grew thick and muddy on her shoes as she marched back toward downtown, but she didn't care.

14

"Miss Evans," the nurse called out from the doorway on the opposite side of the waiting room. "*Miss* Danielle Evans."

Dani felt her face grow warm as she crossed the room.

"*Miss* Evans?"

"Yes."

The nurse's eyes roamed over her. She was a buxom woman with stout legs. She had pulled her dark hair into a tight bun at the nape of her neck beneath a crisp white cap. She first obtained Dani's height and weight and then escorted her into a tiny room. Dani noted she hadn't yet gained a single pound with her pregnancy; in fact, she'd lost five. Probably stress.

"And why are we here today?" the nurse asked tersely.

"Dr. Nash recommended Dr. O'Hare."

"For what?"

"He's an obstetrician, isn't he?"

"Ah. So you're pregnant, *Miss* Evans."

"Yes," Dani answered. "I'm told that I am."

"Dr. Nash told you?"

"Yes."

She fiddled with her nameplate, which identified her as Mrs. Murphy. Whether she was attempting to insinuate something, Dani didn't know. After a moment, she opened a cabinet and pulled out a starched white gown. "Take everything off," she said. "Put this on, so it opens in the front."

"The front," Dani repeated. "Not the back?"

"That's what I said. Dr. O'Hare will be right with you."

She was tempted to leave once the nurse had departed, and the door had closed behind her. The room smelled of potent antiseptic. There were only two tiny chairs, a corner counter, and the exam table, but the furniture dwarfed the room. She quickly shed her clothes, folding them neatly into one chair, before donning the cold, thin gown. She sat on the edge of the exam table. Her fingers wrapped around the edges of the coarse material, pulling the two sides closer.

The minutes ticked past, and then an hour. Dani made up her mind that this was a bad idea. She'd just stepped down from the exam table when the door opened.

"Dr. O'Hare," the man said, reaching out to shake her hand. "Please." He gestured to the exam table. He was a tall man and lithe, and his white jacket opened casually to reveal a checked shirt. Beneath his dress slacks were a pair of battered tennis shoes that looked like they'd seen better days. He was young; as Dani settled back onto the exam table, she concluded that he couldn't be much older than Rich. She felt a wave of embarrassment roll over her. This was a terrible idea, indeed.

"So you are Danielle?" he said as he flipped through a thin chart. "Dr. Nash sent you?"

"Yes."

"I'll have to thank him for referring you." After a moment, he set the chart on the counter in the corner. "Congratulations on your pregnancy."

"I'm not sure congratulations are in order."

"Oh?" He seated himself in a chair and rolled it closer. "A surprise, was it?"

"Yes. A surprise."

Half an hour later, Dani was dressed once more and waiting in the tiny exam room for Dr. O'Hare's return. The examination itself had been humiliating. Mrs. Murphy—Mistress Murphy was what Dani wanted to call her—held a piece of cloth over Dani's private parts as if the sight of them would arouse the doctor. She didn't know how he'd managed to get the speculum inside her without taking the cloth with it. And the entire time she was splayed out on the table, Mistress Murphy glared at her. She should have gone through with the procedure the other night, she thought. It was less degrading.

But when Dr. O'Hare returned, he was alone. He closed the door behind him. "Well, Miss Evans, Dr. Nash was right. You are expecting."

He smiled at her, but Dani could only groan in disappointment.

"Your due date is November 7, give or take a week."

Dani stared at her hands in her lap. She heard the sound of the chair and looked up to see Dr. O'Hare leaning forward as he sat, his eyes on her.

"Why do I have the impression you don't want this baby?" he asked. His voice was soft and compassionate.

"I don't. It's a long story," Dani added hastily.

"Do you want me to discuss options with you?"

"Options?"

"Medically and ethically, I can't steer you in one way or the other unless your health is in question, and it appears you are very healthy... But I can point you in the right direction if you want alternatives." The last word hung in the air.

"What choice do I have?" Her heart began to beat a little faster. Maybe it wasn't a mistake coming here, after all.

"If you don't want the child, it can be put up for adoption. Some establishments will allow you to stay with them until you give birth."

"What kind of establishments?"

"Mostly religious. You'd have to work to cover your room and board, of course."

"Religious." She gripped her hands. "They tend to be judgmental."

"Some are. I can give you a few to check out if you'd like."

She nodded. "Are there other possibilities?"

"Abortion is illegal in Mississippi." His eyes were gray, so light they appeared like glass. He seemed to be looking right through to her soul.

"I know."

"Some of my patients go to Memphis. I can give you the name of a doctor there. He delivers babies, and he—assists with miscarriages."

"Miscarriages. Abortions, you mean."

He nodded. "Legally, I can refer you to another physician. He can go over options with you. But I can't refer you to one that does abortions…"

"Ah," Dani said. "But he can assist with a miscarriage."

Dr. O'Hare nodded. "He is nonjudgmental."

Dani forced a smile. "Thank you."

The doctor stood. "Do you have any further questions for me?"

"I don't think so."

"Then the receptionist will give you the materials as you leave. If you change your mind, I'd like to see you in another month."

Dani nodded. She was barely aware of the doctor leaving. She waited a moment to regain what little composure she felt she had left. When she stepped into the hall, Mistress Murphy was with another patient that looked like a child herself, though she was visibly expecting. She wondered if she appeared that way to the staff as well, like a child having a child.

She stopped at the desk and paid her bill, counting out yet more money taken from her college fund. At this rate, she wouldn't have the means to attend a university. The receptionist handed her a receipt, Dr. O'Hare's card and another card to a clinic in Memphis, and a list of adoption agencies. The Little Acorn Orphanage seemed to pop off the page at her. The receptionist didn't meet Dani's eyes as she handed them over, and a ringing telephone further distracted her. As she turned to answer it, Dani took the opportunity to hurry out the door.

15

Dani sat in the front row of the classroom at a chair attached to a desk barely large enough for a notebook. She couldn't help but peer down at the distance between her belly and the desk. She had no doubt it would not accommodate a growing abdomen.

The classroom was abuzz as the other students filed into the hallway. The cacophony of voices quickly became muffled as Mrs. Johnston closed the door. Dani felt her eyes upon her as the teacher crossed to her desk and settled behind it.

The seconds ticked past, and Dani squirmed uncomfortably.

"Do you know why I asked you to stay?" Mrs. Johnston asked. She was a short woman, barely five feet if that, and Dani suspected she had a cushion in her chair to seat her higher. She taught Dani's mother when she had attended the same high school, and judging by her gray hair and her kind but crumpled face, Dani wouldn't have been surprised to learn she'd taught Grandma Dottie, too.

"No, ma'am," she answered.

"How are you feeling?"

"Feeling?" Dani repeated.

"Since your accident. You look like you've healed up."

"Oh. That." She crossed her ankles and then uncrossed them. "My injuries are healed, for the most part."

"Listen, Dani… You were a straight-A student before your accident."

Dani nodded. She'd been at the top of her class. In the previous semester, her overall score had been 108 due to extracurricular projects.

"I know you've been planning to go to college. Are you still interested in journalism?"

"Yes," she answered quickly. She sat up a little straighter. "Do you have—?"

"No," Mrs. Johnston replied. "In fact, since the accident, your grades have fallen sharply."

She looked down at her desk. The books in front of her held no interest.

"I understand you were badly injured. You lost over a month's worth of school work."

"I can make it up."

Mrs. Johnston hesitated. Taking a deep breath, she said, "I thought so, at first. But since you've been back, it's like something else is on your mind. Your grades have taken a nosedive."

"I'm sorry."

"Is there anything going on at home?"

"No, ma'am."

"I understand you're staying with the Bransons."

"Yes, ma'am."

"Are you and Janie studying together?"

"I think you know the answer to that."

"I do."

"Well."

"Well," Mrs. Johnston repeated. "You have always been above average, Dani. Janie is... average. But now, her scores are head and shoulders above yours."

Dani nodded.

"And you're not making up for the time you lost."

"No, ma'am."

A long silence ensued. Then Mrs. Johnston stood and rested her hands on the desk. "I want you to know I've requested a meeting with your parents."

"Why?" Dani breathed.

"You're failing, Dani."

"Failing?" Her jaw dropped, and she struggled to close it. She felt exposed, and she didn't know why.

"I can't pass you. The thing is, you're so smart. You have so much potential. But you haven't caught up since your accident. Even things I could have sworn you already knew, you're getting wrong on the tests."

"I'll try harder."

"I'm going to suggest to your parents that you attend summer school. You can't graduate with the rest of your class, but you can graduate in time to attend college next fall."

"No! Please don't do that. I'll work night and day to catch up."

"Are you still working at the newspaper?"

"Yes—I'll—" She hesitated, unable to commit to quitting. "I can handle both."

"I don't believe you can, Dani." Mrs. Johnston's voice was kind but firm. "I wonder if the fall resulted in a bit of a brain injury, something they haven't yet diagnosed? I'm going to suggest your parents have that possibility checked out. It might sound cruel, but you'd have better chances of getting into college if it can be shown the reason for your failing grades was due to an injury. Especially given your previous grades," she hastily added.

"I can catch up," she repeated.

"Another thing. You're cutting a lot of classes. You never did that before."

"I've had things," she stumbled. "My health. Doctors' appointments."

Another silence ensued. The room felt stifling as Dani glanced toward the windows. They were all open, but there was no sign of a breeze outside. The classroom felt smaller than usual, though the students that regularly filled it were on the sidewalk or crossing the parking lot. Mrs. Johnston was still talking, but her words were lost on Dani as if they were disintegrating between them. She tried to concentrate, but she saw only her teacher's large eyes, her head tilting further toward her with an expression of concern, her mouth moving, but the words jumbled.

She bolted out of the chair, nearly knocking over the desk. Grabbing her books, she raced for the door, slinging it open. She could still hear Mrs. Johnston's voice as she ran down the hall toward the front doors and freedom.

~~~~~

The Greyhound Bus Station sat at the junction of two roads, its rounded Art Deco entrance facing the corner. "Greyhound" glowed in vertical neon lights, evoking a sense of travel and movement, even upward mobility. It was built in the 1930s, no doubt eliciting excitement and fanfare. Now, it was beginning to look dated and worn, a relic, Dani supposed, of all the people that had crossed through, never to permanently return. Long before Dani's birth, the Delta had been a hubbub of activity between the cottonfields and other agriculture and the manufacturing plants that had dotted the landscape. But as the Industrial Revolution took hold in all facets of life, mechanized harvesters replaced scores of families in the fields. Automation removed workers accustomed to repetitive work on the manufacturing line. There was no place to go but poverty or out. The Greyhound Bus Station symbolized those that managed to escape.

At one time, the Clarksdale station was purported to be one of the busiest in the nation, rivaling New York, if one could believe the rumors. The busses arrived day and night, empty when arriving, and full as they left the Deep South for points north. Memphis was the early choice, but as jobs became harder to come by there, travelers migrated further north to St. Louis and Chicago, eventually branching out to points both east and west. There was even a bus regularly leaving for New York City.

Around five million people had left the Deep South between 1940 and 1970 in search of a better future. Textbooks called it "The Second Black Migration," the first having happened decades earlier, but it was anyone with no viable future, which meant the poor and oppressed. The poorest of the poor remained behind, unable to afford a bus ticket north. As Dani drove past the terminal, she wondered if they'd ever found the opportunities they craved. Occasionally, she spotted a spit-shined Cadillac roaming into a poor neighborhood; no doubt, someone that had discovered success coming home to show friends and families how they'd fared.

Those that hadn't prospered probably never wanted to return, Dani thought. And then some might have succeeded but never wanted to see the rural south again.

She began to wonder which category she might fall into if she ventured out of Mississippi in search of her future. But she found her thoughts abruptly halted as she turned the corner. Sitting at the stoplight in a shiny bronze Dodge Charger was her rapist. She nearly ran into him as shock took over, and as she veered her Spitfire into the correct lane, she tried to suppress any sign of recognition. Maybe she didn't have to glance at him; perhaps she could have kept her eyes on the road, but she felt compelled to look at his face.

He smiled.

Dani felt the heat rising in her cheeks as she steered her vehicle into her lane. As she put her foot more firmly on the gas pedal, she heard his laughter through the unopened windows. She thought she was going to vomit. She could have, right there in the intersection, she could have opened her door, and projectile vomited at his shiny door. That would stop his laughter and smirk, surely. But she didn't. Shaking, she managed to drive another mile until she pulled her car into the newspaper's parking lot.

Beauregard called out to her from the loading dock. "Jimmy Bob is looking for you! You're late again!" She half-waved her hand to let him know she'd heard him and parked under a magnolia tree at the edge of the lot. She consciously attempted to calm herself as she tried to replace the rapist's face with something mundane, boring, even. She reminded herself to roll down her windows. Summer seemed to last a good eight months in these parts, and finding a parking spot under a shade tree was invaluable.

Keeping the windows open prevented her from frying when she came back out.

She could hear Jimmy Bob shouting even before she reached the door, shattering her vain attempts to remain serene. Through the glass, she spotted everyone running in different directions. As she entered, the receptionist, Mary Jane, rolled her eyes.

"What's going on?" Dani asked.

"Newspaper printed late today. Everyone's scrambling to get it out the door."

"Why? Did a machine break down?"

Mary Jane shook her head. "Jimmy Bob's looking for you."

"Why?" She straightened her back. "Does he have an assignment for me?"

"Does he ever." She opened her mouth to say more but was interrupted by Jimmy Bob.

"Evans!" he shouted. "In my office! Now!"

Dani hurried to the corner office. Jimmy Bob's tantrums were the stuff of legend. Most reporters didn't last more than a year or two under his insults. "I'm sorry I'm late," she said as she entered. "It won't happen again—"

"How could you have withheld information from us?" Jimmy Bob yelled.

"What are you talking about?"

"Close that door behind you!"

Even as she closed the door, she knew it wouldn't make a difference. The walls were not drywall but paneling, so thin that even the bathroom was seldom used due to the acoustics. She had no doubt everyone had heard her vomiting over the toilet.

"You knew we were working on a story," Jimmy Bob shouted in an accusatory tone.

Dani stared at him. He was short and squat like a fireplug, his head so smooth that the light bounced off it. Now he glared at her with beady eyes. And she was sick of being treated like an ignorant child. "How could I have known that when you keep me busy cleaning instead of reporting?"

He stepped back as if momentarily stunned before he came back in like a boxer in a ring. "Your father!" he said, wagging his finger.

"My father what?"

"Your father!" He wagged his finger again as if at a loss for words. "You had to have known!"

"Known what?"

The door opened slightly, and Tom stepped in, closing the door behind him. Tom was only in his twenties. He followed a long line of lead reporters at the paper; they were generally recruited shortly after graduation, and they moved on as quickly as possible. Besides Jimmy Bob's ferocious temper, the area was small potatoes compared to the major cities within a day's drive.

Now Tom sat in a chair and beckoned for Dani to sit opposite him. "Dani," he began softly, "I want to be the one to tell you."

"Tell me what?"

Jimmy Bob huffed in the background, and Tom locked his eyes onto Dani's as if to direct her attention away from their boss. They were clear and green, like Grandma Dottie's etched iced tea glasses. It occurred to her that he was Jimmy Bob's opposite: slender, authoritative but more soft-spoken, steady.

"I've written a front-page story," Tom was saying. "It took me a long time to research, to get it right. It's about something that took place a couple of months back."

Dani felt her hands grow as cold as ice as she remembered their conversation. She'd never approached her father for the interview Tom had wanted. "What does that have to do with me?" she asked. Her throat constricted as she spoke.

"Not you," Tom said. "It's your dad."

"What about him?" She shot a sideways glance at Jimmy Bob. "Will someone please tell me what is going on?"

Tom reached for Dani's hand. The touch unexpectedly sent a jolt through her. He seemed to have felt it, too, and he hesitated before he continued. "I want you to know I wrote a story that isn't favorable to your daddy."

She laughed. She knew she sounded on the verge of being maniacal, but she didn't care. "You wouldn't be the first."

Tom appeared to relax a bit. He settled back in his chair but kept his hand lightly on hers. "It's just that—well, a couple of months back, he won a court case. I didn't hear about it at the courthouse. I heard through—other sources. It took me a while to check it out. The judge had ordered the case sealed. I tried to get his side of it," he added hastily. "I tried to get an interview. But the gatekeepers at his office blocked me, every step of the way."

"I see," Dani said. "That's why you wanted me to approach him."

"It was wrong of me, I know," Tom said.

Jimmy Bob snorted.

"But I thought, maybe you could have…" His voice faded off as he peered curiously at her.

Dani's mind darted back to the evening of the rape. Her parents—in fact, the entire law firm—was celebrating a big win. With the events that occurred later, she never discovered the significance of that case over the others he regularly won. She supposed, now that she considered it, she had never been that interested in his work or Rich's future in the firm.

"You're going to hear a lot about this, that's all," Tom was saying. "And the shit might hit the fan here at the paper. And I wanted you to be prepared for it." He paused as he watched her reaction. "There might not be a lot of nice things said about him."

Dani forced a chuckle. "That's real nice of you, Tom, but my daddy's work has nothing to do with me."

"Yeah. I just wanted to make sure."

The room fell silent. Jimmy Bob was still glaring at Dani as if she'd committed a crime. "So," she said, "what's the big deal about this case?"

She hadn't realized that Tom carried a newspaper with him until his hand left hers to grasped it in his lap. It was in a roll so tight that she wondered if he'd been squeezing it with his free hand. "It's big, Dani. It's real big."

"So tell me."

"Oh, for God's sake," Jimmy Bob interrupted. "Last year, your daddy represented a man accused of rape. The details were salacious. We covered every day of the trial."

"I remember," Dani said slowly. "It was Willadeene Carter, wasn't it? She was a grade ahead of me in school. But I thought it wasn't rape —"

"That's on account of your daddy won the case. He raked that girl over the coals, made her out to be a trailer park slut. The jury decided it was Willadeene's fault, and they let the boy go."

"It wasn't exactly a boy, Jimmy Bob," Tom said.

"But that was last year. What does that have to do with today?" Dani tried to peer at the article, but

Tom kept it clasped in his hands.

"Dani," Tom said quietly, "they went back to court."

"Willadeene and the rapist?"

"Man named Dele Mason. He's not officially the rapist, on account of—"

"My daddy representing him."

"Yeah. So, Willadeene had a child—"

"She did?"

"You didn't know?"

Dani shook her head. "I guess, well, I didn't see her after the trial. I thought, I don't know, that they moved away."

"They were right here in Coahoma County. She lived with her parents."

"And the child?"

"The child was his—Dele Mason's." He paused. "Dele took Willadeene to court."

"Why?"

"He claimed the baby was his. And he wanted parental rights."

Dani looked from Tom to Jimmy Bob and back again. "So, let me get this straight. Willadeene said this guy Dele raped her. My daddy defended Dele, so he was not convicted of rape. Then Willadeene had his child?"

"You got it," Jimmy Bob spat. "Your daddy had the judge seal the records. We had to jump through some legal hoops to get access to it."

"So, that's what you've written about? How a man accused of rape—did what, precisely?"

"He got parental rights, Dani," Tom said. "If he was, indeed, Willadeene's rapist—well, she was ordered to hand over the little girl every other weekend to Dele."

"It was a little girl?" Dani repeated. She felt as if she was in a daze, yet every word imprinted permanently on her mind. "If he was guilty of rape, it meant Willadeene had to see him—"

"Every other weekend, and on Wednesdays, too."

"And this little girl, she was alone with this guy?"

Tom nodded. His eyes grew dark and sad.

"There's more," Jimmy Bob said. "And I don't mind telling you; I am mighty disgusted with your daddy. Mighty disgusted."

Tom handed the paper to Dani. "I'm sorry, Dani. I know he's your daddy and all. But I just had to write it like I saw it."

She slowly flattened out the paper from where Tom had rolled it. The story was front-page news, above the fold. There was a large picture accompanying the article, but it wasn't her daddy's picture as she'd anticipated.

"I was sitting on the story," Tom said. "I just had a few more things to check, but—" He swallowed.

"But what?"

"Willadeene killed her little girl and committed suicide this afternoon."

The words had trouble penetrating through to her. She could no longer picture Willadeene, the neighbor that had attended school one year ahead of her. The court cases surrounding the rape and Dele's petition for parental rights blurred into one. "Dele Mason," she mumbled as if in a stupor.

"What did you say?" Tom asked, leaning closer.

She couldn't answer. Her mouth had gone dry, and her brain empty as she stared at the picture of Dele Mason. The scars were there—one that crossed the brow and another that split his lip. Even without the disfigurement, she would know his face anywhere. It almost seemed as though it was contorting into a smirk and evil laughter. And he was laughing at her.

16

The Branson family lived on a quiet, tree-lined street. Their house sat back from the road, a one-story red brick rancher with four small columns along the front porch that matched those that held up the adjoining carport. The giant magnolia tree that dwarfed the front yard had transformed the lawn into moss and exposed tree roots.

There was an unseasonable crispness in the air as Dani parked her car adjacent to the curb. The storm had subsided, leaving in its wake cooler weather but just as humid. She used the side entrance from the carport, which led her directly into the kitchen. Like many of the newer homes, the Branson's house was decorated in the latest colors. Dani's eyes panned over the harvest gold refrigerator and matching stovetop and oven, coming to rest briefly on Mrs. Branson as she prepared dinner.

"Dani," she exclaimed when she saw her. "I'm so glad you're back. Your folks called and—"

"Hi, Mrs. Branson," Dani mumbled as she quickly passed through the kitchen into the dining room.

"Dani, stop."

At the sound of Mrs. Branson's stern voice, she hesitated at the door as she peered into the hallway.

Mrs. Branson was standing behind her at the head of the oblong table, a spatula in her hand. "Mr. Branson and I need to speak to you this evening. It's non-negotiable."

"Yes, ma'am."

"Supper is at seven o'clock. Don't miss it. Afterward, you and I and Mr. Branson will sit right here and talk."

"Yes, ma'am."

Mrs. Branson peered at her for a moment as if she wanted to say more. She was a petite woman with shoulder-length brunette hair and enormous eyes. Dani supposed Janie's hair would have been the same color if she hadn't bleached it. But after a moment, Mrs. Branson retreated into the kitchen, and Dani entered the hallway.

The sound of James Taylor's "Fire and Rain" filtered into the hall. She pounded on the first door so she could be heard above the music.

After a moment, Brandon opened the door. "Dani," he said, surprised. Over his shoulder, she spotted his best friend, Stu. Like Brandon, Stu was seventeen. He was tall and lanky, his strawberry blond hair straight and silky as it flowed past his shoulders.

"What's up?" Janie opened her bedroom door across the hall.

Dani glanced at her friend and then back at Brandon. "I need to go shooting."

His eyes widened, but he immediately responded, "Sure thing, Dani. Rifles?"

"Pistols."

"I want to go," Janie said.

"Well, come on, then," Brandon said, moving to the closet in the bedroom. "Stu, you coming?"

"You bet."

A short time later, the four piled into Brandon's vintage Jeep. It was a Willys CJ2, a civilian vehicle manufactured shortly after World War II. The undercarriage was rusting, the paint now speckled, but the engine roared to life as Brandon and Stu settled into the front while Janie and Dani sat behind them, the pistols and ammunition box between them. She still held the newspaper clenched in her hand, much as Tom had kept it in his. As she relaxed her grip, the articles underneath the main story peered out at her. Charles Manson had been sentenced to death for the murders of two people and orchestrating the murders of seven more, all of which had happened nearly two years ago. Beside Manson's picture was another of his most famous victim. Sharon Tate had been eight months pregnant at the time of her slaying. It seemed no matter which way Dani turned, she could not escape tragedies staring her in the face. Well, she had just encountered her last straw. She would not be another victim.

~~~~~

Bullet holes riddled cans that once held beer or soft drinks. Brandon picked up a handful and repositioned them on a row of uprooted tree trunks they'd lined up along the edge of the cottonfield. "You got 'em good," he called back to Dani. "Now try 'em at twenty yards."

Dani backed up until she was even with Janie and Stu. "This it?"

"A bit further back."

"She won't be able to see the cans if she keeps backing up," Janie said.

"Right there," Brandon directed. "Wait till I get back there with you. Remember, that gun doesn't have a safety lever."

Dani pointed the Beretta 950 toward the ground as he approached. It was a short pistol designed to carry in a woman's purse or a man's pocket, giving rise to its reputation as a pocket pistol. It was a beautiful gun, sleek and black. It had a magazine to accommodate eight bullets plus one in the tip-up barrel, unlike her father's old-fashioned revolvers. It also fit easily into the palm of her petite hand.

"Alright," Brandon said as he rejoined the group.

Stu stood beside her, his legs spread wide and his arms crossing his chest as he watched her. Janie absent-mindedly pulled her long hair into a twist at her neck as she kept her eyes on the cans. "They look too far away," she said to no one in particular.

Dani held the pistol with both hands and carefully aimed it through the sight.

"Remember," Brandon said quietly, "don't hold it too tight. It'll bite you if you do."

She relaxed her grip, conscious of the barrel. Then she aimed, fired, and missed.

"I think she's too far away," Janie said.

"Try again," Stu directed.

Dani aimed at another can, took her time, fired, and missed again.

"Want to move closer?" Brandon asked.

"How far away was I last time?" Dani asked.

"About ten yards, give or take."

"Thirty feet," she mumbled. She tried a third time and missed.

"You need a larger target at that range," Stu said.

Dani stepped forward a few paces, aimed, and fired. This time, one of the cans bounced off the trunk and into the cotton.

"That was real good, Dani," Brandon said.

"Guys, we need to wrap it up," Janie said. "Mama said to be home in time for dinner."

"I need more practice," Dani said, frowning.

Brandon held out his hand. Dani deposited the pistol in his palm and watched as he unloaded it. "Why shooting, Dani?" he asked.

"What do you mean?"

"Why do you want to shoot? You never did before."

Dani's eyes panned her friends' faces. Brandon's eyes focused on the pistol. Stu watched her intently, and Janie's eyes were wide as though her friend's secret was about to be revealed. "Protection," she said.

"From what?" Stu asked.

Brandon returned to the Jeep and placed the pistol into the case, lovingly arranging it on the foam as though it was a baby.

Dani and Janie knocked the mud off their boots before slipping inside the open back. Stu slid into the passenger seat in front of them and turned around to peer at Dani. "Protection from what?" he repeated.

Dani sighed. "I was assaulted."

"When? By who?" Stu's voice rose.

Brandon positioned himself behind the wheel and started the engine.

"It doesn't matter. I just want to be ready if I see the jerk again."

"I thought something seemed different about you today," Stu said.

"How so?"

He shrugged and turned back around. "Something about your eyes," he said vaguely.

"Standing in a field shooting somebody else's gun won't do it, Dani," Brandon said, glancing at her in the rearview mirror. They rocked as the vehicle rolled over the rough ground at the edge of the field.

"Why not?"

"You need a gun of your own." Brandon's eyes remained on her this time until the rocking caused him to avert his attention back to the vehicle.

"You got one I can use?"

"Like the one you just fired?" He shook his head. "Not one you can borrow indefinitely. Besides, you need more practice." He stopped and pointed. "Look at that."

They followed his gaze to a doe standing along the woodline with two fawns. Had he not pointed them out, Dani might have missed them entirely. The doe stood straight and regal; her long neck turned, so she was gazing directly at them. As they studied one another, one ear twitched. The fawns were much smaller but the same light color, though white dots speckled their coats. After a few brief seconds, the doe sprinted into the woods, followed immediately by her fawns. In another brief moment, they were gone without a trace.

"See," Brandon said with a knowing smile. "It happens just that fast. One minute, you think you're completely alone. The next, there's the assailant. You've got to be ready. That means carrying."

"I know somebody with pistols for sale," Stu offered.

Brandon eased the vehicle forward until they reached the dirt road.

"Who?" Dani asked.

"Darrell Eddy."

"I know him."

"Yeah, he lives a few doors down from us," Janie said.

"What kind of guns does he have?"

"Last I saw," Stu said, "he had about three dozen. Mostly Smith and Wesson, Colt, a couple of Berettas like the one you just shot. He also has hunting rifles."

"Do we have time to stop by?" Dani asked.

"You got the money?"

"How much would he want?"

Stu smiled. "We got time, Janie?"

~~~~~

Darrell Eddy was a burly fellow. He was overweight like his father, and though he was only twenty years old, the scraggly beard that reached below his neck made him appear more aged. His bedroom had red, white, and blue striped walls and a Confederate flag draped from the ceiling, held in place by tacks. The combination caused the room to feel small, the single bulb from a bedside lamp providing inadequate illumination.

Janie and Brandon remained in the hallway as Darrell spun the combination lock on the gun cabinet.

"Whoa," Dani breathed as the thick cabinet door opened wide. "Are you preparing for another civil war?"

"You never know," Darrell said. He reached below the rack of rifles and slid open a drawer. "Any of these appeal to you?"

Dani's fingers went straight to a Beretta that appeared nearly identical to the one she'd just shot. She held it in one hand as if weighing it. "This one."

"Need a pocketbook for it?"

Janie laughed as she peered in through the open door. "What, you sell women's accessories now?"

"I do when they've got a hidden compartment." Darrell lifted one off the top shelf in his closet. It was light tan leather and appeared much like others Dani had seen in stores, with two zippered compartments and shoulder straps. But as she watched, Darrell opened a hidden sleeve between the two sections and slid his beefy hand inside. "See, you put the pistol in here, slide your hand in, and your finger could be resting on the trigger. Nobody would even know."

"Don't get her in trouble now," Janie admonished.

"Only if she fires it," Darrell answered.

"I'll take it. Bullets, too."

"Hey," Darrell said as if just remembering something. "You're eighteen, right?"

"I will be soon."

"How soon?"

"A few days," Brandon offered.

"Soon enough. I'll set you up," Darrell grinned.

"We've gotta go," Janie said. "It's a quarter till now."

"You still staying at their house?" Darrell asked, nodding toward Brandon and Janie.

"Yes."

"I'll get everything together and bring it by later."

Dani wanted to snatch the pocketbook and pistol out of his hands, toss him the money, and be done with it, but she held back. "Sure. How much for everything?"

He watched her expression intently as he gave her a price.

"Come on," Janie urged.

"It's a deal," Dani said. Then she quickly backed out of the room and followed her friends to the car. The sun had dipped closer to the horizon, its light waning as a copse of trees shielded it. On the opposite side, the moon was just starting to crest full and bright. It felt like a message to Dani. Settling into the open rear, she peered into the skies as Brandon drove them the half-block to the Evans's house. She thought perhaps the message was that one chapter was ending while another was only beginning. With the full moon staring down at her, she hoped the future would be brighter than her recent past.

"Hey, listen," Brandon said as he parked along the street. "I wouldn't mention to my mom and dad that you're buying a gun, okay?"

"Sure," Dani said. "But why not?"

"They don't care for them."

"That's because they haven't been in my position."

As Dani climbed out, she caught a glimpse of the quizzical expression on Brandon's face. Janie was opening the house door, and Dani hesitated only momentarily before following her.

17

The only remnants of dinner that remained on the dining table were the vintage green glass salt and pepper shakers and a few pecan pie crumbs. The aroma of deep-fried chicken permeated the small house. Along with the Branson family, Dani had quickly consumed the mashed potatoes and gravy, snap peas, and fried okra. She felt split in two. One side urged her to eat more, even as she devoured the homemade pie. The other half felt ill with the knowledge that a baby was growing inside her. She'd felt Mrs. Branson's eyes on her during dinner, though Mr. Branson had remained focused on his plate of food.

Now they sat on the other side of the table from Dani. Janie's and Brandon's voices were muffled as they washed dishes in the kitchen, now that Mr. Branson had closed the door between the two rooms.

Dani sat with her hands in her lap. The wall clock sounded loud and rude as it ticked the seconds.

"Dani," Mrs. Branson began, her voice soft, "your mama called me at work today." She paused as if expecting Dani to respond. When she didn't, she continued, "You know we love having you here. We all do."

"It's true," Mr. Branson said. "You've always been like a daughter to us."

"But you want me to leave," Dani said. Her jaw trembled.

"No," they both said in unison. "Dani, we want you to stay," Mrs. Branson added. "But—"

As the silence fell on the room, Dani glanced up to meet her eyes. They appeared sad, the outer corners downturned.

"Dani, we had an agreement with your folks," Mr. Branson said. "You had to go to school; your grades couldn't drop."

"Is that it?" Dani mused. "It's all about my grades?"

"No," Mrs. Branson responded. "It's all about your future."

"So, my teacher told you that I was failing."

"She told your mama, and your mama told me. And it came as such a shock—your grades, and the fact that you've been skipping school—that, well, one thing led to another."

The room grew quiet again as if they were expecting Dani to respond. After a few moments, she said, "So, you know."

"Is it Rich's?"

"No."

Mr. Branson sucked in his breath.

"Will you tell us whose it is?" Mrs. Branson asked.

"My mama didn't tell you?"

"No. We were interrupted."

"Yeah. Right." She pictured her mother on the phone in the kitchen with a drink in her hand. She wouldn't have cared if Mae or Grandma Dottie was listening. She suspected that she didn't want to admit the accident had been a lie. "I was raped," she heard herself saying. Her voice sounded far away.

"You were what?" Mrs. Branson breathed.

"I didn't have an accident on the night of the storm. It was a lie to cover up the rape."

The room was deathly still as Janie's parents stared at her in stunned silence. Finally, Mrs. Branson said, "Why would your parents lie about something like that?"

"I suppose they don't want to be embarrassed."

Mrs. Branson pushed her chair away from the table. She stared at Dani. "Do you swear you're telling us the truth?"

Dani locked eyes with her. "I swear it's the truth."

"But," Mrs. Branson began and then stopped. A moment later, she said, "Okay. Let's start from the beginning. Do you know this person, the child's father?"

"I didn't before he attacked me. Today, I found out his identity. It's one of my father's clients, as it turns out."

"Oh, my God," Mr. Branson said. "Should I—do you two want to be left alone? I mean, would you feel more comfortable, Dani?"

She shook her head. Tears began to well up in her eyes, but she pushed them back. "I'm just thankful that you both care."

"Of course, we care."

"That's why your grades plummeted," Mr. Branson said.

Dani nodded. "I've been having problems focusing."

"It's no wonder."

"Okay, first things first. What do you plan to do with the child?"

"I don't know. I really don't."

"Well, you have options—"

"I know. I've considered all of them—illegal abortion, legal abortion. Giving the child up for adoption. Raising the child alone—"

"But, what about Rich? Aren't you two planning to marry this summer?"

"He won't marry me if I have the child."

Mr. and Mrs. Branson looked at one another with incredulous expressions. Mr. Branson shook his head sadly.

"I know I have to make a decision soon," Dani said. "And tonight's newspaper is going to make things worse if I decide to have the baby."

"I'll get the paper," Mr. Branson said, abruptly leaving the room.

"Why?" Mrs. Branson asked.

"Because, as it turns out, my father represented the same man—the guy that raped me—in a paternity lawsuit."

Mr. Branson returned and settled into his chair, unrolling the newspaper. "This is the guy that assaulted you?" He held up the paper.

Dani felt as though she might vomit. Just glancing at Dele's picture on the front page sickened her. She nodded.

"He sued a woman that claimed he raped her," he said as he skimmed the article. "He sued her for the right to help raise her child—his child?"

Dani nodded. "That's right. And I have every reason to suspect he'd do the same to me."

"And your parents know this is the man that raped you?" Mrs. Branson said, shivering as she peered at the picture.

"I don't know. I just found out today."

"Surely, your daddy wouldn't have continued to represent this thug."

"I don't know."

Mr. Branson set the paper on the table. "You're not in this alone, Dani. I want you to know that."

"That's right." Mrs. Branson reached across the table to grasp Dani's hand. "We're going to be here for you every step of the way."

"Thank you," Dani said as she again fought back the tears. "But will you feel the same way, regardless of my decision?"

"We will. I promise you; we will."

"Does Janie know?" Mr. Branson asked.

"Yes."

"Well, she honored your secret," Mrs. Branson said. "We need to come up with a plan."

"A plan?" Dani asked.

"Well, you're still a minor. As long as you're living with us, we're responsible for you. You have school to finish, and—"

"I'm not going to finish school."

"Dani, you can't mean that," Mr. Branson said, leaning forward. "Your future—you want to be a journalist—"

"I still want that. But I've decided to get my GED."

"Why?" Mrs. Branson asked. "You're so close to finishing—"

"But I can't finish, at least not with my class. And if I go to summer school, and I decide to have this child,

I'll be—it'll be obvious."

"Okay," Mr. Branson said. "A GED is possible. You could take the test at any time, even before your class graduates. You won't receive the certificate until they do. You know that, right?"

"I didn't," Dani admitted. "But that's okay."

"It would mean," he continued, "you couldn't apply to the best universities."

She swallowed. "I don't even know if I'm going to college now."

"But you must!" Mrs. Branson exclaimed.

"I have to figure out what to do first."

Mr. Branson rose. "I need to have a chat with your folks, Dani."

"Do you have to?"

"I'm afraid so. Your parents do love you, even if sometimes it doesn't seem that way."

"But what will you tell them?"

He looked at his wife for a moment before answering. "I'll tell them that we've spoken to you, and the reason your grades have slipped is due to the physical trauma of your… accident."

"You're not going to tell them you know the truth?"

"I don't think so. I'll give them the opportunity to tell me what really happened."

"And if they don't?"

"Then, we figure out a way forward together—the five of us."

"You and Mrs. Branson and—?"

"Janie and Brandon. Brandon won't have to be told, but if you have the child—well, he's not blind."

"But we have to show your parents that you're working toward your high school diploma," Mrs. Branson said.

"But my GED—"

"Get it," she said. "And when you receive your score, we'll cross that bridge when we come to it."

"One step at a time," Mr. Branson said.

Dani swallowed. Nothing was going as she'd planned it—not her wedding to Rich, her high school graduation, or her college plans. And least of all, an unplanned pregnancy.

18

Darrell rang the doorbell at half-past nine. Dani was in Janie's bedroom when they heard his voice at the door. As they peered around the corner, she discovered Mrs. Branson in the doorway. At the sight of Dani, Darrell leaned around Janie's mother. "You forgot your pocketbook, Dani."

"Oh, thank you," she said, rushing forward. She grasped the pocketbook and nearly dropped it from the unexpected weight. "I'm glad you're here. I have something of yours, too."

They both stole a questioning glance at Mrs. Branson.

"Go ahead," she said, stepping away from the door. "But no more visitors and lights out at ten o'clock. I won't tell you twice."

"Yes, ma'am," they said in unison.

It took less than five minutes for them to converge in Janie's room and complete their business. Dani handed the money to Darrell. "The ammunition?"

"It's all there," Darrell said. "You know where I hang if you need anything else."

"Thank you," Dani said.

He nodded. "Oh, and I threw in an extra magazine."

"I—" she started.

"I don't need to know." With that, he was back down the hall, disappearing through the door and into the night.

Janie waited until she heard the front door open and close before she closed the bedroom door and leaned against it. "So, you bought yourself a birthday gift."

Dani climbed onto the bed and tucked her legs under herself, pulling the pocketbook into her lap. "Birthday gift?"

"Have you really forgotten? It's just a couple of days away. It's only the most important birthday of our lives—all three of us!"

Dani frowned at her friend. "Oh," she exclaimed. "We'll be eighteen!"

"You betcha. And then, you don't have to ask for permission to do anything."

"Except drink."

"Who pays attention to that?" Janie smiled as she grabbed her hairbrush and began to run it through her long locks. "I'm pretty sure your parents and mine are planning a joint party."

"They always do." Dani hesitated with a box of ammunition in her hands as she recalled the annual event. They always held it at the Evans' home; it was large enough to accommodate the crowd, and Mae customarily outdid herself with a formal buffet. It had never mattered to Dani before now that two-thirds of the attendees were her parents' friends. Tonight, for some reason, it did bother her—a lot.

"So, everything is there?" Janie asked.

"Two boxes of ammunition, two magazines, the pistol, and the purse…"

"What are you going to do with it?"

"Practice every chance I get." She loaded the pistol, returned it to the secret compartment, and set the pocketbook on the nightstand.

"Maybe I should get one, too."

"It wouldn't hurt, I suppose."

"Or, I could just use Brandon's." She slipped out of her blouse and shimmied into her nightgown, sliding her slacks onto the floor. "I wonder what my dad is saying to your folks right now," she said as she pulled back the covers on her side of the bed.

"In a few days," Dani said as she also changed into her nightclothes, "it won't matter."

~~~~~

The sun was already burning through the morning haze as Dani drove to school. Her schoolbooks rested beside her, with the new pocketbook sitting atop them. Her night had been filled with restless dreams of shooting cans off tree trunks. Then Dele Mason appeared in the field behind her, and she turned abruptly and shot him dead.

Now, in the harsh light of day, she wasn't so sure she would have those killer instincts. When the time came—*if* it came—Dani knew she could not hesitate. She could not waste time talking to him, explaining why she planned to kill him, as Hollywood always depicted. Instead, she must simply pull the trigger, again and again and again, until the magazine was spent. And if he somehow managed to survive that, she had to replace the magazine and empty that one. That's the way it had to be.

As she drove past Parchman, she caught a glimpse of the inmates in the cottonfields and adjacent cornfields, working like modern-day slaves as the guards stood over them with rifles and shotguns. She wondered if Mae's son was among them, watching her drive past while yearning for freedom.

A few years earlier, the comedian Jerry Lewis had flown over Mississippi; he told an audience later that it had looked like a toilet bowl. She hadn't actually heard him say it; she was far too busy with her life to pay any attention to things like that. But her schoolteacher had heard it, and Mrs. Cochelli had gone on quite a rant. She threatened to fail any student that uttered the comedian's name in her presence.

He must have seen it in the winter, Dani surmised. In the winter months, the summer grasses turned brown and blended into the Mississippi clay. The farmers had harvested the cotton and most vegetables except for a scattered patch of winter cabbage or zucchini. They would not have turned over the soil just yet, leaving a residue of stalks and stubble to tackle come spring. From the air, it would look like acre upon acre of decay.

There truly was no spring in the Deep South insofar as Mother Nature was concerned. There was hot and hotter, pure and simple. But the farmers acted as though there were four proper seasons, and they were already hard at work turning the soil, plowing the rows, and planting their crops.

Had Jerry Lewis flown over the state in late August, he might have had a different impression. By then, the cotton was high with seas of white waving in the breeze, and the summer grass tall and green. The cornstalks would have reached beyond a man's head, and vegetable stands and farmers' markets would have been overflowing. He might have seen a mosaic of color then, as pumpkin fields and autumn crops competed against the waning summer crops.

She turned the corner and neared the high school. She would play the part expected of her for a few more days, at least. But between classes, she would meet with the librarian, who could surely inform her of the next GED testing. A plan was beginning to form. With the age of eighteen looming before her, it meant emancipation. It was time to take her life back.

19

Dani pulled her vehicle alongside her father's shiny Lincoln Continental. It seemed like a lifetime ago when she'd last ridden in his car. It had been the night of the assault. She vaguely remembered the ride to Dr. Nash's clinic, but she did not recall the drive back home. Now it felt as though it had all happened to someone else—or it would, she thought wryly, if she didn't have Dele Mason's baby growing inside her. Had it not been for this little life, she might have turned a corner now, able perhaps in varying degrees to convince herself it had all been a nightmare. She might be planning her wedding to Rich, preparing to graduate high school, and already lining up interviews for more substantial journalism positions while she worked on her degree.

She turned off the ignition and sat for a moment, reluctant to leave the relative serenity of the car for the tumult that surely awaited her inside. The house appeared as it always had; she supposed it had remained mostly unchanged for generations. The trees were taller than those of her youth, some now reaching to the roof and beyond. The copses were filled with underbrush, the trail leading to Grandma Dottie's house lined with encroaching wildflowers.

Yet, it felt different somehow. It seemed foreign, as if Dani hadn't spent her life growing up here. The energy had shifted. Or perhaps, she thought, it was her energy that had changed. Maybe she was no longer that innocent little girl climbing onto her father's lap or the teenager borrowing her mother's lipstick.

Dani caught a glimpse of her grandmother nearly skipping along the path. She carried a basket in her hands as though she'd been picking wildflowers. She was dressed only in her bra and panties. Dani groaned and leaned her head against the headrest. That was an image she didn't need to see.

The top was down on her convertible Spitfire, and when she inhaled deeply, she could detect the alluring aroma of wild honeysuckle in the evening breeze. The pungent odor of boxwood mingled with it, combining the bouquet of carefully cultivated hedges with wild plants. Beneath it all was the unique fragrance of Mississippi soil.

She sighed and removed her keys from the ignition. She'd best get this over with.

~~~~~

Dani pushed back from the table. Whether it was nerves or her pregnancy, she was famished when she entered the house and caught a whiff of Mae's cooking. Now she realized she'd probably overeaten, but she didn't care. Every bite from the pot roast and vegetables to the homemade biscuits and gravy had been delicious.

She might not miss her life in this house, but she sure had missed Mae's home-cooked meals. A large crystal bowl rested on the side table, its contents half-eaten. The remainder of the banana pudding called to her for a second and third helping, and she barely resisted the temptation. Mae knew how to make the classic dessert like no other, with the perfect blend of overripe bananas, creamy homemade pudding, vanilla wafers softened just right, and freshly whipped cream.

At each end of the table were two vases, each filled with a haphazard mixture of wildflowers and weeds, the root balls still clinging to some.

As Mae returned to the room to gather the used dishes, Jilly Anne stood. She held her whiskey glass in the air for all to see its forlorn emptiness and announced she was retiring to the study. It escaped no one that her destination held the expansive liquor cabinet.

"It was delicious, as usual," Grandma Dottie said. She was dressed now in a light pink shift covered in a small floral pattern. As her eyes turned from Mae to Dani, she added, "Even if I was seated across from a harlot."

Cole sucked in his breath. "Dottie—" he began.

"Are you happy, Grandma?" Dani interrupted. "Really happy?"

"Never been happier." Dottie rose from her seat. She was barefoot.

"Then good for you," Dani said, her voice firm. "I've concluded that some people aren't meant to spend their lives pursuing happiness."

"Now, Dani—" her father began.

"Some people," Dani continued, "might be here to pursue justice instead. Some of us might encounter bumps in the road so we can smooth it over for those that come behind us."

"Bumps in the road, 'ey?" Dottie grimaced. "Looks more like a bump in the stomach to me." Without waiting for a response, she crossed the room and picked up the dessert bowl. "I'm taking this home if nobody else wants it," she announced. Then she abruptly left the room, crossed the hall, and entered the formal living room. Mae stopped at the doorway and watched as Dottie reentered the corridor a moment later. The older woman looked toward the front door and then the back before peering at Mae.

"The path to your place is through that door," Mae said, nodding in the direction of the back door.

"I know that!" she retorted. "Don't you get insolent with me!" Then she padded off down the hallway, slamming the screen door behind her as she exited.

Cole shook his head. "Your grandmother…" He left his words to hang in the air.

"Is she getting worse, or is it my imagination?" Dani asked.

"Who knows?" He sipped the last of his wine as he watched Mae. "Don't mind her. She doesn't know what she's saying half the time."

"Or maybe, societal filters have slipped away, so she's saying precisely what she means."

"You sure you got plenty to eat, Miss Dani?" Mae asked, her voice defusing Dani's rising temperature. "Mister Cole?"

"Plenty," Dani answered. "It was fabulous, Mae. You're the best cook in the world."

She cackled. "I don't know about all that now, but I tries my best." She loaded a tray with the dishes, lifted it to her waist, and carried it out of the room.

"I'm glad you came by," Cole said. He picked up the bottle of wine from the table and poured the last of it into his glass.

"Did I have a choice?" Dani quipped. Realizing her voice had taken on a sharpness she hadn't intended, she added, "The Bransons told me you wanted to see me."

"Actually, your mother and I…"

The sound of glass bottles clinking against one another sounded from the study. "It's okay, Dad. It's best it's you and me, anyway."

He wrapped his hand around the glass stem. "I know things haven't been easy for you."

Dani waited for him to continue. When he didn't, she said, "No. They haven't."

"You were always so good at school."

"At times, it was all I had."

He glanced up, his eyebrows rising in surprise. "I was working, Dani. Somebody had to keep a roof over your head and food on the table." He gestured toward the ceiling and the tabletop as if to drive home his point.

"I know."

"We've never minded you visiting with Janie," he went on. "But maybe, sometime, and maybe this is the right time, you and Janie should consider staying here."

"Yeah. I don't think so."

"There's more space here. Janie could have her own room."

"She likes the room she's got."

"And what about you? You don't miss your place here?"

"Of course I do."

"And Mae's cooking?"

"I miss that, too."

"Then come home, Dani. It's time. Soon, you'll be out of the house for good—married to Rich—and we miss you. I miss you."

Dani grew conscious of the pocketbook she'd placed in the seat beside hers. The pistol seemed like it had taken on an energy of its own, the gleaming metal calling out to her. She stared at the table with her hands folded into her lap. "Everyone grows up," she heard herself saying, "sooner or later."

"I'd rather it be later." He swished the wine around in the glass before taking a hearty swig.

"And what of this child I'm carrying?" she asked.

He looked at her, surprised. "Oh. That."

"You say that like you'd forgotten."

"No. I just… I've had a lot on my mind."

"I know."

He cocked his head. "I don't think you do."

"I work at the newspaper, Dad. I saw the article as it was leaving the press."

He nodded. "I see."

"Why didn't you tell me you represented Dele Mason?"

His brows knit together. "I never discuss my clients at home. You know that."

"But you could have told me you represented a rapist."

"He was never convicted of rape."

"Thanks to you."

He took a deep breath. "Look, Dani, I'm sorry about what happened to you, but every case is different—"

"You also fought for his right to see his victim's child."

"It was his child, too."

"What does that matter, if it was rape?"

"He's the father, Dani. I won't discuss it further with you."

"Okay. So let's discuss me."

"Let's."

"You just set a precedent in the State Supreme Court."

"It doesn't affect you."

"How do you know that?"

He finished off the wine and rose. He carried his glass to the side table and set it down on a beverage tray. Then he opened the double doors below it and retrieved another bottle. "Care for some?" he asked.

"I'm a minor."

He glanced at his watch. "Only for another thirty hours or so."

"No, thanks. I'll pass."

He uncorked it and left it to breathe.

"How do you know that your representation of Dele Mason won't end up binding your daughter to him forever?"

"What the hell are you talking about?" He lifted the bottle.

"It was your client, Dad. It was Dele Mason."

"What are you saying?"

"He was the man that attacked me."

Cole slammed the bottle to the table with such a jar that it spilled across the neat white doily. "What?"

Dani grabbed for her pocketbook, pulling it into her lap as if it could protect her. "That's right. I saw him standing outside your office the night I dropped off Mama. You remember that night, don't you? It was the night of your big win. It was the night you forever bound a rapist to his victim—and her child."

His jaw had dropped. As he remained speechless, Dani continued, "You gave him exactly what he wanted, Dad. I suppose maybe he felt emboldened, don't you think? I wonder if he knew about me even before that night. Maybe he saw pictures of me scattered around your office—"

"Are you telling me Dele Mason raped you?"

"That is exactly what I'm telling you."

"Why didn't you say something?"

"I didn't know until I saw his picture in the paper. You never asked, Dad." Tears of anger rose. "You never asked me to describe the attacker. If you had, you would have known—"

"I'll kill him."

"Before or after he pays you?"

He spread his hands wide. "Mason is a piece of shit. He's not worth—"

"—defending? And yet you did, Dad. You did."

Cole took a deep breath. "Life isn't always simple, Dani. Mason is connected to some big names in St. Louis—"

"Then why didn't they defend him?"

"They did. They hired me."

"So, you sold yourself out?"

"I did what I needed to do." He carried the bottle and his glass back to the table. His hand shook as he poured another drink. "I will kill him," he repeated.

"Then, who will defend you?" Dani clutched the pocketbook closer to her.

He waved his hand in dismissal. "You presume I'd get caught."

"Yes. I do." She took a deep breath. "And what if you were? You and Mama have been pretty adamant that we avoid the appearance of impropriety."

"I wouldn't do it myself."

"Oh?"

"Look, Dani, you don't want to know the details. Trust me; you don't."

"Killing him doesn't solve the dilemma I'm in."

He stared at his drink. "No. It doesn't."

"I've been going over my options, again and again." She hesitated. "You spoke to Rich, didn't you?"

He nodded. "He'll do right by you."

Dani tried to chuckle sardonically but fell short, and it came out like a cackle. "I am having second thoughts about Rich."

His head popped up. "What? Why?"

"I can't imagine a situation where I needed him more," Dani said thoughtfully. "And his kneejerk reactions aren't what I would have expected from someone that says he loves me."

"He does love you. He was just surprised, that's all."

"He couldn't have been more surprised than me."

"Don't call off the wedding, Dani."

"Why? So you and Mama could have the wedding? So you could hire Rich at your law firm?" She sighed. Her voice had a flat tone of resignation, not the indignation she'd intended.

"Trust me on this, Dani. Finish school, get married—"

"Yeah. About that."

He paused. His eyes were tired and sad. "Work on your grades. Promise me you'll buckle down and work hard."

Dani stared at him. His only child was sitting in front of him, pregnant with a rapist's child. Her father had made it possible—even probable—that the man who had brutally assaulted her would have rights to the baby she carried. What if the child was a girl? What if he brutalized his daughter? She couldn't put anything past Dele Mason. All this time, she'd worried that she carried a boy and he would be the spitting image of his father. Now she realized if she carried a girl, she could become prey to the same man that assaulted her.

Yet, Cole Evans was still concerned about keeping up appearances. God forbid that his daughter should be anything less than the perfect high school student. "Yeah. I'm taking care of that, Dad."

"Promise me?"

"I promise. I won't fail." She stood. Her bones felt heavy as if she had aged in the time she'd been back home. "I gotta go."

"Stay, Dani."

"I can't." She lifted the pocketbook strap onto her shoulder. The bag felt heavy, weightier than it should with just a weapon inside. It was almost as though the pistol had taken on a life of its own and was growing inside. "I promised Janie…"

He nodded.

She made her way into the hallway and through the front door. She was already stepping off the porch when she heard the door open behind her.

"I'll take care of it, Dani," her father called out. "Just trust me."

She turned at the sound of his voice. Trust you, she thought as she stared at him. Trust you to take care of me. "Sure, Dad."

Before he could respond, she made her way to her car. A moment later, she was pulling onto the rural road. She felt her father's presence as he remained in the doorway, but she didn't look back. The time for trust was over.

20

Dani closed the telephone booth's accordion glass door and fumbled in her pocket for the business card Dr. O'Hare had given her. The booth reeked of old potato chips and spilled soft drinks, and just above her head was a spider-webbed pit that appeared suspiciously like a bullet hole. She fed in her dime and dialed the number. An operator came on the line, directing her to deposit more money for the long-distance call. As she emptied her coin purse, she decided she could drive to Memphis for less money than this call was costing.

Finally, a pleasant voice answered on the other end. "Bianci and Romano Obstetrics and Gynecology."

"Hello," Dani said, her voice strained. "I'd like to make an appointment with Dr. Bianci, please."

"Are you a patient?"

She swallowed. "Not yet. Dr. O'Hare recommended that I see him."

"Dr. O'Hare. You're in Mississippi?"

"Yes."

"I see. The purpose of your visit?"

"I'm expecting."

"Congratulations. So you'll be wanting Dr. Bianci to handle the delivery here in Memphis?"

"No." She took a breath. "I want an abortion. I understand you do that there."

The woman hesitated. "We assist in miscarriages. How far along are you?"

"About six weeks. Seven," Dani corrected herself.

"Age?"

"Eighteen."

"Date of birth?"

Dani rattled off her date of birth.

"Happy birthday," the receptionist said. "Eighteen today, 'ey?"

"Thanks."

"Are you available the day after tomorrow?"

"Yes."

"Nine o'clock?"

"Yes."

"Do you have the address?"

"I think so." Dani read off the address from the card.

"That's right. You can eat a normal breakfast that morning. No alcohol. Bring a list of medications you're taking."

"Okay."

"We'll see you then. Oh, and — if you want it done during this visit, you'll need your husband's permission."

"My husband's permission?" Dani felt the heat beginning to rise in her cheeks, and her heart quickened.

"Your husband's or your parent's. Are you married?"

"Yes," Dani lied. "But why does my husband have to give his permission? It's my body," she continued, her voice rising.

"But it's his baby. Right?"

"I'll be there the day after tomorrow."

"But remember—"

"Right. I got it."

She hung up the phone. Then she removed it from the hook, slammed it back down twice more for effect, and then three more times. She tried to catch her breath as her heart pounded, her chest visibly rising and falling.

The door to the adjacent convenience store swung open, and it barely registered that someone was exiting. It was a quarter till three. Dani's last class of the day had ended fifteen minutes earlier, and she had scheduled the school's librarian for three o'clock. She supposed that any other time, she might have noticed the beautiful day, the warmth of the sun, or the breeze that barely kept the humidity from sticking to her skin. But now, the words from the doctor's office reverberated in her mind.

A rap on the door startled her.

"Hey, Dani!"

She turned, surprised to see Brandon smiling at her in a curious sort of way.

"Hey, what gives?" he asked.

She opened the door and grabbed her bag. "Nothing. Just… I've gotta go."

"Want to hang with me and Stu?"

She glanced toward the parking lot, where Stu had exited the Jeep and was leaning over the hood as he watched them.

"I can't," she said. "I've gotta meet with the school librarian."

"The librarian? Why?"

She shook her head. "Just… testing."

"Hey, good luck with that." He took a couple of steps toward the car. "I am done with testing for the whole week."

"Oh, yeah?"

"Yep. And there's a teacher conference tomorrow and Friday, so I am done for four days." He held up his fingers for emphasis. "Hey, Dani, happy birthday!"

"Thanks. Happy birthday to you and Janie, too!"

"Birthday party's Saturday night."

"At my place," she said. "Same as always."

"Nope," he corrected. "Not the same. We're eighteen!" He let out a celebratory howl as he got into the driver's seat and cranked the car.

"Hey, Dani," Stu called.

She came to stand beside the driver's door. "Hey, Stu," she called back through the open window as Stu settled into the passenger seat.

"See you Saturday, Dani." Brandon glanced behind him and then placed the car in reverse.

"Hey, Bran." Dani held onto the window jamb.

"Yeah?" He put his foot on the brake.

"You want to go with me to Memphis on Friday?"

~~~~~

The library was in stark contrast with the medley of voices Dani had passed in the corridor. Once the heavy double doors swung closed behind her, it was as though she had entered into a different world.

It was a small space, particularly for a high school. Cinderblocks comprised the walls, the paint so thick that it bespoke of years in varying colors. Shelves reached from the floor to the ceiling along the back wall, but the top shelf was covered in construction paper cut out to appear like spring flowers and budding trees. The center of the room consisted of aisles arranged like spokes of a wheel, in which shelving no taller than four feet ran its length. A rumor circulated that Earline Delmont and Dwayne Pervis were caught making out two years ago, hidden by the more towering shelves in use at the time. The librarian, the same widowed Mrs. Daisy Saggory that Dani was there to meet, turned the corner with an armful of books and nearly fainted at the sight of Earline on her knees and Dwayne in the throws of ejaculating.

The library hadn't been the same since.

Mrs. Saggory had rearranged the long rows that had afforded so much privacy into spokes, allowing the librarian to view every aisle from the comfort of her desk. As if that hadn't been enough, she'd torn down the upper shelves, having forced Dwayne to cut them with his daddy's chainsaw as penance for his poor judgment. Earline was ruined even as she became the most popular girl among the football team. A year later, the Delmont family left. It was rumored they'd fled to Baton Rouge in shame, but Dani suspected her reputation had preceded them. It was just the way of the South.

Now, she peered down the aisles as she stood in front of the checkout desk. Mrs. Saggory had spotted her, and she was now on her way to greet her.

"How are you, Dani?" she asked. She was a pleasant lady, and her name fit. Her hair was an unnatural shade of blond, a flat color that might as well have been from a piece of yellow construction paper. She styled it high and stiff. Everybody knew she had a standing appointment at Stella's Styles every Saturday. It meant her hair was fairly erect on Monday, but as the week went on, it became more lopsided as she slept on one side. By the time Friday rolled around, it often looked like the Leaning Tower of Pisa.

"I'm good," Dani answered.

"How's your mama and daddy?"

"They're good."

The door opened, and two giggling girls stepped in, their arms filled with books.

"Can we go someplace private?" Dani asked.

"My office."

They stepped behind the desk to another room. The front wall consisted of a large plate glass window that overlooked the library, but Dani suspected it was about as private as things were going to get.

"What's on your mind, Dani?"

"I want to take the GED test, and I've been told you're the one that administers it."

She frowned. "Your class is graduating in one more month."

"Yes, ma'am. But I'm not."

Her eyes went straight to Dani's belly. "You didn't get yourself in trouble, did you?"

"No, ma'am." As Mrs. Saggory continued to stare at her, Dani self-consciously covered her stomach with her bag and continued, "I lost a lot of time due to my accident."

"Yes, I heard about that. Are you feeling better nowadays?" Her eyes moved back to Dani's face. She appeared somewhat disappointed.

"Yes, ma'am. I'm almost back to normal. But I wasn't able to catch up on my schoolwork. So Mrs. Johnston says I'd need to attend summer school."

"Summer school's not so bad," Mrs. Saggory said.

"It's filled with kids that don't learn during the school year."

"I imagine you'd be in a class of your own, no pun intended," Mrs. Saggory said, chuckling at her attempt at witticism. "Half days, I bet, and maybe a bit of homework."

"Yes, ma'am. But I'm getting married this summer, and—"

"You're marrying Rich, aren't you?"

"Yes, ma'am."

"You couldn't do better. He's studying to be a lawyer, isn't he?"

Dani nodded.

"So, you're afraid that summer school will interfere with your wedding?"

"And the honeymoon."

"Where are you going?"

"New Orleans." She wanted to choke as she said it. They had made their plans in more innocent times. Dani had already purchased the lingerie she'd intended to wear on her wedding night. It was white and lacy and showed her curves. When they weren't in the hotel room, they'd made plans to visit Madame Tussauds' Wax Museum, take a romantic carriage ride from Jackson Square, visit the Chalmette Battlefield, and maybe even take a swamp tour. She forced her focus away from those plans.

"What do your mama and daddy say about that?" Mrs. Saggory was saying.

"About New Orleans?"

"About your idea to take the GED, child."

The word hung in the air. Dani swallowed. "I'm eighteen today."

"Happy birthday."

"Thank you."

"Now, answer my question."

"Well, seeing as how I'm eighteen and I'm not living at home, I didn't think I needed their permission."

Mrs. Saggory sighed and straightened her back as she peered at her. "You don't. Anybody can drop out of school on their own, even if you weren't eighteen."

"Then why did you ask it?"

She shrugged. "Just curious. So, Dani, you can't take the GED if you're still attending school. Did you know that?"

Dani shook her head.

"Here's what it looks like to me. You could drop out, take the test, and when your class graduates—provided you passed the test—you'd get your GED certificate."

"That's what I want to do."

"Or, you could stay in school, attend this summer, and have a regular high school diploma."

"What does it matter?"

Mrs. Saggory rubbed her chin. "Honest to God, Dani, it won't make a hill of beans because you're a young woman. If you were a man, I'd suggest staying in school so you would qualify for the better universities."

"But because I'm a girl, it doesn't matter?"

She shook her head. "It won't matter one whit."

Dani's lower lip trembled. "So, when is the next test given?"

"This Saturday. It means you'd have to drop out before then."

"How do I do that?"

"Just tell me that's what you want."

"That's it?"

"That's it. Your mama and daddy aren't going to be mad at me, are they?"

"No, ma'am."

"You're sure this is what you want to do?"

Dani nodded. "Mrs. Saggory, I've got to go." She stood. "Do I need to sign anything? A form or—"

"No. You've told me. That's all that's needed." She hesitated. "So, I'll see you Saturday?"

"Yes, ma'am."

"Eight o'clock sharp, right here in the library."

Dani nodded. As she exited the office, the two classmates were approaching the checkout desk. Mrs. Saggory engaged them in conversation, asking about their parents as she'd asked about Dani's.

Dani slipped through the library doors into the corridor. The halls were quiet now as most students couldn't wait to get off the school grounds once the final bell had sounded. She hurried to the side door that emptied into the student parking lot. Her Spitfire looked forlorn in the empty lot.

She slipped behind the wheel and set her bag on the passenger seat, and began to cry.

21

Memphis appeared grimy and noisy compared to rural Mississippi, and despite the detailed map she held in her lap, Dani had managed to get them turned around no less than five times. A crease had begun to form between Brandon's brows as he navigated Janie's 1965 Corvair through the mounting traffic. It was a vehicle Ralph Nader had recently labeled unsafe at any speed, Brandon having determined that his Jeep was unsuited for the interstate.

Janie had wanted to come along also, eager for an infrequent trip out of state. But she was still in the midst of final testing, as was Stu.

"There it is," Dani said excitedly, pointing at a one-story whitewashed brick building. It was situated in a shopping center in what appeared to be an old grocery store. Above plate glass windows, letters spelled out 'Bianci and Romano Obstetrics and Gynecology' in neon that glowed through the mist that had begun to form.

They'd left the Branson home before seven o'clock that morning, though the drive to Memphis should have taken less than an hour and a half. With the detours she'd inadvertently taken them on, they pulled into the parking lot with just five minutes to spare.

"So, this is it," Brandon said, turning off the ignition and silencing Led Zeppelin.

Four people marched along the sidewalk in front of the clinic. Each was holding a sign, but from this distance and through the mist, Dani was unable to read them. "Thanks for doing this," she said nervously.

"I wasn't doing anything today anyway," Brandon said with a sheepish smile. He opened his car door as Dani opened hers. They met in front of the vehicle and made their way to the clinic.

Before they'd reached the sidewalk, one of the sign-holders blocked their path. The man appeared to be in his mid-30s. Unlike Brandon's long hair, his was a neat buzzcut, and his face was shiny as though he spent a fair bit of time polishing it. He reeked of Old Spice aftershave as if he had soaked his polyester plaid shirt and crisp trousers in it. Dani drew her eyes upward to the sign he held: 'Babykiller' it proclaimed in bold red letters.

"Don't go in there," he warned. In his other hand, he held a Bible. "Jesus will forgive you if you turn around now."

"Forgive us for what?" Brandon retorted.

"Don't talk to him," Dani said, trying to sidestep him.

"They murder babies in there," he said, his clean-shaven face contorting. "Do you want to spend eternity in hell?"

"We have an appointment," Dani said curtly, reaching out her arm to brush past him.

"You're a sinner!" the man yelled. The other three marchers formed a barricade in front of them.

Dani stopped in her tracks but did not turn around. "You know nothing about me!"

"Are you giving birth to your baby?" a woman pressed. Her hair was styled in a beehive, the highly teased strands beginning to appear like a spiderweb as the mist formed tiny balls like dew upon it.

"That's none of your business," Brandon said. He was taller than the others, and his voice had taken on a deeper tone.

"You're going in there so they can kill it!" the woman exclaimed.

"Murderer!" another chanted. The others picked up the chant. "Murderer! Murderer!"

Dani and Brandon tried again to move past them. When that failed, she turned to the man carrying the Bible. "What do you care what I do here?"

"We're here to save your baby," he said.

"I bet it will have blond hair just like yours," a short young lady said. She had a cherubic face and round body. "And big blue eyes."

"Why do you want to save my baby—assuming I'm even pregnant?"

"It's God's will!" the man exclaimed. "Jesus put that baby into your womb!"

"I don't think Jesus had anything to do with it," Dani answered.

"Jesus wants you to have it!" the beehive woman said, pressing her face closer.

"Then he can show up and take it," Dani said. Her growing impatience was causing her cheeks to warm. "Do you want it? Will you raise it?" She turned to each. "Will you adopt it?" As she spoke, each took a step back. "I didn't think so. You want to force me to have a baby, but you won't take responsibility to raise it yourself."

"It's your responsibility," the cherubic woman purred. "You did the deed; now pay the piper."

"Is that what this is?" Brandon snapped. "Judgment on the sidewalk? Get the fuck out of her face before I wipe the pavement with you." He wrapped an arm around Dani. "Come on." They moved past the others as the strangers' chants began again.

"Babykillers! Babykillers!"

"Don't listen to them, Dani," Brandon whispered hoarsely. "They're holy rollers, is all they are."

A nurse appeared at the door to usher them in. "I'm sorry," she said. "We can't get rid of them."

"You have to put up with this every day?" Brandon said, his face reddening in anger.

"Every. Single. Day." She led them to the front desk. "It's reached the point where we park a block away and walk through the woods out back just to avoid them. We can't leave for lunch, or they'll accost us. Last month, we lost our receptionist when they pushed her to the ground. Broke two ribs. Two bucks an hour isn't worth it."

"That's what your receptionist earned?" Dani asked.

"You want the job?"

She shook her head. "I live in Mississippi."

"If you change your mind, we're accepting applications." The nurse stole a glance at the large windows, where the four had begun marching again. "It's been difficult keeping employees. Anyway," she said, forcing a smile, "do you have an appointment?"

"Yes," Dani said, "with Dr. Bianci."

"I'm Cora." She handed her a clipboard. "Fill this out, please. Let me know when you're done, and I'll take you right back."

~~~~~

'Right back' turned out to be an hour, during which time they watched as three more women entered the building. Two had bulging midsections; with those, the man with the Bible opened the door and smiled pleasantly. The third came alone, her eyes averted, a thick sweater covering her. Dani watched as they verbally accosted her.

Brandon reached over and grasped Dani's hand. "It's going to be okay," he said.

Dani squeezed his hand. She'd told him everything on the drive to Memphis. Brandon had listened intently, asking a few questions here and there. As he took it all in, he seemed wiser than his years. "I guess at some point, they'll ask your permission," Dani mumbled.

"A good husband always supports his wife," he whispered with a gentle smile. He hesitated, his lips moving ever so slightly as if he was weighing his words.

"We didn't think to put on rings," she said suddenly, looking at their hands.

"I bet they don't care," he said. "Listen, Dani; there's something I need to tell you."

"Well, I've bent your ear all morning about me." She nodded. "I'm all ears."

"Dani, ever since—well,—I know we were young, but I knew—I just could feel—"

Nurse Cora called Dani's name.

A myriad of emotions crossed Brandon's face as he was stopped midsentence. He rose with Dani. "Do you want me to go with you?" he asked, his eyes searching hers.

Dani stole a glance at Cora.

"They don't usually," Cora said.

Brandon's face registered disappointment as he settled back into his seat. Dani crossed the small waiting area. The clinic smelled of antiseptic, and the temperature was too cold. She hesitated at the door to glance back at Brandon. He smiled reassuringly.

"Mister Evans," another nurse called out.

Brandon was still smiling at Dani.

"Mister Evans," she said again, "you'll need to sign this."

"Oh," he said, realizing she was referring to him. "Absolutely. That's me. Brandon Evans."

As he moved toward the reception desk, Cora took Dani through the first door on the right, where Cora recorded her height and weight. Then the nurse directed her to sit in a chair beside a dark desk. As the nurse took her blood pressure, she nodded toward the front window. Though the blinds were drawn, they continued to hear the demonstrators outside.

"Does that go on all day?" Dani asked.

"All day, every day." Cora sighed. "It's like these people have no other life but here. These used to be exam rooms," she continued. "This is one of the rooms where we did the procedures. But the heckling was too much for some patients." She peered at Dani. "Are you okay?"

"I'm fine."

"Your blood pressure is a little high," she said. "Not too much to worry about," she added hastily. "It's probably the visit."

"If seeing a doctor wasn't enough, those protesters would certainly do it," Dani said with a forced chuckle.

"Come with me."

Cora led her down a corridor, rounding a corner until they had reached the back of the clinic. It was so quiet here that their shoe soles echoed as they tapped across the tile. They entered a room with blinding lights, an exam table, and three chairs. "Have a seat," Cora said. As Dani settled into a chair, Cora opened a folder and pulled out a pen. "How far along are you?"

"About seven weeks."

"About. No more than twelve weeks, though?"

"No. Definitely not. Seven weeks. Why? What does it matter?"

A younger nurse with darker skin and large brown eyes joined them. She smiled as she sat beside Cora.

"This is Jasmine," Cora said.

"Hi, Danielle," Jasmine said. Though her English was flawless, she spoke with a heavy accent. "Sometimes, people like to have two perspectives before they continue."

"Two perspectives," Dani mumbled. "You're not going to try and talk me out of this, are you? My circumstances—"

"No," Jasmine said. Her smile was comfortable and reassuring. "But tell us your circumstances, if you'd like. It won't affect your treatment."

Dani glanced down at her hands, held neatly in her lap. "I was raped."

"By the young man outside?" Cora asked, her brows knitting.

"No. That's Brandon. He would never—no. The assailant broke into my house—our house. I was the only one at home."

"I'm so sorry," Jasmine said. Her eyes appeared genuinely saddened.

"We often recommend therapy," Cora said. "Women come here for all kinds of reasons, and often they are traumatized."

"By the procedure?" Dani asked quietly.

Cora shook her head. "No. They tend to be traumatized by the pregnancy itself. If their circumstances were better, they would have the baby, wouldn't they?"

"So," Jasmine said, "what we'd like to do is chat with you about the pregnancy. We want you to make the right decision."

"My mind is already made up."

"So it is. But often, afterward, the patient has doubts. We'll give you everything in writing, but we want to make sure we answer any questions you might have." Cora pulled a brochure out of the folder. "This is for you."

Dani opened the brochure.

"Right now, the fetus is about the size of a blueberry," Jasmine said.

"A blueberry. Is that all?" She envisioned Mae's blueberry cobbler served with ice cream. She'd never look at it the same way again.

Cora and Jasmine nodded. Cora added, "We want you to understand that at this point—seven weeks in—we're not talking about a fully-formed baby. It doesn't yet have a heart; it is tissue that is beginning to form. Technically, it's an embryo until you're about nine weeks along."

"I really don't need to hear this," Dani said. "My mind is made up."

"We know," Jasmine said gently. "But later, you'll be glad we discussed this."

"You see," Cora said, "the folks outside our clinic, they want you to believe you have a fully-formed baby inside you right now and that when your pregnancy is terminated, it will look just like giving birth to a newborn."

"And that isn't true," Jasmine added. "If you've had heavy periods, you've already expelled as much as aborted tissue at this stage. There are no eyes, no ears, not even a heart yet. There are no arms and no legs."

"But don't you listen to the baby's heart?" Dani asked.

"At this stage, the umbilical cord is keeping the embryo alive. The heartbeat is the mother's. The fetus won't begin a heartbeat of its own until it's around four or five months along."

Dani nodded. She placed a hand over her belly.

"I am from India," Jasmine continued. "Our beliefs are a bit different from many Americans. We believe the soul does not enter the fetus until it is nearing the end of gestation."

"And Christians?" Dani asked. She felt as though she was going to be nauseous.

"Officially, it's considered to be somewhere between the second and third months," Cora answered. "Evangelicals—like those out front—think it's the moment the sperm enters the egg."

"And is there evidence of that?"

They both shook their heads. "But, who can measure a soul?" Jasmine asked. "We can measure brain activity…"

"At what stage?"

"Well, as much as we can tell, it's automatic," Cora said. "The brain begins with electrical impulses. Cells begin to replicate. That's what eventually forms the body."

"And pain?" Dani heard herself asking. Her voice sounded disconnected from her, as if she was somewhere outside looking in. "Will it feel pain?"

"We anesthetize the womb," Cora explained. They both appeared to observe Dani's expressions. "We can't truly tell if they feel pain, so the anesthesia is similar to performing an operation on you. The fetus then doesn't feel anything, just like you can't feel anything during an operation."

"We do have a chapel," Jasmine added. "Before you have this procedure, if you'd like to pray or meditate—or afterward, it's right next door. You don't have to go outside; it's just down the hallway. Literally, the next door over."

Dani swallowed.

"Do you have any questions for us?" Cora asked.

Dani shook her head.

The nurses' voices droned on, but she no longer heard their words. Something about the doctor, an exam, a few minutes—she thought they were explaining the procedure to her. But her mind was somewhere else entirely. She'd traveled back to the dirty kitchen, the coat hanger stuck into the fire, the funnel ready... What if she had gone through with it then? She would never have thought of anesthesia, despite the fact that the fetus didn't yet have organs.

"So, you want to go through with this?" Cora asked.

Dani nodded. "I haven't changed my mind."

"Okay then. Change into this gown," Cora was saying as they both stood up. "Remove all your clothes. Sit on the table, and we'll be back in shortly with the doctor."

Jasmine squeezed her hand. "Our little chat took longer than the procedure will take. Do you need to go to the chapel first?"

Dani shook her head. "Do you need Brandon's?"

"Your husband's approval? Yes, I think he's signed it. The fact that he's here with you says a lot."

They left then, the door sliding shut behind them. Yes, Dani thought. It did say a lot about Brandon. Perhaps it said even more about Rich.

22

Oddly, now that Dani was here, she was unhurried. She didn't leave the exam room for the chapel, but she sat for a long moment in contemplation. Dani knew this was the right decision. Once this was over, this entire ordeal would be behind her, and her life could move forward. It wouldn't be the same as the one she and Rich had planned; that time seemed so long ago, and everything felt so different now. But one thing Dani did know: this was not the time or place for a newborn. For the first time since learning she was pregnant, she realized that she might not be able to give up the child for adoption without the father's consent, and she could not, would not, bring a child into the world to be abused or molested by a serial rapist.

She had just begun to unbutton her blouse when the explosion rocked the building.

One moment, Dani was standing in the middle of the exam room with her fingers on a button, and in the next instant, she found herself lying in the middle of the floor. An excruciating pain shot through her ears. The entire building shook uncontrollably like an angry giant aroused. She lay on the floor, her hands over her ears in a vain attempt to stop the ringing. Her vision blurred; she tried to focus on the ceiling above her. Once comprised of pristine white panels, now half of them were missing, the metal grid dangling above her.

It took a moment for things to register. When they did, the sound of screaming reached her battered ears, followed by shouting. Dani felt her body lose coordination as she tried to rise onto her elbow. The missing ceiling tiles were scattered around the floor, broken into smaller pieces that looked like loose cardboard. A thick layer of dust covered everything, and as she struggled to her knees and grabbed the exam table for support, she ran a hand over her head. Grimy clumps of drywall and insulation covered her hair, but as she peered at her hand afterward through glazed eyes, there was no blood. A cursory examination of her body revealed no outward injuries.

The screams and shouting grew louder, and she forced herself onto wobbly feet. She tried several times to catch her breath; her torso felt constricted.

Brandon.

The thought of her friend raced through her mind, forcing adrenaline through her body. She tried to leap toward the door, but it felt more like a clumsy hurdle, her body not yet coordinated.

When she managed to heave the door open, the corridor was a pile of rubble. Thick dust was everywhere, even floating in the air. Somehow it registered that the drywall and ceiling had disintegrated, revealing jagged holes in the roof above her. It no longer appeared like the hall she had walked down only moments earlier; now, it was foreign and otherworldly.

Dani stumbled into the hall and followed the sound of voices. As she neared the front of the clinic, thick acrid smoke overtook the floating debris. Through the ringing in her ears, she thought she heard sirens, but they sounded too faint and far away.

"Brandon!" Dani tried to scream, but her throat was dry. She realized for the first time that dust filled her mouth. Inhaling to shout louder, she began to dry retch as particles poured into her throat. She pulled her blouse over her face as she staggered forward. Her eyes began to burn as the smoke grew more oppressive.

There was no corridor here; the exam rooms were gone. Dani tried to see ahead to the waiting room, but smoke and flames obscured it. "Brandon!" she called again, her voice raspy.

She thought she heard her name called, but it sounded too distant. She called for Brandon again. Dani held the blouse against her mouth and nose with one hand. The other searched along the wall for the way out, dipping as the wall gave way.

"Dani! Dani!"

Brandon plunged out of the smoke like an apparition, his head and shirt bloodied and his face pasty. His eyes appeared wild and wide as though he was trying not to blink. They locked eyes in an instant, and he grasped her by her blouse, pulling her to him. "This way!" he yelled, taking her back the way she'd just come.

At the end of the first corridor, Brandon pulled her into a room where a rush of air met them. The sirens were louder here, the shouting making it through to her ringing ears, though she couldn't make out the words. A stranger stepped into the debris, his face obscured by a helmet and face covering. Then another appeared, followed by another. Two pulled them to the safety of the parking lot while others rushed past them into the burning building.

They were shouting at her now. It took Dani a moment to understand that they were asking about others in the building. With Brandon's help, they told them of the nurses and other patients, but Dani felt woefully inept. How could she have known she should have memorized where everyone had been?

Dani didn't know how she arrived at the ambulance. She didn't remember walking there, and she knew she had not been carried. Yet there she was, sitting in the open door, a paramedic carefully examining her. She realized he was asking questions at the same time that it registered Brandon was gone.

"Where is Brandon?" she asked. Her voice sounded muffled.

"The guy that was with you? Over there," the paramedic answered. He nodded toward another ambulance, where two people were bandaging Brandon's head.

She tried to come to her feet, but they gave out beneath her.

"Whoa," the medic said, rescuing her from a fall. "He's okay. Can you tell me your name?"

"Where is everybody?" she asked.

The question was ludicrous, of course. Dani knew it even before the medic stared at her as though she'd lost her mind. The parking lot was teeming with people. The lights from fire trucks, ambulances, and police cars all melded together into a flashing mosaic that seared into her eyes. Everyone was shouting.

The windows in the front of the building were gone. Left behind were gaping, black holes. Fire licked at the edges as firefighters aimed their hoses. Bitter black smoke rolled out, choking everyone around them.

Dani realized they were at the outer edge of the parking lot, and people were staring. Someone carried a camera with a bulky lens. He wore a placard around his neck, and despite the fogginess that threatened to take over, she knew he was with the media. A wave of horror swept over her as it occurred to her that they could be on the evening news.

"I'm fine," she said, rising to her feet. This time, they held her.

"You need to be checked out," the paramedic insisted.

She made her way to Brandon. "Are you okay?"

He nodded. "It's nothing duct tape won't fix." He smiled a bit shakily.

"We've got to get out of here."

"In what?" He pointed toward the lot. Janie's car was parked oddly; the first thing that occurred to her was that someone had moved it. Then she realized the tires were smoldering, and the windows were blown out. "Janie's gonna kill me."

"Oh, my God."

"That your car?" one of the medics asked.

"Yeah," Brandon answered. "My sister's."

"Were you in it?"

He shook his head and pointed to the corner of the building. "I was in the waiting room." As Dani followed his gaze, her eyes fell upon the crumbled corner.

A firefighter emerged out of the window opening closest to the waiting room where Cora had taken her vitals. At first, it appeared as though the firefighter was missing his arms. Then Dani quickly realized he was carrying a stretcher behind him. Another firefighter had the rear.

Two paramedics raced forward, one on either side. As they ran past them, Dani caught a glimpse of one of the pregnant women. She laid flat on her back, her large abdomen like a round hill beneath a white sheet. She was not moving. Her eyes stared at the skies, unblinking.

"Stay with us," one of the paramedics was saying. "We've got you. Stay with us."

Everything began to unfurl around her in slow motion. Officers led the man that had waved the Bible at her to a police car, his wrists handcuffed behind his back, a silly grin on his face. The marchers waved their signs and shouted words of support until they, too, were arrested. Another pregnant woman stumbled out, supported by a firefighter, before collapsing into a medic's arms. Dani did not see Cora or Jasmine.

Then Brandon and Dani were climbing into an ambulance. She sat on a bench along the side while they laid Brandon on the stretcher. They pulled off his bloody shirt as the siren began, and someone shoved a bottle of water at her, folding her hand around it.

As the ambulance pulled away, she caught a glimpse of photographers, their camera lights popping as they sped past. As a medic placed a blood pressure cuff on her, her eyes moved upward to peer out the window. The mist had stopped. The skies were blue and clear. It was a beautiful day.

23

Dani watched the clock tick closer to the two o'clock hour. The hospital waiting room was too cold. She and Brandon had moved twice in vain to escape the air conditioner vents, but the chilly air had permeated everything. Now she rubbed her arm where goosebumps had appeared.

She noticed that goosebumps also dotted Brandon's arms, but he appeared to be oblivious. He'd spent the last hour staring into space, deep in thought. A slow but steady stream of people had entered the hospital's emergency room throughout the day, and most were still waiting for the nurse to call them. The clinic bombing had impacted the average flow.

Rescue personnel had transported others from the clinic, and Dani's emotions were all over the place. She had been examined and released relatively quickly. Her location had saved her from physical injury, though her ears continued to ring. Then she spent several hours with Brandon, who required several stitches in his head and shoulder from flying debris. They were the lucky ones.

The pregnant woman was declared dead at the hospital, and there had been a frantic attempt to save the baby. Her inconsolable husband had rushed to her side. She had watched him from her seat near the curtain at the foot of Brandon's bed. He was young, perhaps in his twenties. He paced the emergency room floor, running his hands through his hair. He tried to sit, but he popped up immediately. The minutes ticked past until a doctor still in scrubs approached him. They were too far away for her to hear the conversation, but the message was unmistakable. The doctor had shaken his head, and after a few seconds, the husband had dropped to his knees. The baby was gone.

Dani caught a glimpse of Jasmine as a code blue was announced over the PA, and medical personnel scrambled to gather around her. Jasmine was covered in blood while a doctor stood over her with a defibrillator. Then the curtain was closed around her. A few moments later, she was wheeled quickly out of the emergency room, a host of nurses rushing alongside her. She was alive and heading into surgery.

Cora had not yet arrived, though Dani and Brandon were there for hours. The bomb had crushed several areas, and the rumor was that rescue personnel were still searching for survivors.

When the doctor released Dani and Brandon, they found themselves in the waiting room. Brandon used the payphone to call his father, and while they waited for him to drive to Memphis, they were interviewed several times by various police officers, who didn't appear to care that they'd told their story to someone else. Dani had thought the morning appointment would be discreet, and now it felt as if she had broadcast her circumstances to the entire world. The hospital banned the press from approaching them inside the hospital, but journalists waited on the sidewalk outside, occasionally peering through the windows. Dani and Brandon kept their backs to them.

When Mr. Branson arrived, Dani felt a mixture of relief and apprehension. He rushed into the waiting room, his wide eyes taking in Brandon's injuries. "Come on," he ordered.

They didn't question his directive but followed him down a corridor and then another. They finally stopped in a smaller waiting room away from prying eyes.

"What happened?" Mr. Branson asked as he motioned for them to sit.

"It's all my fault," Dani began.

"It's nobody's fault," he corrected. "I just want to know what happened."

"I asked Brandon to drive me," she said. "I didn't know if I would be able to drive myself home afterward."

"I heard the news on the radio while I was driving up here," Mr. Branson said. "The clinic handles abortions?"

She swallowed hard. "They also deliver babies." She tried not to think about the pregnant woman that had lost her life and that of her baby.

"Were you there for a checkup, Dani, or for an abortion?"

Her face grew flushed. "An abortion."

He nodded and placed his arm around her shoulder. "I would have driven you, Dani. All you had to do was ask."

"I'm sorry, Mr. Branson."

He peered past her at Brandon. "I spoke to the

doctor before I left my office. You took some shrapnel, did you?"

Brandon nodded. He still had a faraway look in his eyes.

"You two were very fortunate," Mr. Branson said. "I hope you know that."

"We do," Dani said.

"Janie's car is totaled, Dad."

"Where is it?"

"The clinic."

"It's probably part of the crime scene now. Did either of you receive any prescriptions?"

"I did," Brandon said. "Something for the pain."

"Let me see it." Brandon handed the bottle to him, and he read the label and then handed it back. "Are you two ready to leave?"

"Yes," they both said in relieved unison.

"There are reporters at the emergency room entrance. I parked in the outpatient lot. We can get there through here, so they won't see you leave."

They all rose. Dani hadn't realized until then just how exhausted she had become. Brandon looked like he was ready to collapse.

"Have either of you eaten anything?"

They both shook their heads.

"Let's get out of here," Mr. Branson said. "We'll find a burger joint before we head back home. Your parents are worried about you, Dani. And so's your mother," he added as he looked at Brandon.

24

Dani had not expected to awaken in her own room. Of course, it made sense that Mr. and Mrs. Branson would phone her parents with the news. Her birthday had come and gone, and she was now legally an adult, yet they seemed set in their ways to treat her like a child.

They did not leave Memphis until nearly six o'clock, after an interminably long time learning the Corvair's ultimate fate and getting the insurance company involved. Then there was another stop at the police department to answer any additional questions the investigators might have. Through it all, she was forced to answer time and again why she was there. What did it matter? She had an appointment. Brandon drove her in his sister's car. They were inside, and the car was outside when the explosion occurred. End of story. Only it wasn't.

The detectives brought Brandon and Dani into a tiny room, where they peered through plate glass to identify the four people that had stopped them on the way into the clinic. She quickly picked out the man with the Bible. The others appeared to blend into one another, and she was afraid of making a mistake. Brandon's memory was better; he'd had the advantage of watching them through the windows of the waiting room.

It was the man's second arrest; Jackson, Tennessee police had arrested him a month prior. He was a suspect in an attempted bombing, which was planted under a doctor's vehicle but didn't detonate. He was awaiting trial and was out on bail. It was the others' first arrests. They all claimed they'd been led to do what they did by Jesus, who told them through third-party clergy that the people who worked at the clinic were murderers. Dani didn't know how they reconciled having killed a woman and her unborn child, a child she was looking forward to birthing in another month or two. Now, the Memphis police held all four of the demonstrators on premeditated murder charges.

They ate lunch somewhere in the blur between the police and the insurance agent. Or rather, Dani stared at her food. It had been a quiet diner. The wait staff and patrons didn't appear to know about the bombing, and the atmosphere was surreal in its normalcy. Dani felt as though they should all have known of their ordeal as she and Brandon sat in clothes soiled with dust, debris, and blood in Brandon's case. She felt exposed and vulnerable as if everyone should have known that she was pregnant with a rapist's child, and she'd been at the clinic attempting to end the pregnancy and get on with her life.

By the time she arrived home, her parents were out for the evening—God forbid her ordeal should stand in the way of a cocktail party—and Mae had been quietly reassuring as she'd cooked her dinner and taken her dirty clothes to wash. When her parents arrived home, she'd been in bed, faking sleep to avoid dealing with them.

She sighed. No such luck this morning.

She placed her hand over her belly as if she could feel the little life there. The size of a blueberry, the nurse had said. This world was too violent for a child, she thought.

She remembered the GED testing scheduled for this morning and glanced at the clock. There was plenty of time for her to get dressed, have a few cursory words with her parents, and get out the door.

Or so she thought.

~~~~~

Her father called to her as she tried to slip around the newel post. Dani had known when she reached the bottom of the stairs, she would be visible for mere seconds, and she'd hoped to slip past undetected. At the sound of her father's voice, she stifled a groan and turned toward the dining room.

Cole waved her closer.

"I can't, Dad," she said. "I'll be late for school."

"It's Saturday," he answered curtly. He set down the newspaper and picked up his coffee cup.

"I have a test," Dani answered, stopping in the doorway. Grandma Dottie sat in her usual spot. She wore her nightgown and one slipper. God only knew where the other one had gone, and Dani had a brief vision of her grandmother strolling through the woods to the big house with one foot bare and the other in a furry slipper. Jilly Anne sat next to her, dressed to the nines.

Dottie buttered a homemade biscuit. "You will burn in hell, Danielle Evans," she said as calmly as if she was discussing the weather.

"Really, Dani," Jilly Anne sighed as she set her fork down, "Memphis? Everybody goes to Memphis. If you were going to do something so scandalous, you should have gone where nobody knew us!"

"God meant for you to have that child," Dottie continued. "He wanted you to have a reminder of your heathen ways! Now there's no denying what a sinner you are."

"What test are they giving on a Saturday?" Cole asked skeptically.

Dani shrugged nonchalantly. "You said you wanted me to try harder. Well, if I don't leave now, I'll miss it. And it won't be my fault." She adjusted her purse strap on her shoulder.

"You could go to New York," Jilly Anne continued. "There are doctors that bundle the price of airfare with the cost of the abortion. New York is so big that you'd never run into anybody that knows you."

"She is not getting an abortion!" Dottie plopped her biscuit down on her plate so forcefully that bits flew across the table.

"Well, I never!" Jilly Anne exclaimed, staring at her mother.

"There will be no abortions in this family," Dottie continued. "I will tie you to your bedposts myself."

Dani felt the blood rush out of her face as the image of her body tied to the bedposts raced through her mind, followed immediately by Dele Mason's scarred face. She turned on her heels and headed for the front door.

"Wait, Dani," Cole said.

She didn't stop. She hurried out the front door and was on the final step onto the lawn when Cole called to her from the front porch.

"Dani, stop," he said. His voice had lost its commanding presence and sounded as if he was pleading with her instead.

She hesitated, half-turning.

"If you want to go through with it," he said, stepping closer, "I'll drive you. Wherever you want to go."

She nodded. She opened her mouth, but the words wouldn't form. Finally, she started toward the Triumph once more. "I'll be late," she managed to choke out.

"Tonight's your birthday party," he called after her. "Happy birthday!"

She didn't bother putting the top down but started the engine as soon as she was seated. As it whirred to life, she closed the car door. As she turned the Spitfire around to get onto the rural road, she caught a glimpse of her father standing just outside the screen door, his table napkin still in his hand. It was too far away for her to see his expression clearly, and yet as she drove away, she felt an overwhelming sadness emanating from him.

Or maybe, she thought, it was her own sadness she was feeling. It had deepened to the point where it was turning into depression, a hollowness that threatened to suck her in and take her soul.

New York seemed as far away as London, Paris, or Moscow. It was not an option, and she wondered why her mother even mentioned it—or, for that matter, how she knew about abortions there. New York was about as foreign as one could get from the Mississippi

Delta. It was filled with rude people hurrying everywhere, congested roads and sidewalks, graffiti, and winos.

And it was the home of the *New York Times* and countless universities.

25

Clouds were forming as Dani parked her car in front of a small clapboard house that had seen better times. Now that the GED test was complete, she couldn't recall a single question on it, and she was sure she had failed it.

The radio played "Here Comes the Sun" by George Harrison, and she listened for a moment to his mesmerizing voice and gentle guitar as she waited for the sun to peek through the clouds. A tiny stream of light struggled to flicker through but was overwhelmed by the volume of thick, gray clouds. It was a metaphor for her life, she thought. But if the sun refused to arrive on its own accord, perhaps she could manufacture a little bit of sunshine in her own life—if not now, then surely, in the foreseeable future. She had to hope it could be there.

She turned off the ignition and gazed at the house for a long moment. The neighborhood was built in the

1940s when manufacturing and agriculture were booming. A family of five lived comfortably in a thousand square feet with a bathroom barely large enough to turn around. Now the house was subdivided into three units. A steep staircase led to the second floor, where the landlord had turned the bedrooms and bath into a tiny apartment. The downstairs side door led to a second unit and the front door to a third. She'd been there several times before, and she'd always marveled at the way additional kitchens and baths had been added to accommodate multiple families. It felt haphazard, as though somebody had a friend that claimed to know how to do the renovations but had never actually done it before.

She climbed out of the Spitfire and made her way to the side door, passing the front porch as a stooped woman with a walker emerged to water a few straggly hanging plants. They nodded to one another, but Dani didn't stop to chat. If she did, she might lose her nerve.

She rapped on the screen door, the flimsy wood causing the door to sway and echo with each knock. Almost immediately, the inner door opened, and an astonished Tom stared back at her.

"Dani," he breathed. "So strange to see you outside the newsroom. What are you doing here?" Without waiting for her reply, he opened the screen door. "Come in, come in."

She stepped into the living room and waited for her eyes to adjust to the dim light. It was a tiny space that smelled of dampness and mold and remnants of last night's dinner. A console television dwarfed the wall under the window; the sound low while the black and white screen flickered under duct-taped rabbit ears. A battered brown sofa was against the opposite wall, and as her eyes adjusted, she discovered a young man sitting there, watching her. As their eyes met, he rose, setting a bottle of Coca-Cola on the makeshift coffee table in front of him.

"I'm sorry," Dani said, turning back to Tom. "I didn't realize you had company—"

Tom was closing the door, casting them into deeper darkness. "Nonsense, Dani. You know you're welcome here any time. This is my friend, Josh. He's visiting from New York."

Josh held out his hand. "I've heard a lot about you, Dani."

"New York?" she said. "You're a long way from home."

"That I am." He was a tall fellow with long, lanky limbs and a wide smile. He had closely cropped hair, but she couldn't quite make out its color in the dim light. Shadows obscured the details in his face, with only his pearly white teeth clearly visible.

"Josh is from Birmingham," Tom was saying. "We were dorm mates in college; that's how we met."

"But you live in New York now?"

Josh nodded. "Newspaperman, like Tom."

"The *New York Times*?" Dani breathed as if she was speaking to royalty.

Josh laughed. It was a boisterous laugh whose warmth wrapped itself around Dani. "Not hardly," he said. "I work in Delaware County, just north of Poughkeepsie."

"Poughkeepsie," she repeated. "I've heard of that."

"FDR's home," Tom said. He gestured toward the sofa. "Have a seat, Dani."

"It's a museum now, his home," Josh said. He waited until Dani sat before resuming his seat at the opposite end.

"And you remember my granny," Tom said.

Dani turned to find a stout woman in the doorway just a few feet away. The light emanating from the kitchen framed her, her shift nearly see-through as she clutched a walker.

"Babula," Dani said, using the Polish term for a grandmother as she rose with Josh to greet her.

"Sit, sit, all of you," she said, gesturing toward the sofa. Yet they remained standing until she had settled into a worn chair in the corner and covered her legs with a frayed afghan. Her accent was heavy, though she had been in the United States for nearly thirty years. She had regaled Dani of her history one wet, chilly day; her grandparents had immigrated to Poland from Ireland searching for job opportunities. They'd raised seven children in the shadow of the Carpathian Mountains as they managed to transform themselves from poor immigrants into proprietors of goat cheese. Among Babula's fondest memories was visiting her grandparents and hustling the goats into the house when heavy storms arose.

She'd moved in with Tom a couple of years prior, after Tom's mother, Babula's daughter, passed away from cancer. Tom's father had been killed in an accident at the cotton gin when Tom was just a tyke. Dani never knew how they managed to make their living arrangements work, as Tom's tiny apartment had only one bedroom, but she was too polite to ask. She supposed Tom slept on the sofa each night, which made her feel less at ease when she sat back down.

"Granny Malor—" Josh began.

"Malgorzata," she corrected. "But, child, that is why everyone calls me Babula." She smiled then. Her face appeared to glow as she sat beside the only lamp in the room. Her skin appeared as translucent and delicate as vellum beneath shimmering white hair.

"Babula," Josh began again, "had been giving me some advice."

"Advice?" Dani asked.

Tom sat in a corner opposite them on a wobbly wood chair. "We should fill Dani in on the conversation," he said. "And to do that, I suppose we have to go back a few years."

"Tom's granny is the reason I live in New York," Josh said, turning to Dani.

"Oh?"

"I'll never forget her words. Do you remember them, Babula?"

"I remember everything," she said. She leaned forward, though her voice carried in the small room. "You two gents had just graduated from the university. You were assessing your futures. And I gave you both the same advice: geography determines your destiny."

"Geography determines your destiny," Dani repeated, allowing the words to sink in.

"And she was right," Josh said.

"It was a lesson I learned myself, having been handed down to me from my mother and her mother before her," Babula said. "It was the reason my ancestors left Ireland for Eastern Europe and the reason I left Europe for America."

"How old were you?" Tom asked though Dani suspected he knew his grandmother's stories by heart.

"I do believe I was forty-three. My daughter Saoirse, Tom's mother, was preparing to marry an oat farmer. Our isolation allowed us to escape from the Nazi's most horrific acts of genocide." She sighed. "For a time, at least."

"They fled the Carpathian Mountains, didn't you, Babula?" Tom filled in when the room became silent as if they were all envisioning World War II.

"My parents never said we were fleeing. They looked ahead and knew our futures were not in Poland. They were excited for my sisters and brothers and me to move to a country where there were endless opportunities." She met each of their gazes. "It wasn't until much later that I realized we had indeed fled."

"And did Saoirse's fiancée come to America as well?" Dani asked.

Babula shook her head. "He would not leave. He wanted to stand his ground. The land had been in his family for generations…"

"Whatever happened to him?"

"We heard after the war that the Nazis had rounded him up with others in neighboring villages. Killed. The lot of them."

The room grew quiet. Babula remained forward in her seat, her eyes moving from one to the other. "Geography determines your destiny," she said again with a finality in her voice.

"If your family was originally from Ireland," Dani asked, "why didn't you return there? The Nazis never made it that far west. It just seems like it would have been much closer," she added lamely.

"Ah." Her eyes took on a distant look. "Sometimes, what appears as the easiest route isn't always the best one. It would have been easy for us to move there, yes. Ireland had declared itself a neutral country. But those times were filled with uncertainty. All times," she said, waggling one finger for emphasis, "are filled with uncertainty."

She leaned further forward and fixed each of them with her gaze before continuing. "We can look back upon those times now and see how history unfolded to the very end. But when you're living it, nothing is certain; nothing is guaranteed. You see, Nazi Germany had entered into an agreement with Russia, and yet they invaded her. Chamberlain, too, had sought to appease Hitler. Under Churchill, the United Kingdom was the only country between the Nazis and Ireland. If they fell, so would the Irish. We could not escape to the east nor the west. Our best course of action was to flee the continent altogether. It was Australia or America, and my parents chose the latter."

"My mom spent the war waiting for her fiancée," Tom said. His voice had taken on a quiet, reflective tone. "She said she wrote to him every week. She never learned where her mail had gone; after the war, she discovered the Nazis had taken him within a week of her leaving for America. He'd been dead the whole time..." He paused before adding, "She met my dad a few years after the war. His family was from Mississippi, which is how she ended up here." He smiled shyly. "And how I came to be born here."

"I've been trying to convince Tom and Babula to move to New York," Josh said.

"Oh?" Surprised, Dani looked at Tom.

"And he should go," Babula said. Her voice was gentle but firm. "There are more opportunities for you there, child."

"But she won't come with him," Josh said quietly. "And, understandably, Tom won't go without her."

"But what about geography and destiny?" Dani teased.

Babula laughed. "Ah, yes. Tom's destiny is before him; my destiny is behind me."

"But your destinies are tied together," Josh said.

"You don't sound like you're from the south," Dani said abruptly, turning to Josh. She realized her comment sounded rude, and she tried to backpedal, but Josh stopped her.

"No," he said. "I don't." He took a breath. "I attended language school to rid myself of a southern drawl."

"Why on earth would you do that?" Dani breathed.

Josh smiled sadly. "Those outside of the Deep South interpret a slow Mississippi drawl to mean—well, that you're slow-witted."

"No."

"Don't look so shocked. It's a big world out there," Josh continued. "And the choice is to fit in or stand out."

"And you chose to fit in."

He nodded. "For the right reason, I hope. I'd like to stand out for the right reason as well."

"And there are schools for that?"

He laughed again, that boisterous laugh that seemed to come from deep inside him. "There are."

"It probably helped him to land a job," Tom added.

"And your advice, Babula?" Dani turned to Tom's grandmother. "I'm sorry I interrupted."

"You didn't, child," Babula said. She continued to lean forward as she peered at her. Under the light of the lamp, her blue eyes appeared vivid and sharp, as if she was able to look through Dani to her deepest secrets. "I told Tom to go and find his future there."

"But I won't leave you," Tom said. "Besides, we'd already talked it through. I'm trying to land a job in Jackson at the *Clarion-Ledger*. With a better-paying job, I can afford a larger place for us." He turned to Dani.

"Anyway, we've been chatting on, and I haven't asked you why you stopped by."

~~~~~

The first drops of rain darkened the soil beside the porch stoop as Dani and Tom huddled under the small awning. They'd stepped outside to have a bit of privacy, but through the thin door, they could hear Josh and Babula's voices, sprinkled here and there with laughter.

"What is it, Dani?" Tom asked.

"You asked me for help once," Dani said. "You wanted an interview with my father."

He shook his head. "I shouldn't have asked that of you. Forget I ever mentioned it."

"What if I could give you his files?"

Tom's eyes narrowed, and his brow furrowed. "What are you saying?"

She swallowed. "He has an office at the house. He often keeps files there."

"And he'd allow you to have them?" He cocked his head in disbelief.

"Not exactly."

"You'd steal the files from your own father? Why?"

"Borrow them," she corrected. "I want Dele Mason put away. Forever," she added emphatically.

"Why?"

"He's a bad guy, isn't he? I read your story—great journalism, by the way."

"Thanks. And yes. But there are other ways to get to him."

"Like what?"

Tom grew silent.

"I thought so. You have nothing."

"I printed everything I knew—for now."

"But you're still investigating?"

"Yes. But, Dani, this doesn't concern you. And if you took your dad's files, I think you'd live to regret it."

The rain began in earnest then, causing her to move closer to the stoop center and closer to Tom to avoid the droplets. She hesitated momentarily as her eyes wandered to the side yard and then across the street, where the rain had nearly obscured her car. It was a typical storm in the Mississippi Delta; the flat land stretched for miles with nothing to stop the storm clouds from gathering strength overhead. Afterward, the humidity was not diminished but thicker than it had been before the storm.

Now she watched the water swiftly rise along the street curb; the storm drains unable to keep up with the deluge. "But it does concern me," she heard herself say quietly. When she turned back to Tom, he was studying her curiously. "He attacked me, too, Tom."

A look of shock crossed his face, and for a moment, he stared at her with wide eyes. "Dele Mason?" he breathed.

She nodded.

"But—what—?" He took a step back, seemingly unaware as the rain pelted him.

She pulled him closer to the center and out of the rain. "I'm pregnant, Tom. And it's Dele Mason's baby."

Tom's lips parted as though he might respond, but the words seemed to freeze on his lips.

"It happened the night of the tornadoes, back in February," she continued, lowering her chin.

"You don't have to tell me—"

"I'm telling you as a friend, Tom, not as a reporter."

He nodded. "You're sure it's not Rich's child?"

"Positive. It isn't possible."

He half-nodded, averting his eyes as if he was thinking.

"Rich won't marry me if I have the child," she said.

He sucked in his breath. "The cad —"

"And the abortion clinic was bombed while I was there."

"You were in Memphis? To get an abortion?"

Dani wasn't sure whether he was expressing surprise that she'd been a victim of the bombing or he was shocked that she'd considered an abortion.

"Dani," he said. His voice took on a gentler tone, and he pulled her to him, wrapping his arms around her. "Dani, I've something to tell you."

She rested her chin on his shoulder. She hadn't realized how long it had been since she'd felt arms around her. She tried to remember if Rich or her parents had held her since that awful night. She realized with a start that she'd needed their comforting arms, even if they could do nothing about her situation. Dani squeezed Tom and felt his arms tighten in response. His cologne smelled of lime and musk, and she closed her eyes as she inhaled the fragrance. His hair tickled her face as she snuggled against him; it was surprisingly soft and silky.

"Dani," he whispered hoarsely, "let me take care of you. You won't need to get rid of the baby. I'll take care of you both."

His words startled her, and she opened her eyes, her expression shielded by their embrace. His arms tightened once more, one hand moving to her hair to grasp it ever so gently.

"I've felt something for you since I first laid eyes on you," Tom continued. "But you were with Rich, and I—I couldn't do anything to cause you distress. But now, if Rich—"

"But how?" she asked, pulling away to look him in the eye. Her peripheral vision caught the dingy white clapboard and the screen door in need of repair. "How could you possibly take on two more? This place is barely large enough for the two of you—"

"You haven't been listening, Dani. I'm not staying here. I've got friends in Jackson; that's where I want to be."

"Jackson," she said woodenly.

"It's the big city," he said, his voice growing in enthusiasm. "There's lots happening there. The job will pay more, and I'll find a place where you'll be happy. A nice rancher with a nursery for the baby—"

"But it's Dele Mason's child. Don't you see, Tom? You exposed the lawsuit. Dele Mason can come after this child. As its father, he can exercise his rights—"

"Only if he's acknowledged as the father."

"But—"

"Listen to me, Dani." He placed a hand on each shoulder and held her half an arm's length from him so he could lock his eyes on hers. "Marry me, Dani. I'm in love with you. We'll claim the child is ours. I'll love him—or her—as if they're my own."

Her mind raced. "But—for you to be the father, it would mean—last February—while Rich and I were engaged—"

He placed a finger against her lips. He smiled reassuringly. "No one needs to know all that, Dani. Don't you hear what I'm saying? We'll get away from here, out of the Delta. We'll go where no one knows us, and we'll start over—as a family."

She rested her head against his neck once more. She didn't trust her expressions as a myriad of thoughts raced through her mind. "What if the child doesn't look like either of us?"

He chuckled. "You mean, what if it doesn't have my red hair or your fair skin? What if the child looks like Dele?"

She nodded.

"Who cares what it looks like?" he murmured, hugging her. "We'd be a family, Dani. A family filled with love—"

At the mention of the word, she stiffened. "I can't."

"Why not?" He chuckled. "Do you have a better offer?"

"I don't love you, Tom. I like you—a lot—but we've never even dated."

"So we'll date. I don't care if I'm wooing you when you're nine months pregnant, Dani. I don't care if you have to waddle down the aisle."

"But Tom," she said, placing her hand against his cheek. "You deserve someone that loves you."

"Give me time. I'm told I can grow on a person." His smile was so warm and so genuine that she felt like a heel.

"It's all so sudden," she said, her voice barely above a whisper. "I had no idea you felt this way."

"How could you not have known? I've been worried that everybody at the newspaper must've known the way I felt about you."

"Will you give me time—time to think it over?"

"Of course I will. Hey," he said abruptly, "aren't you supposed to be getting ready for your big party?

Aren't you the birthday girl?"

She smiled. "A couple of days ago. Eighteen."

"I'm sorry I didn't see you on your birthday. But," Tom added, "I've been looking forward to tonight's party." His face darkened. "Will Rich be there?"

"I assume he will be. You're coming, aren't you, Tom?"

"I wouldn't miss it for the world."

"And Babula?"

"I doubt it. She's usually in bed by dusk."

"I better be going." She started to extricate herself from him when he pulled her against him. His lips found hers before she understood what was happening. They were full and moist and insistent with a passion she'd never experienced with Rich. She closed her eyes and melted into him, allowing herself to be carried away. Wasn't this what she wanted? Someone to make all her problems vanish, someone that loved her and would care for her, someone that would share her burden?

When at last he stopped, their hearts were beating almost in rhythm. Dani took a moment to catch her breath. "I'll see you in a few hours," she managed to say as she gently pulled away. "Bring Josh, won't you? Plan on staying a while." She didn't know why she'd added that last part, and as Dani gathered her thin jacket above her head to shield it from the rain, she realized she didn't know how to say goodbye to him. A moment later, she was sprinting toward her car as the storm drenched her. When she managed to squeeze behind the steering wheel, turn the ignition, and start the wiper blades, he was still standing on the stoop, watching her.

26

Brandon and Stu hopped out of the Jeep as soon as Brandon pulled the key from the ignition. They watched as Janie and Dani pulled in behind them in Dani's Spitfire. Janie had been surprisingly unworried about her Corvair, focusing more on any harm that might have befallen Brandon or Dani.

"Hey, you coming?" Brandon asked impatiently.

"We're right behind you," Janie called out as Mr. and Mrs. Branson pulled alongside them both.

"It's a girl thing," Stu ribbed. "They have to put on more lipstick—or something like that."

Janie turned to Dani as the guys strolled toward the house. It appeared as if every light was on, and Dani could hear the music, although the car doors were shut and the windows rolled up. In a nod to her parents' older friends, she recognized Frank Sinatra's song "Watertown." She rolled her eyes. If they didn't put something hipper on the turntable, her friends would leave in record time.

Her friends, she thought. They didn't feel much like friends anymore. And she hadn't felt like herself in a very long time. It felt as though those easy friendships had all happened to someone else.

"Is everything okay?" Janie's voice was soft.

Dani glanced at her friend to find her staring at Dani's hands. "Oh, this." She held up the note. "I'd forgotten I was still holding it."

"You had a strange look on your face when Mom handed it to you."

"Yeah." She sighed and turned off the ignition. "Just a message that the abortion clinic called while I was out. They're not reopening for several weeks." She crumpled the note. "They're going to mail a list of other clinics to me, on account of, well, it would be too late..."

"I'm sorry, Dani."

"What the hell?" she asked. She half-waved as Mr. and Mrs. Branson turned back from the front door as if reassuring themselves that they were following them inside. "Twice I've gone, and twice I've left with—" She stopped abruptly. She couldn't bring herself to disparage the blueberry inside her.

"Maybe it's a sign." Janie waved at her parents, and they continued inside to join the other revelers.

"A sign of what?"

"Maybe... is it kicking yet? Can you feel it inside?"

Dani laughed wryly despite her mood. "It's the size of a peanut, Janie."

Janie looked toward the door. Some of the older partiers were hanging out on the wide veranda. The lawn was filled with cars parked in every direction. "Rich is inside. I recognize his car." She pointed.

"I think everybody I know is here," Dani added.

"Are you ready to celebrate our birthdays?" Janie giggled. "Come on. Forget your troubles just for this one night."

"No, I'm not ready. And yes, you're right. Of course." Sighing heavily, she opened the door and climbed out.

"Let's find the guys," Janie said, joining her arm-in-arm as they headed toward the door.

The partiers were too busy to pay any attention to them as they passed them by on the way to the door. Dani recognized all of them. It was an odd mixture of their church family, as Jilly Anne preferred to call them, Cole's business associates, and the social who's who. Several called out well wishes for both girls' birthdays as Dani and Janie nodded and smiled on their way to the door.

Once inside, the music blared so loudly that people were shouting at one another to be heard over the ruckus. Her shoulder bag weighed down her body, and she became acutely aware of the pistol tucked inside. She slung it across her torso, using her forearm to bolster it.

The music abruptly stopped, emphasizing the voices clamoring over one another. A moment later, it began again with Janis Joplin's "Me and Bobby Magee." The mood shifted as the older partiers moved further from the music and those that were Dani's age began an impromptu dance floor, pushing back the furniture in the living room.

She caught a glimpse of Stu and Brandon. Brandon cupped his hands to his mouth and shouted something at her, but she couldn't make out his words. She waved and kept moving, ignoring his motion to join him. "I'll be back!" she shouted, though she knew her words were lost as well as they floated along with the racket.

Somewhere along the way, she became separated from Janie as her friend stopped to chat with fellow classmates.

Dani eventually found Rich on the back sun porch, surrounded by her parents' friends. The men wore black or dark blue suits, crisp white shirts, and staid ties as though they were all headed into a courtroom. The women were dressed in their finery, with dainty heels peeking out from under sequined gowns, unlike the chunky platform shoes Dani's friends wore. Their hair, too, was different; it was teased and coaxed into stiff updo's while the younger set mimicked the longer, freer hairstyles of their role models.

Dani stopped at the entrance to the porch. She stood alone as she watched Rich. He was a younger version of her father; his hair cropped short and proper. He held a glass of wine in his hand, but from the looks of it, it was more a prop than a drink. His suit was immaculate as if he'd had it tailored for him. There was a time when she'd been drawn to his persona, the South's version of Ivy League prep. Even during casual moments, she realized he'd been anything but casual, and she'd wanted that. She'd been drawn to that. But now, it felt as though she was looking through a lens at another life.

She became acutely aware of her own outfit. She wore a patterned top of hot pink and neon orange in a paisley design like one of her idols, Goldie Hawn, wore on "Rowan & Martin's Laugh-In." Underneath were jeans, the bell-bottoms frayed at the bottom, which was all the rage, despite the horror their parents showed and their protests that only "poor people" wore ragged clothes. Like her friends, she wore thick platform shoes that made her appear three inches taller. She wasn't drawn to a dainty glass of wine that she'd hold with her pinky out like her mother's generation, but to a bottle of beer.

"There's the birthday girl!" Her father's exclamation brought her abruptly back to the present. She must have been standing there longer than she'd realized because the music had changed again, the Rolling Stones' "Good Time Woman" replacing Janis Joplin's full-throated voice.

"Darling, it's your birthday," her mother cooed as she moved closer to her. In a lower voice, she admonished, "Get out of those rags, for God's sake."

"Everybody, wish my little girl a happy birthday!" Cole shouted, holding his glass in the air as if giving a toast. Almost in unison, their friends chimed in with a dutiful birthday greeting before returning to their topics of conversation.

Dani made her way to Rich. His eyes raked her from top to bottom, his cheeks becoming flushed, and she realized her clothing had embarrassed him. "Can we talk?" she asked.

"Sure," he answered, taking such a tiny sip of his wine that it barely brushed his lips.

"I mean, someplace where it's quiet. Private," Dani added when he didn't budge.

He set his drink onto a nearby table and took her hand, leading her through the back door onto the brick patio. They strolled for a moment until the music, the din of laughter, and the chat began to wane.

It was different here, among the trees. The rain had moved through, leaving behind the heavy scent of wild honeysuckle mingled with fresh pine and pungent boxwood. The walk beyond her grandmother's cottage glowed from the lights within, finding wildflowers blooming alongside the meandering path like a moonlit garden. The bullfrogs were rowdy, the rain having brought them out in a baritone chorus.

Dani shivered from the cool night air, and Rich removed his suit jacket to place around her shoulders.

"Are you okay, Dani?" he asked. His inquisitive, celestial blue eyes were clearly visible under the gentle moonlight.

"I will be," she answered.

"Your dad told me what happened." He ran his thumb along her shoulder blade. "You know. The bombing. I've been trying to get hold of you."

"I've been at Janie's house."

"I've called there," he answered. His tone was flat. "And you weren't there."

She took a breath. "I had a test this morning."

"On a Saturday?" he frowned dubiously.

"My life is taking different turns." She hesitated, expecting him to interject, but he stared back at her as if waiting for her to continue. After a moment, she took a deep breath.

"Have you made another appointment?" he asked as she began to speak.

"Not yet."

"But you're going to."

Perhaps it was a trick of the moonlight that made his eyes appear so narrow and dark, as though his face foreshadowed darkness within him. "I need some time, Rich."

"Time is running out. You can't procrastinate about something like this."

"I can't rush into it, either."

Silence fell between them. It was heavy as if the clouds had begun to descend around them.

Finally, he broke the silence. "Are we talking about the same thing?"

"No, Rich," she said, trying to force away the tremor in her voice. "We're not." A movement caught her eye. Startled, she jerked her head in that direction. It had come from the woods beyond them. They appeared dark and foreboding, the shadows twisting in the light as the moon ducked behind fast-moving clouds. Her heart skipped a beat and then two, and then the blood rushed into her head. "We need to go inside."

She took a step, but he grabbed her arm, forcing her to stop. "Look at me, Danielle."

Dani might have laughed at the use of her proper name had it not been for the sternness in his face. She tilted her chin upward when she stared back at him.

"Yes, we're going back inside. You're going to change out of that ridiculous outfit. Put on that pink chiffon number and your black heels. Do something with your hair. Put it up. Then you're going to play the gracious hostess, offering the guests drinks and hors d'oeuvres and chatting them up. Get that crap off the turntable and ensure the music is subtle. Classical should do it."

"Pardon me?" She asked, wrenching her arm free of him. "This is my birthday party."

"Really?" He smirked. "You think that's what this is? This is a showcase for your parents. Grow up. They're networking in there. Your birthday was just an excuse. It always has been."

She turned fully to him. "And am I just an excuse, Rich?"

"What are you talking about?"

"Don't you really want the big house, the partnership at the law firm—?"

"Of course I do. I'm an ambitious man. You should be proud of that." He straightened his tie.

"And what am I? Am I 'just the excuse' so you can cozy up to my father?"

He drew back his hand but then allowed it to lower to his side. His eyes darted to the windows.

"Afraid someone is watching us?" Dani asked. She took a step toward him. "Yes, Rich. They are. So here's what we're going to do. I am stepping away from you, now and forever. I'm calling off the wedding."

He sneered. "And then what? What will you do, saddled with a brat you never wanted?"

She drew up her shoulders. "That is none of your concern. I'm only glad I discovered who is really lurking inside you."

She turned to leave, and she felt the weight of his jacket unceremoniously yanked off her. She paused. He chuckled as she heard a rustling behind her. Assuming he was putting his suit jacket back on, she started forward again.

"Dani!" The voice came from the corner of the house, and she hesitated while she tried to make out the figures in the dark. As the two men came into view, she caught a glimpse of Rich rushing past her, heading back into the house.

"Everything okay?" Tom asked as he and Josh drew near.

"It will be," she said. "I just broke up with Rich." She managed to avoid Tom's eyes.

"Dani and Rich were engaged," Tom said to his friend in a hushed tone.

"And it was your decision to call it off?" Josh asked.

Dani laughed. "Are you ever not a reporter?" Growing serious, she added, "It's what my parents always wanted for me. Marriage to someone in upper-crust society. Status. Money. But it isn't me. It was never me."

"You're cold," Tom said. "You're shivering."

Dani glanced behind her. "Did you see anything a moment ago?"

"You mean, you and Rich—?"

"No. Out there." She nodded her head toward the woods.

"I wasn't looking in that direction," Tom said. "We parked the car, and as we were heading to the house, we heard voices over here."

"Could you make out the words?"

"I'm afraid so. It's kind of quiet out here. Your voices carried."

"I am cold," she said suddenly. "Come on. The party's inside." As she led Tom and Josh toward the back entrance, she couldn't shake the feeling that someone was watching them, boring holes into her back. She told herself it couldn't be Dele Mason; he wouldn't be so brazen as to show up at her home when half the county was there. But if it was him, her frantic mind realized that he, too, might have overheard their conversation, and now he knew she was pregnant with his child.

27

Creedence Clearwater Revival belted out "Green River" in between The Rolling Stones and David Bowie. Someone had brought strobe lights and lava lamps and turned the living room into something resembling a nightclub. The music became louder and more anti-establishment as the night progressed, much to Dani's encouragement.

Dani hadn't seen Rich since she'd returned to the house hours earlier, though she hadn't truly looked for him. Her parents' guests had retreated to the other, calmer, side of the house, the men at one point gathered in Cole's study for drinks and discussion, while Jilly Anne's friends gathered in the drawing-room with the door closed. Escaping the music was futile, for the house shook from the hard bass and dancing feet.

Dani leaned against the door jamb, still dressed in her jeans. She smiled now and then, gesturing and laughing to jokes she didn't hear as she kept one eye on the hallway. It would be impossible to get into her father's study and remove Dele Mason's file—if it was even there. What had she been thinking?

The room swam with images that changed colors with the lights. Brandon beckoned her to dance with him, but she waved him away with a smile glued to her face. Meanwhile, a line of high school girls was trying vainly to get his attention.

Stu was propped against a door jamb, studying her as though he knew something was up. A strange smile would start across his face before he subdued it, his eyes morphing from amusement to concern and back again.

Tom and Josh appeared out of place, stuck somewhere between the teenagers and her parents' generation. As the night wore on, Tom's expression became more concerned, but each time he attempted to approach her, someone stepped between them and chatted up Dani. The two journalists ended up finding a relatively quieter space where they could watch the drama playing out around them, each nursing a cold beer. Dani's parents were so absorbed with their friends that they hadn't recognized the reporter that had written the front page article—if they'd ever known what Tom looked like.

Janie alternated between hovering, repeatedly asking what was wrong, and assuming the hostess's role while Dani remained emotionally checked out. Birthday greetings flowed to Brandon and Janie, who each appeared to relish the good wishes.

The buffet table in the dining room was overflowing with gifts for Dani, Janie, and Brandon. The wrappings ranged from purple paisley to staid solid colors. She could glance at each one and know whether one of her parents' friends purchased the item or a student bought and wrapped it. They wouldn't unwrap them in front of their guests, as Jilly Anne thought that was low-class. They would be unwrapped on Sunday morning before or after brunch, in relative silence and privacy.

"Do we have any more ice?" Janie shouted to be heard.

"What?" Dani said as she tried to awaken from her thoughts.

Janie repeated herself. "I checked the kitchen, but—"

"I'll find Mae. She'll know," Dani answered. Thankful for something to do, she weaved her way through the crowd in the hallway. The throng dissipated as she neared the back of the house until she was alone at the swinging kitchen door. She was just about to place her hand on the door to push it open when she caught a strange mixture of odors.

She was instantly transported back to that fateful night. Her heart pounded relentlessly, and she felt the blood rush to her head. She had an overwhelming desire to run and run and run—until no one could find her.

"Did she have it?"

Dani whirled around and came face to face with Janie. "Have what?"

"The ice." Janie's eyebrows knit together. "Are you okay?"

"He's here."

"Who?"

"*Him*. Dele Mason."

"He isn't, Dani."

"I can smell him."

"Smell—what do you smell?"

"Stale liquor, and—"

"Your whole house smells like liquor. Come on, let's find Mae—"

"Not this liquor. It's—it's whiskey. I think it's whiskey."

"Do you even know what whiskey smells like?" Janie forced a smile.

"It doesn't smell like wine or beer." Dani snapped the words as her eyes frantically scanned the hallway. "There's something else. It's like body odor—"

"Do you know how many people are in your house?" Janie reached her arm through Dani's. "I'd be surprised if you didn't smell body odor."

"Not like this. It's him, Janie. He's here."

"You're just having a case of anxiety," Janie said. "Come on, let's—"

At that moment, the door swung open, nearly hitting the two friends.

"Oh, Miss Dani," Mae said, trying to keep a large bucket overflowing with ice from tumbling onto the floor. "I'm sorry, Miss Janie. I didn't know either of you—"

"Here," Janie said, reaching for the bucket. "I'll take it. We were just looking for ice."

"It goes—"

"With the beer?" Janie smiled reassuringly. "Yep. The bottles are floating in water right now."

As Janie took the bucket and disappeared down the hall, Dionne found Mae. She pulled her mother toward the dining room, asking her about the birthday cake. Dani found herself alone.

Janie was right. It was only her imagination. Dele Mason would not have come back here, especially when everybody who was anybody was there. All Dani had to do was point at him and tell the crowd that he was her attacker, and they'd—

They'd what? She thought. She liked to think they'd attack him and beat him until he never thought of touching another woman again. But as she stared down the hall at familiar faces she'd known since childhood, she realized they'd likely do nothing more than stare at him.

Dani readjusted the shoulder strap to her bag. She was armed now, she told herself, and she hadn't been armed before. He'd caught her unawares, and she would never be unaware again. She had once been the victim, but now she was the pursuer. The thought gave her an unsteady kind of comfort. Yes, that was it, she realized. She would not rest until she'd found him and eliminated his threat to her. What that meant, she didn't know. Would she have the courage to pull the trigger? Or would she stand there, woodenly holding the pistol, while he calmly approached her and removed it from her fingers?

The coat closet door swung open, and she took a step back, her hand instinctively moving to the bulk in her bag. Mabelle and Huck Bobby Woods emerged from the closet. Mabelle was giggling, her sprayed hair wadded up in back like she'd been pressed against the coats. She caught sight of Dani just as she tried to adjust her panties under her short dress.

Dani's eyes met hers across the hall.

"You didn't see nothing, Dani," Huck Bobby said. Laughing, he pulled Mabelle into his embrace, and they wandered toward the front of the house. Mabelle stole a glance over her shoulder at Dani just before disappearing around the stair railing.

Dani's mind raced with the knowledge that a little boy was growing up believing that Mabelle was his sister, and he'd been a surprise to a menopausal mother. And there were his parents, all of seventeen years old, in a coat closet trying to make another baby. No doubt it hadn't been the first time since Mabelle had been back in town.

Her hand moved to her belly. A blueberry, she thought. She felt strangely protective of it at that moment, and in the next, she felt a wave of nausea.

Dani's mind wandered to her party one year prior. She'd felt a camaraderie with her schoolmates. She'd laughed and danced and gossiped as the others were doing now. She'd stood with a group of girls lined against one wall while the guys stood opposite, everyone eyeing one another, trying to play it cool but both sides looking like puppies panting after their owners. Then the air inevitably turned tense, the girls wondering which one would be asked to dance first while no guy wanted to be the initial one to break the line.

All of that changed as the night wore on. By the party's end, at least one couple was in tatters, the girl in tears because her guy had spoken to someone else, or the guy furious because his girl had danced with another. The gossip lasted for days afterward as they all compared notes.

She wandered back toward the crowd, her eyes searching every face in a vain attempt to convince herself that none of them was Dele Mason.

It occurred to her as a group of girls looked her way that they might be wondering why Rich wasn't at her side or why she wasn't joining in. She felt detached tonight, as though these were all strangers in her midst, and she wondered now what she'd ever had in common with them. She felt irrevocably changed, her soul altered by the events that had unfolded during and since that fateful night.

It was nearly midnight when a buzz swept through the house, and the guests were all corralled outside for the party's annual fireworks display. The study and drawing-room doors opened as everyone poured into the hall on their way to the front porch. Dani moved against the flow, finding her way to the staircase just as Cole started past her.

"You can't miss the fireworks," he urged, grasping her arm. "It's all for the birthday girl!" He glanced around him. "Where are Janie and Brandon? It's for them, too."

She gently extricated herself from his grasp. "I've got to go to the ladies' room," she said in a stage whisper. "I'll be right behind you."

"Ah!" Cole exclaimed, spotting the Branson family. "There you are!" Forgetting Dani, he hurried down the hall, chatting with Mr. and Mrs. Branson about this special evening.

As the house emptied, she took the stairs two at a time. She peered downward as she reached the second floor. Mae and a few servants hurried into the rooms to clear out the buffet and clean the mess left behind. Dani knew the annual routine. By the time the fireworks were over, if any guests returned to the house, they'd find the food and bottles of drinks removed, a clear signal that the party was over. The servants would replace the lava lamps and strobe lights with the glare of overhead bulbs, illuminating the mess left behind. Bottles of cleaners would come out, and within minutes the house would be filled with an antiseptic aroma, replacing the stench of split beer and half-eaten food.

Dani raced to her bedroom and grabbed an over-the-shoulder bag from the hook behind the door. It had been all the rage when she purchased it; it was barely two inches thick, but it was tall and wide with streamers of macramé trailing from the bottom. She held it in her hands as she descended the staircase, rushing past Mae as she gave orders to the others in the dining room. Mae had her back to Dani, and the others were already busy removing items from the table. Confident that no one had paid attention to her, she made her way to the study.

The door was ajar. Dani heard voices coming from the kitchen, and as they drew near, she ducked inside the study and quietly closed the door behind her.

Unlike the bright lights in the other rooms, the lighting here was more muted, and she hesitated a moment as her eyes adjusted. Half-empty glasses of wine lay scattered across Cole's desk and bookcases amid plates topped with crumpled napkins.

Someone called out to another as they made their way past the study door.

She had only a brief moment.

She raced to Cole's desk and yanked open first one drawer and then another. There were a scant number of files, and they appeared to be related to household expenses. She rushed to the four-drawer filing cabinet in the corner, pulling open one drawer after another. She found her parents' wills, her birth certificate, the deeds to their properties, but nothing about any of his clients.

Her heart began to sink, and she felt a wave of nausea washing over her. The clock behind Cole's desk ticked incessantly, a constant reminder that she was running out of time.

Then her eyes landed on the safe tucked under her father's desk. Had the light not been precisely as it was, she might have missed the gleam of metal that was barely visible underneath the heavy mahogany that draped three sides of the massive desk. She whirled around to the other side. Dropping to her knees, she leaned into the cubbyhole under the desk.

There was a combination on the safe.

Her mind raced. What had Mae said the night that Jilly Anne had tried to open the safe? She closed her eyes and tried to remember.

In the fraction of a second, it registered that Cole was a logical person not prone to imagination. That meant the combination would have to be a series of numbers that was completely logical. Birth dates. That had to be it. But whose? And how many numbers were required?

She tried Cole's birthdate because both the month and the day were double digits: 103126. The door did not budge. She tried 10311926 but still got nothing.

The study door opened, and she held her breath.

"Anybody working this room?" Dani recognized Dionne's voice.

"Come give me a hand," Mae called from down the hall.

Seconds, Dani thought. She may only have seconds.

She tried Jilly Anne's birthdate in various combinations—6627, 060627, 06061927—until she ran out of options. Then she turned to her own. The combination had remained the same for nigh on eighteen years; wasn't that what Mae had said?

The safe opened on the first try. Dani heard the voices further down the hall, and then there was silence.

There were perhaps a dozen files in the safe, along with two pistols and several packages of ammunition. Dani opened one file after another until she found Dele Mason's file. He lived in Pine Acres; she knew the subdivision well. How many times had she driven past his house, not knowing there was a predator inside?

She shivered and stuffed the file into the macramé bag. There was another one—something to do with St. Louis. Hadn't Cole told her that Mason knew powerful people there, that he was 'connected'? On a whim, she took that file, too. Then Dani closed the safe, whirled the combination lock, and checked it for good measure. It was closed as tight as when she'd found it.

Dani froze. There, under the heavy table with her head inches from the safe, she smelled it again. It was stale whiskey, and yet her father didn't drink whiskey and never had. Jilly Anne wouldn't touch the stuff because of its telltale odor; after all, she had a reputation to uphold as a stalwart Southern woman.

Had Dele Mason been to her father's office? Is that how he knew where Dani lived? And he would have known her parents were celebrating Cole's big legal win—Mason's win—and the house would be empty for hours. Had he followed her home from Clarksdale that fateful night?

There was something else mixed in with the odor. It had terrified her on the night of the attack, and now it sent shockwaves through her body. It was a peculiar kind of musk, something far more potent than cologne.

Shaking, Dani climbed out from under the desk. He had been there. He'd stood right there where she was standing now. She rammed her right hand into the pocket in the center of her purse and pulled out the pistol. He would never touch her again.

She heard a faint noise behind her, and Dani whirled around to face the door, her finger on the trigger.

Mae stood in the doorway, and it registered in Dani's mind that the sound she'd heard was Mae gasping. They stood barely four yards from one another, and though shadows obscured details in the older woman's face, Dani knew she was staring at her.

The clock ticked loudly, the pendulum steadily swinging in the otherwise still room. Dani felt riveted to the spot, one hand grasping the pistol while the other held the files.

Someone outside the windows called for the birthday girl.

Then the first firework exploded over the night sky.

28

Dionne's voice seemed to echo in the nearly empty hallway, followed by another.

"Y'all get those chairs put back in the parlor yet?" Mae's voice sounded clipped.

"No, Mama, we—"

"Then you'd better get y'selves back in yonder," she ordered. Footsteps faded down the hall, and Mae turned back to Dani. "You got one minute. One minute," she waggled her finger for emphasis, "to get your scrawny ass out of this room. And put that gun away before you hurt somebody."

Mae had barely cleared the door before Dani rushed through it. The hallway was deserted except for Mae's broad back as she moved toward the parlor. Dani turned in the opposite direction. A moment later, she moved onto the back porch, and then her foot touched down upon the soft grass. The pistol was back in her purse, and she'd stuffed the files unceremoniously into the macramé bag.

All faces were turned toward the skies as one firework after another exploded. With the crowd illuminated, Dani made her way behind them until she found Tom and Josh.

Tom noticed her as she approached. He opened his mouth, perhaps to announce her presence, but her frown and a shake of her head stopped the words from forming. She brushed against him, forcing the macramé bag into his hands.

"Get it out of here," she whispered.

Tom did not hesitate. "Josh," he said, his voice firmly out of cadence with the *oohs* and *aahs* surrounding the fireworks.

"There she is!" Dani recognized Cole's voice somewhere in the crowd. "There's the birthday girl!"

The crowd erupted in applause, parting to provide a path from Dani to her father. As she moved past them, she caught a glimpse of Tom rushing toward his car, the bag barely visible under his arm, most of the macramé tucked up and away. Josh was on his heels.

"Come join the other birthday guests!" Cole's face broadened into a smile as Janie and Brandon joined them in the center. Then all eyes were once again on the skies as the finale began.

~~~~~

"What's got into you?" Janie asked as Dani found herself surrounded by her best friend, Brandon and Stu.

"He's here," Dani said, peering into the darkness.

The woods were far from quiet, the fireworks having awakened every dog for miles around. The hounds were baying as frantically as though they were after a fox, stirred on by the howls of others acres away. But the birthday crowd had mainly disbursed. The last of the cars eased their way off the grounds and onto the rural road. Cole and Jilly Anne stood dutifully in the front yard, waving until the last guest was down the road.

Mae had not looked at Dani since their brief encounter. Now she busily directed other servants as they cleared debris. Only moments earlier, they'd arrived on the scene as the last of the fireworks died away, offering slices of birthday cake and cups of coffee. There was no blowing out of the candles; there never were. The cake and coffee were signals that the evening had come to an end. The confection was on paper plates, the coffee in clear plastic cups, better for transporting. Now all that remained was finding every last bit of litter and plunking it into giant green trash bags.

"Who's here?" Brandon asked. Noticing Dani shiver, he removed his jean jacket and wrapped it around her.

"You know who." Dani met his eyes. She saw the recognition flash through his eyes as her meaning penetrated. "Has anyone see my grandma?"

"Grandma Dottie?" Janie frowned. "She never attends your party."

"You know she thinks dancing and drinking is Satan's work," Stu said.

"Yeah," Brandon added, "she'll be in church in a few hours, praying for our souls."

Cole and Jilly Anne joined them. "What's going on?" Cole asked.

"Grandma Dottie," Dani said. "Has anyone seen her?"

Jilly Anne sniffed. "Hours ago. Mae brought her an early dinner like she always does."

"Why?" Cole asked. In the light of the moon, Dani made out the lines across his forehead.

"Something isn't right," Dani answered.

"Like what?" Janie prodded. "You're spooking us."

"Something's not right with Grandma."

"What are you talking about?" Jilly Anne said, her words slurring. "She's doing what she always does. You know she hates our parties, always has. She ate her dinner, put to bed early, and she'll be up at dawn getting ready for church."

"No," Dani said. "Not this time."

"Dani—" Cole began.

"Oh, for heaven's sake," Jilly Anne puffed. "I'll go inside and phone her. She'll be mighty upset that we woke her, and I'm blaming it all on you. You ruin everything."

As Jilly Anne moved toward the back door, Dani took a deep stride forward. "I'm not waiting. I'm going down there."

"Then I'm going with you," Brandon said.

"Me, too," Stu offered.

"You're not leaving me standing here in the dark," Janie said. "I'm going inside with your mama."

As Janie moved toward the house, the others made their way down the dark path to Dottie's cottage. Cole followed, muttering something about supervising them. An owl hooted overhead, and the top of a tree rustled as birds flew into the night sky. The dogs continued to howl in the distance, their voices seeming to emanate from every direction.

Dani found her way impeded by tree roots that rose in her path, threatening to trip her. "Watch your step," she called to the others behind her. She felt the weight of her pistol in her bag. She clutched it in front of her, slipping her hand inside the concealed pocket. Her heart began to beat faster. She could feel *him* in the air.

The cottage shone in the moonlight, the white-washed walls broken only by trellises and vines. The scent of roses intermingled with honeysuckle as the wind kicked up. Another odor penetrated through the idyllic garden scents, gaining in intensity as she drew nearer. It was the unmistakable smell of smoke.

She could see the dance of orange and red fingers through the sheers covering the living room window. The fireplace was in the living room corner, she reminded herself. She'd traveled that path countless times, often on cold days when the warmth of the fire beckoned to her.

But tonight was different.

Dani was mere steps from the cottage door when she felt her skin begin to prickle and grow hot. She had difficulty breathing, and she placed a hand on her heart to calm her.

The door was slightly ajar.

"She's not answering!" Janie's and Lilly Anne's voices melded into one as they made their way from the big house onto the path. "She's not answering her phone!"

"Wait," Cole directed, pushing past Dani's friends to reach the door first. He pulled a pistol from underneath his suit jacket.

"Dad—" Dani breathed when she saw it.

"Stay here," he said. "All of you."

He planted his palm on the door and slowly pushed it inward as his other hand aimed the pistol. Smoke billowed outward, choking them all.

"Don't shoot Mama!" Jilly Anne called from behind.

"The back door!" Dani shouted to no one in particular. She spotted Brandon and Stu racing around the side of the house toward the back.

Once inside, Cole tried to flick on an overhead light, but it sputtered and died. "Don't anybody go in!" he shouted as he ignored his own advice. He quickly shed his suit jacket and placed it over his mouth and nose as he entered.

Dani stepped to the threshold. The worn leather recliner sported a knitted throw laid neatly across the top. Both were now in flames. The console television against the wall displayed a myriad of photographs in various sizes and frames. They appeared otherworldly now as the blaze licked at them. She grasped at the throw, catching it by a corner, and began to beat it against the chair, vainly trying to put out the fire. She knew it was futile as the flames licked up the wallpaper, causing it to melt in sheets around her. She coughed and pulled her shirt up to cover her nose and mouth.

Somewhere in the dark and smoke-filled hallway Cole called out to Dottie, his voice muffled.

Despite the screams of her mother behind her, urging her to come out, Dani moved deeper into the house, her mind barely registering Janie's voice joining the chorus. She could sense *him* there; she recognized his evil. Her heart began to race as Dani made her way down the hall. She was unable to feel her way along the wall; it was too hot. Sweat broke out across her brow as the smoke intensified.

Dani hesitated at a bedroom door, the room transformed into Dottie's sewing room. The Singer quieted, a swath of cloth laid across it as if waiting for the morning. They were now both engulfed in flames. On the other side of the hall was a guest room that might have been used twice in twenty years, the bed neatly made in yellow gingham, the matching shams perfectly arranged, the dresser dust-free. Everything was engulfed in flames.

She heard shouting now at the back of the house, and she knew that Brandon and Stu were trying to break down the door leading into the kitchen. She heard wood splintering, and a draft of air cut through the hall, intensifying the smoke and flames. Voices tumbled over one another, calling for Dani to escape.

"Dottie!" Cole's voice cut through the maelstrom; unaware Dani had followed him, his voice was growing ever more urgent. "Dottie!"

29

Jilly Anne shook her mother until her head lolled to the side, her blue lips parting from the jolt. Cole pulled her away, forcing her to drop Dottie's head back onto the bed of pine needles outside the house. Dani stood at her feet, feeling as though her spirit was somehow detaching from her body. Crammed behind her stood Janie, Brandon, and Stu.

"Stop it, Jilly Anne," Cole was saying as he wiped a tear from his eye. "She's gone."

"She can't be," Jilly Anne moaned. "She's not burned. See? Her gown is just like the day she bought it."

Cole turned to the others. "Smoke inhalation, most likely," he said. "Stu, run up to the house and call the fire department, will you? And ask them to send—I don't know, an ambulance, I guess." He turned back toward the house. "It'll be a total loss, I suspect. They need to get here before the woods catch fire."

As Stu raced for the house and Cole returned to Jilly Anne's side, Dani said, "Aren't you going to call the sheriff, Dad?

He looked at her with sad and weary eyes. "The sheriff isn't necessary, Dani. There's no sign of foul play."

Dani's eyes darted between her mother's grief and her father's set jaw. "How do you know?" she pressed.

"She died in her sleep, Dani, most likely of smoke inhalation," he repeated. "She died peacefully. Now help me comfort your mother."

"He was here," Dani repeated. As Cole turned his back to her to concentrate on his wife, she turned to her friends. "He was here."

"Dani," Janie said, brushing a tear from her eye, "I know what you've been through. I know. But, your dad's right. There's no sign he did this—"

"How do we know? How do we know that he didn't force his way into her house? How do we know he didn't set the fire? How do we—?"

Brandon stepped forward and put his arms around her. "Walk this through, Dani. The fire department will investigate the cause…"

"They're on their way," Stu called from the back door. He continued as he rushed back to them. "They're volunteers, so it'll take a few minutes—but they're coming."

Cole pulled Jilly Anne away from Dottie. "We've got to move away from the house," he said. "The fire's out of control." He turned to Stu. "Help me move Dottie, will you?"

"Why was the door open?" Dani pressed.

"Maybe she forgot to latch it," Janie offered.

"She never forgot. Not ever."

"Dani," Brandon said, hugging her tighter, "Dottie's mind was going. Sometimes she didn't remember where she was or how she'd gotten there—"

"What does that have to do—?"

"She honest-to-God could've forgotten to close the door before she went to bed."

"She would have closed it to keep the music out," Dani answered stubbornly.

"—And maybe she started a fire without opening the damper."

"On a night like this? It's not even cold out here!"

Brandon opened his mouth to respond when a car engine roared to life, the sudden sound cutting through the night air. Simultaneously, as if acting as one, all eyes darted toward the big house. The woods obscured all but the taillights as they cut through the darkness.

~~~~~

Dani reached the side yard first, bursting out of the woods. She must have appeared frantic because Mae, who had been directing several others, stopped in mid-sentence.

"Did you see someone leave?" Dani demanded, dashing over to her.

"Everyone left a half an hour ago," Mae said. "I'm sending everyone over with the garden hose. We'll turn it up full blast and—"

"And none of the workers—?"

"Child, we'll be working on this cleanup 'til 3 o'clock in the morning, long after y'all have gone to bed. Just like always," she added. Her eyes raked Dani up and down before moving to Janie and Brandon. "What y'all got goin' on here? What's happening at Miz Dottie's?"

"Dottie's passed," Janie blurted as several servants darted past her, dragging the garden hose behind them.

"Passed?" Mae's face went ashen. "Miss Dottie done gone? Where's your mama and daddy?" She turned to Dani.

"They're with Grandma," Dani said.

"How did she die? They sure she's gone? Sometimes people, they sleep so soundly—"

"She's gone." Dani forced back tears. "Did you see anybody around here, Mae? Somebody in the woods?"

"You tellin' me somebody—no," Mae said, grasping at her breast, over her heart, "Not Miss Dottie. Please tell me, not Miss Dottie. Did the fire done burn her up?"

"Smoke inhalation's what Mr. Evans thinks," Brandon said firmly, stepping in between Mae and Dani. He cast a withering glance at Dani. "She passed in her sleep, Mae. She wasn't burned."

"But how—?" Mae tried to peer around Brandon to look at Dani, but he continued to block her. The other workers were shouting instructions. The hose was too short, and the water wasn't reaching Dottie's cottage. Somewhere in the back of her mind, it registered that her father was carrying Dottie into the house. Mae was rushing to his side to assist.

Dani's heart was racing. She'd seen it; she knew she hadn't imagined the roar of the engine and the distinct horizontal taillights glowing amidst the trees. A movement caught her eye. It came not from the familiar path to Dottie's cottage but from several yards to the left, further from the big house. "There!" she screamed.

As all eyes watched, Stu emerged from the woods. His hands were brushing against his face and skin as though he was being eaten alive by Mississippi's notorious mosquitoes. "She's right!" he called when he was within shouting distance of them.

"What did you find?" Brandon asked as Stu joined them.

"Tire tracks, fresh ones, they're filling up fast from the muck."

"Where did he go?" Dani's voice was hoarse.

Stu pointed behind them. "There's an old trail leading to the county road; looks like he took that."

Before he'd finished speaking, Dani had turned toward her car. Her walk became a sprint, the voice behind her becoming one with the wind. She hadn't realized that Brandon was on her heels until she jerked open her car door and found him grasping the door to keep it open.

"Where are you going?" he demanded.

"I have to find him. I have to stop him."

"You don't have to do anything. Help is on the way. You can tell them."

"They're coming to put out the fire, Brandon. That's all. There's no one coming to help us. No one."

"Then I'm coming with you."

"No, you're not."

"I'm driving. Get out of the way."

"I'm driving. It's my car."

Abruptly, Brandon let go of the door. Almost before Dani could get into the driver's seat and start the car, he was piling into the passenger seat beside her. The car engine roared to life, and she threw it into reverse.

"Tell Mama I'm with Dani!" Brandon managed to shout. He tossed the Jeep keys to Janie and Stu, who scrambled for them in the grass.

The car zigzagged across the driveway and lawn until they ended up on the road, where Dani threw the gearshift into drive.

Her foot was heavy on the pedal as she envisioned the old trail leading to the county road. She might have forgotten it was passable, as rarely as it was used. As they sped forward, she considered the last time, which must have been during the flood. It was common for the Mississippi River to flood in the spring. The Delta rains combined with the snow that melted in the north, raising the river levels, so they customarily overflowed their banks. It was what helped to make the Delta soil so fertile. It usually didn't affect them, but a few years back, the waters had come dangerously close to the house and cottage. As the ground grew saturated, the tree roots became unstable. She vaguely remembered when the water had receded, her father hiring a landscaping crew to clear out the trees that leaned dangerously close to toppling. They must have cleared the old trail to park the logging trucks closer to the trees they felled.

If Dele Mason had used that road, she thought, he could have driven close to Dottie's cottage. He would have gone undetected if he kept the headlights off. With everyone inside and the music blaring, no one would have noticed. Dani felt sickened.

She pulled onto the shoulder of the road as flashing lights came into view ahead. She recognized the driver, Tanya Brown, gripping the wheel as she sped the ambulance past them. Tanya glanced at them as she passed, her face pale and her eyes wide. Brandon and Dani each made a halfwave to reassure her that they were okay. Dani doubted Tanya would have stopped on the rural road in the dead of night, but she might have called their position into the sheriff's office.

Tanya was barely on the other side of them before Dani pulled the Spitfire back onto the road, gaining speed as she pushed the pedal to the floor.

"So," Brandon said, turning to look at her. "Where are we going?"

30

Pine Acres was aptly named, as the homes appeared to have been built within a loblolly pine forest. She doubted there was a proper lawn in the entire subdivision. The oldest of the trees were the height of a ten-story office building, their trunks bare but the treetops looming over the neighborhood like the shadows of nightwatchmen. Their needles scattered the ground like a carpet, the trees managing to propagate at an alarming rate.

Dele Mason's house was a corner lot at the end of the street. A narrow driveway wound its way around hundreds of loblolly offshoots of heights varying from a couple of feet to shoulder height under the canopy of the older trees. The house itself sat at an angle, so it didn't face either road directly and couldn't be seen from either street.

Dani crouched in the darkness as her eyes adjusted to the dark lot. Somewhere in the distance, an owl hooted, and another answered. There had been a moon earlier, but now it was obscured by the treetops. The house became a hulking shadow, the brown brick blending almost seamlessly into the forest, the pitched, dark roof nearly invisible. The windows were dark.

"I don't think he's there," Brandon whispered as he joined her. "There's a Coupe Deville in the carport. The engine's cold."

"That's not his car," Dani said. Her voice sounded oddly calm, though she was shivering. "The lights are different. What I saw were more like a Dodge Charger's taillights."

"Are you sure this is his house?"

"Positive. I saw his address in my dad's file."

"You went through your dad's files?"

Dani sent him a sideways glance. "I did more than that."

Brandon stared at her for a moment. "Dani, we've got to get out of here."

"In a minute. I need time to think."

"He could come back at any minute, Dani. Your car's too recognizable sitting on the street."

"Yeah," she said. "You're right." Her eyes scanned the terrain. "Where can we go where we can watch the driveway?"

Brandon sighed. After a moment, he said, "There's a cotton gin on the other side of this neighborhood. We could pull your car in back of it. But we'd have to be on foot to keep an eye on the driveway if you don't want him to see us."

Dani nodded. "Can you move it?"

"Sure, but—Dani, think this through."

"It's all I've been doing."

"What will you do when you see him?"

She patted her bag. "You still have your gun?"

He pulled back his jean jacket to display a pistol. "I never go anywhere without it."

"Yeah. Well, neither do I."

"You plan to shoot him, Dani?" He shook his head. "You can't go to prison, Dani. You can't have your baby behind bars. That's a life sentence you're talking about."

"If you don't want any part of it, I don't blame you. Park the car and stay in it."

"No, Dani. I can't let you do this."

She turned to face him. Her voice was hoarse as the cool air chilled her. "Then who is going to do it, Brandon?"

"The sheriff."

"They've arrested him before. He's got a rap sheet a mile long."

"Then he should be in Parchman."

"Yeah. But he's not. He's got somebody protecting him, somebody willing to pay my dad tens of thousands to keep him out of prison."

"But your dad won't represent him against you, Dani. I can't believe he'd do that."

"Then he just finds some other lawyer." She sighed heavily. "Are you going to move the car, or do I need to do it?"

"I'll do it," he said grudgingly. "But I'm coming back. I'm not leaving you out here alone."

"Well, you'd better hurry. Like you said, he could come back any minute."

~~~~~

It was nearing dawn before the gruff engine of the Dodge Charger cut through the silence. Dani was shaking now from a night spent in the cold, huddled against a tree trunk with Brandon for warmth. They crouched behind the smaller trees as the flashy bronze car with a black racing stripe and vented engine made its way down the winding driveway. They watched as it pulled beside the Cadillac.

The door opened and out stepped Dele Mason.

Dani stood. Though she was still visibly trembling from the night air, she forced herself to stand tall and straight.

Brandon grabbed her arm, trying to pull her back to a crouched position. "He'll see you!"

A strange calm swept over Dani. Watching Dele take his time moving from his car to the carport door leading into the house, he looked like any other average man. He didn't have horns or a deep red face as her church portrayed the devil. He wasn't overly tall, as she'd remembered. Instead, he was somewhat shorter than average and wirier than she'd recalled. She realized he had taken on a superhuman status in her mind. But this demon of a man had hurt her; he had not only harmed her physically, but he had taken away the life she had planned.

The carport door opened before Dele reached it. From her vantage point, she could not clearly see the shadowy figure in the doorway, but she heard the high-pitched voice carry across the yards between them.

"Where you been?" An arm reached out and slapped him across the face. "I told you to be in this house by ten o'clock!" More slaps ensued, drowning out the rest of the conversation as he was yanked inside. The door slammed shut behind them.

"Well, that's not what I expected," Brandon said.

"That couldn't have been a wife?"

"Sounded more like his mother."

"Well, this changes things."

"How?" Brandon stood, pulling her closer to the nearest trunk to conceal them from the house.

"I don't want to hurt anyone else," Dani said quietly, her hands wrapped around her bag carrying the pistol. She looked into Brandon's eyes, which were filled with genuine concern. Dark circles revealed his poor night's sleep. "I just want to get Dele Mason out of my life. Permanently," she added for emphasis.

"I understand, Dani. But is this the way to do it?"

The door opened again, and the woman's voice carried across the yard to them. Despite her demands that Dele return to the house, he kept walking toward the Charger. The woman slammed the door shut and retreated into the house.

It all happened in slow motion, and yet Dani knew it had taken only seconds to retrieve her pistol. Before Dele had reached his car door, she fired.

Dele ducked, his hand instantly moving inside his jean jacket. A mere second later, he returned fire. Chunks of the tree next to them flew off, and Brandon yanked Dani to the ground. "Stay behind the tree!" he urged.

She was shaking now, caught between wanting to stand and fire back until he crumpled onto the ground in a lifeless heap and wishing his bullets would stop flying. She was terrified, and she was angry.

She rose shakily to her feet despite Brandon's urging. She stepped out from behind the tree that had shielded her, and aimed her pistol. But he was gone. He was slamming the car door shut behind him as the engine vroomed to life.

Dani took another step forward and froze. Just inches from where she and Brandon had lain half the night was a long black snake. While most of its body lay coiled on the ground, the uppermost part had corkscrewed up the tree, so its head was nearly even with Dani's chest. Its forked tongue darted out several times as she stared at it.

Brandon reached out slowly to touch her arm. He tugged slightly. "Step back, Dani. As slow as you can."

Her foot felt as though it weighed a ton. As she raised it, Brandon continued, "Don't panic. Don't make any sudden movements."

"It's going to bite me," she said, her voice shaking.

"No," he corrected. "It's just sensing the air with its tongue. You're okay. Just step back. That's it. Take another step…" Despite his calming words, his voice was trembling.

She stepped backward on the uneven ground, feeling the thick carpet of pine needles under her feet.

"It's okay, Dani. It's just a black snake. You're okay." Brandon began to step backward as well, placing himself in between her and the snake. They continued until they were almost to the street.

Once on the paved road, Dani stared in the direction she'd last seen the Charger. "Where did he go?"

"Let's get back to the car, Dani. You're shivering."

She felt her heart sink inside. She had been so close. Yet, even though she'd lost sight of Dele Mason temporarily, she felt strength rising inside her. She was no longer his victim. Now, she was hunting him.

31

Dawn was beginning to peer over the distant horizon. The Delta was as flat as a pancake, as Grandma Dottie used to say. One could see a car coming from two miles away or more until the fields of cotton, tobacco, and corn formed curtains around the roads. But though they tried, they could not pick up Dele Mason's trail.

They'd spent the last hour driving the county roads ten miles out in each direction. As the sun rose, Brandon's argument for abandoning their quest grew more insistent.

"We don't have to do this today," he said for the umpteenth time. "Let's go back to your place. Your mama and daddy must be worried about us, and your mama will need you now that Grandma Dottie…" His last words were left unsaid as if he didn't want to voice her grandmother's passing.

She turned toward town; it was the last place she hadn't looked. Yet, even as she drew closer to the outskirts, she knew there were too many neighborhoods, too many back alleys, where Dele might have gone. With a sinking heart, she knew Brandon was right.

"We'll grab something at the Breakfast Burger, okay? They'll be open now, and I'm famished."

"I wish you'd let me drive. You've got to be tired."

She glanced sideways at him. "Not as tired as you look right now." She smiled. "Thank you, Bran. I don't know what I would have done without you."

"Dani," he said, reaching over to grasp her hand. "I hope you know I'm here for you, every step of the way."

"I do, Bran. I do."

"Have you made any decisions?"

"Decisions?"

He nodded toward her belly. "You know."

"I've been thinking through a lot of options. How about you, Brandon?"

"Me?"

"Where are you going when school is out?" Even as she asked it, the question seemed surreal, the normalcy not escaping her after their terrifying night.

He took a deep breath. "Well, my folks want me to get a four-year degree. I'm not smart like you. But I can't see myself working on a factory line, either."

"No," she said. "You're not factory material."

"What's that supposed to mean?" He gave her a crooked smile.

"Repetitive work, day after day. No air conditioning; giant fans blowing at you while you work the line." She shook her head. "Definitely not you.

Janie's getting her cosmetology license. Have you thought about a trade?"

"I have, actually. I'm thinking about becoming an electrician."

"An electrician?"

"Yeah. I can get into technical college and then get an apprenticeship until I'm a full-fledged electrician."

"There's a call for that?"

"Well, yeah. All those old antebellum homes were wired forty years ago; they need updating. And there are buildings all around that got wired a little bit here, a little bit there. I can stay real busy."

She pulled into the parking lot of the Breakfast Burger and claimed a space right by the door.

"Good morning, y'all. Order when you're ready." The voice crackled through the speaker.

Dani looked at the marquee menu. "Do you know what you want, Brandon?"

"Yeah. Sausage and egg burger, two of 'em. And a milkshake. Chocolate."

"Sounds good." Dani doubled the order.

"Be right out," the voice answered.

Brandon reached over to Dani's hair, brushing his fingers through it. As she turned toward him quizzically, he moved his hand to hers. "Dani," he said, squeezing her hand, "Marry me."

Dani laughed before she was able to catch herself. Fortunately, her laughter brought a glint to Brandon's eye. "Marry you?" she chuckled, squeezing his hand in return. "We haven't even had a date yet."

"So what if we haven't?" he asked. "I've known you, like, forever."

She laughed harder. "I think we met in the nursery."

"I think we did," he agreed. "You were wearing this gorgeous pink number with this cute little knitted cap."

She took a swipe at him. "Like you would remember!"

He pouted. "You don't remember our first meeting?"

"Oh, I do." She closed her eyes for a moment before reopening them. "You were wearing this sexy blue pajama—or, it would have been sexy, had you not just pooped in it."

"Hey!"

"And you had a twinkle in your eye, even then."

Brandon reached over to run his fingers across Dani's jawline. "Who knows you better than I do?"

"It isn't that, Bran." She sighed and grew somber. "Your life hasn't even started yet. You could go to Tech and eventually get your electrician's license—and you could stay with your folks while you did it. You could save your money until you're on a steady footing."

"Yes, but you—"

"—I would drain you of every cent you earned. A wife and baby saddled around your neck? We'd be scraping by from the start. That's not fair to you."

"You're assuming my folks—and yours—won't help us." He moved closer, the tiny confines of the Spitfire feeling more intimate. "We won't be alone, Dani. We'll all take care of you."

He kissed her then, his tongue parting hers almost immediately. Caught by surprise, she recoiled, but he pulled her closer. He smelled of last night's hors d'oevres and tasted of stale Coca-Cola.

They pulled back simultaneously.

"I don't think—" Dani began.

" —maybe the timing wasn't right—" Brandon said.

"Let's just remain friends," they said in concert.

A movement caught Dani's attention. Relieved at the distraction, she rolled her window up a couple of inches to accommodate the food tray. The carhop secured the tray. "Dollar ninety-eight," he said.

Brandon pulled out his wallet and extracted two one-dollar bills. "Keep the change," he said as he reached across Dani to pay for their meals.

Dani shook her head as she pulled a quarter out of the change tray, offering it to the carhop. "Thanks."

"Thank you," he answered. "Let me know if you need anything else."

Dani handed a milkshake to Brandon, followed by his breakfast burgers. They chewed in silence for a while, the only noise an occasional slurp.

"Seriously, Dani," Brandon said after a few minutes. "I want you to know I'll help you."

"Thanks, Brandon. You're a good friend."

"What about your folks?"

Dani shook her head. She'd eaten too quickly, and the food was sitting heavy on her stomach. "Mama's too worried about what the neighbors will think."

"Maybe," Brandon said, perking up, "now that Dottie's cottage is empty —"

Dani cast him a sideways glance.

"Too soon?" he asked. "Too soon," he repeated, turning his attention back to his food.

"If it's even there," Dani said. "It might be burned to the ground by now."

"Hey, speak of the devil," Brandon said, his eyes on the side mirror.

A shiny maroon Lincoln Continental had pulled behind them, blocking their exit. She watched as the door opened and Cole stepped out. He was still wearing his formal suit from the previous night's festivities, but his tie was gone, and his collar loosened. As he approached her window, she caught closer sight of him in her side mirror. He had visible bags under his eyes, and his shoulders slumped.

"Dani," he said in greeting. He bent down to peer across the car seat at Brandon. He reeked of smoke. "Brandon. Your folks are worried about you." He returned his gaze to Dani. "We've all been worried about you."

"How's Grandma Dottie's place?" Dani asked. "You know," she added lamely, "is it gone?"

"Dottie is at Kingdom Mortuary. Fire marshall seems to think Dottie didn't open the damper. She'd been so forgetful... They'll come back as soon as it's good and light and start an investigation."

"And the coroner?"

"Most likely smoke inhalation. She wouldn't have suffered, Dani. She looked like she just never woke up." He cleared his throat. "Anyway, word got out pretty quickly, and the house has been flooded with women wanting to help."

Dani nodded. There would be enough food to feed an army, as women would flock to the house carrying a special dish as if the act of dying made family members ravenous. They'd remain at the house in an attempt to clean or cook or help answer the phone. Knowing Jilly Anne, she would feel obligated to entertain her guests, and Mae would arrive to a houseful of folks in her kitchen trying to find the coffee, cups, and utensils.

"I guess you need me at home?" Dani sighed.

He nodded. "Your mama has taken to her bed. She's inconsolable."

"Mama is?"

"It appears that Dottie simply passed away in her sleep, Dani," he repeated as if in a daze. "She went to bed, and she just didn't wake up." He tried a weak smile. "It's the way we all should want to go, isn't it? She had a good, long life, and she passed away peacefully." He looked from Brandon to Dani as though he was seeking reassurance.

"Sure, Dad."

"Anyway, you need to be the woman of the house right now, with your mama in bed."

"Oh?"

"You need to greet folks at the door and make them feel welcome. I've already called Mae, and she'll be on her way in with the first bus."

"But she probably didn't get home until three or four hours ago," Dani protested. "And it's a Sunday. Is the bus even running?"

"She's a strong woman, and these are extenuating circumstances."

"Why's Mama in bed?"

"She can't face everybody right now. Look, Dani, you need to grow up. You need to put on a brave face and a smile and greet our guests like the woman of the house."

"I need to what?"

Cole continued as if he hadn't heard her. "Forget about Dele Mason. I know you think he had something to do with this, but he didn't—"

"The tire marks are there, Dad. He was there last night."

"Let it go, Dani. Even if he was there—which I doubt—it was pure coincidence."

"Why do you doubt it? Stu and Brandon could show you the tire marks—"

"It won't prove anything."

Dani felt a wave of nausea. The breakfast burger with sausage and egg began to feel like something vile inside her. "I think I have morning sickness," she moaned faintly.

"Get over it," Cole said. "Go home. Clean your face. Put on a fresh dress. And be the good hostess you need to be."

"What?" Dani asked incredulously. "Why can't Mama do it?"

"I told you. She's in bed."

"What about you?"

"Don't question me," Cole snapped. "I have work to do."

"It's Sunday."

"So what if it is? My duty is to keep a roof over your head, young lady." He hesitated. "Sunday," he murmured as if he was just remembering. "That means the whole church will be at the house once service is out. It'll be announced…" His voice faded. His face appeared pale and drawn.

"What about my morning sickness?" Dani reached for her milkshake but set it down again. It seemed too thick now.

Cole blinked. "Get through today. Tomorrow, we'll find a place for you — maybe Birmingham… Someplace where no one knows you. Have the baby, get rid of it, and we'll tell people you were distraught over your grandmother's death."

"That doesn't even make sense, Dad."

But Cole had already stepped away from the vehicle. Dani turned to watch him trudge back to the car. The driver's side door was still open from when he'd left it a few moments ago, but to Dani, it felt as though a lifetime had come and gone, and she was forever altered.

"You gonna eat that?" Brandon said.

"What?" She turned to face him. In the corner of her eye, she saw the Lincoln Continental pull away.

"The other breakfast burger."

"Here," she said, handing it to him. "Take it."

"You need for me to drive? You're looking pretty sick."

"I'm feeling pretty sick."

Her father's car circled the restaurant. As he pulled back toward the road, he was faced straight ahead. She waited for him to glance at her, but he didn't. She felt a sinking feeling inside as though a boulder had crawled inside and was weighing her down. Then she opened her door and vomited on the asphalt.

32

The Spitfire idled at the exit to the restaurant. The street had been nearly deserted when Dani and Brandon pulled into the Breakfast Burger, but in the short space of time they'd been there, the bus station in the next block had begun to come alive. The Little Acorn Orphanage van pulled into the station lot as the station's neon lights sliced through the early morning mist.

"Wonder what they're doing?" Brandon mused.

"Well, they sure aren't there to accept more orphans," she sighed.

"Let's hope not. Maybe they're putting kids on buses," he added excitedly, "so they can go to their forever homes."

"'Forever homes'?" Dani chuckled wryly. "I think that's a term used for dogs."

Brandon shrugged. "For people too. It could happen."

"Or maybe foster homes." Dani glanced down the street. The light was changing, but no one was at the intersection. She peered in the opposite direction and saw her father's Lincoln Continental idling a block away. "What's he doing?"

"Waiting for us, I reckon."

"Why?"

Brandon shrugged. "We've kind of been through a lot lately."

Dani sighed again, a resigned sigh that she felt from the pit of her stomach. She took her foot off the brake and placed it on the gas pedal. The Spitfire moved forward onto the street.

A blaring horn split the air, and her windshield filled with bronze metal. She swerved to avoid the oncoming vehicle, her heart leaping into her throat. "Where did he come from?" she yelled.

"It's him!" Brandon said excitedly, pointing.

The Spitfire swerved on the road, moist from the night's humidity, as Dani jammed her foot to the pedal. Her eyes focused on the bronze Charger as the horn sounded again, this time playing a few notes of Dixie. The sound filled the air, causing the people gathering at the bus station to turn and gawk.

With her foot pressed to the floor, the tiny Triumph felt as though it was leaving the pavement as the speedometer rose to 50, 60, 70, and then 80 miles per hour. She was gaining on the Charger when suddenly it lurched forward. The Spitfire rose to 90 and then 100. Dani and Brandon were pinned to the backs of the seats, but the Charger was outracing them.

Dele passed the last intersection in town, blowing through a red light before hitting the open road. Dani's eyes were riveted to the taillights. "I know where he's going," she said.

"How? Where?"

She swerved the car onto the crossroad at the intersection before taking an immediate jog onto another road as Brandon held on. They were now running somewhat parallel to the country road the Charger was on, still behind but gaining.

"Your dad's back there," Brandon said, staring over his shoulder.

"I can't look," Dani said as she continued her focus on the Charger.

"He didn't follow us," Brandon said. "He didn't take the turn. He's—he's following Dele."

As Brandon spoke the words, Dani could see the Lincoln on the same road as the Charger, but he was falling behind rapidly. In a fraction of a second, she pictured the heavier Lincoln trying to catch up to the swift, outfitted Charger—and her Spitfire racing to cut them both off at the next intersection.

A police siren split the air, but it wasn't visible from Dani's vantage point. The Charger must have swerved onto the shoulder because it kicked up a plume of dust that reached at least ten feet high. A few seconds later, the Lincoln slowed as it encountered the dust devil only to speed up a moment later. Coming up behind the Lincoln was the black and white police car, the lights flashing and siren blaring.

There was a cotton field between the Spitfire and the others, broken sporadically by small copses of trees. She swerved onto a one-lane dirt road that cut between two fields. She was now moving at a forty-five degree angle and cutting off valuable time.

They lurched along the uneven road. With each bump they encountered, Dani wrestled with the steering wheel to keep the vehicle from careening into the cottonfield. The plume of dust she created was circling the small car, beginning to obscure her line of sight. Had the ground not been slightly wet from the night's humidity, the dust might have blinded her vision completely.

"Watch out!" Brandon yelled as they bounced off the dirt road and directly in front of Dele's oncoming Charger.

Dele swerved, barely missing them, the blur of bronze metal once again filling Dani's windshield. They both struggled to maintain control of their vehicles as the Lincoln gained on them. Dani caught a glimpse of her father's face as the Spitfire began to spin around, then lost sight of him as it turned back.

Dele's Charger had lurched onto the same dirt road that Dani had been on, but this leg was angled back in the direction of town. He was slowing now as the ruts became more intense, and the Spitfire found itself right on his bumper. Another rural road was coming up, and he gained speed as they approached it.

Another siren began to screech and then a third; maybe they had been there all along, and Dani had been so focused on the Charger that her mind hadn't fully registered them. They were on separate roads, intent not on overtaking them but on completely cutting them off.

The Charger hit the paved road with such velocity that the front end slammed into the pavement while the rear came off the ground. It appeared that Dele had intended to steer away from town and head further into the rural countryside. Instead, the vehicle swayed jerkily while he struggled to maintain control. Dani was forced to slam on her brakes to keep from hitting him. She moved to cut him off, somehow lurching over the edge of the field to spin onto the road, but he'd managed to regain control and was now heading back toward town.

As she struggled to maneuver her car in the right direction, the Lincoln caught up with them. Cole was hunched over the steering wheel, his face as intense as Dani knew her own must be. She managed to right the Spitfire and joined the procession just as one of the police cars reached her. In her rearview mirror, she caught a glimpse of the patrol car careening from one side to the other in an attempt to pass her.

"Dani," Brandon pleaded. "Just give it up. Please."

She realized she was straddling the center line just as Cole and Dele were doing. At the speed she was traveling, it took only the mildest of adjustments to move to the right. The rough shoulder jarred the car as she adjusted a little too much.

The patrol car swerved past her, the lights filling the windows of the Spitfire as the siren pierced the air. Another patrol vehicle was crossing the cottonfield and appeared ready to intercept the Charger. A third was approaching from the opposite direction.

"Stop," Brandon pleaded. "Please, Dani. Just stop."

The town was coming up quickly. The skies were turning amber as the sun rose, cutting through the final haze of night. Several cars were on the main road into town, pulling over and stopping as they observed Dele throttling back into town with a score of vehicles behind him. The sirens were nearly deafening, the flashing lights amplified in store windows.

Dani felt her foot ease up on the peddle. The Spitfire instantly dropped back, placing more distance between her and the others. Cole had also pulled to the side, allowing the officers to move in on Dele.

The bus station was ablaze in lights, the strong parking lot lights that kept the station illuminated still on despite morning's sleepy presence. Two buses were in the lot, each with an attendant at the door and lines of people piling on. Roughly half a dozen children were being herded onto one of the buses as Dele's Charger swerved toward the station.

Perhaps seeing that he could not outrun all the patrol cars converging on him from different directions, Dele sped the Charger into the parking lot, causing pedestrians to scatter in every direction. The Charger came to a stop just inches from the station's entrance.

The patrol cars were instantly upon him, the cars stopping helter-skelter along the road and the lot, officers shouting for onlookers to take cover.

Dani arrived less than twenty seconds later. She managed to slow the vehicle before coming to a full, abrupt stop a few feet from one of the buses. Everyone that had been in an orderly line was now disbanding. Some hurriedly boarded the bus, while others sought refuge nearer the building.

Dani's door was open before she'd come to a complete stop. She bounded out of the vehicle, grabbing her purse as she rushed to the front of her car. Brandon hurried to her side.

Dele bolted from the Charger. He held a pistol in his hand, and even from this short distance, he was wild-eyed as he looked in her direction. A police officer shouted for him to drop the weapon, and another called orders for him to get on the ground.

Dele stared directly at her. His right arm was stiff as he raised it.

Dani grabbed at her purse, but Brandon held her arm. "Don't do it, Dani," he ordered. "Don't do it."

When Dele fired his gun at her, it sounded almost like a supersonic jet. She heard the bullet whistle past her ear to lodge somewhere behind her. He cackled and kept the pistol raised to fire again.

Then a second shot rang out, blasting through the air like a separate jet, and his hand exploded in blood, the pistol clattering to the ground. The bus driver that had, moments before, been standing a mere foot from Dani was now on his knees, staring at Dele Mason. Dele stood for a moment with an oddly puzzled look on his face before he turned slowly to look at his bloodied wrist.

Dani's eyes panned from Dele to the direction from which the second bullet was fired. Across the lot from her was her father. The Lincoln was stopped, the door open, and Cole stood behind it. Both arms were extended over the door, gripping his pistol.

Dani again grabbed for her pistol. It was now or never.

"Don't!" Brandon yelled.

As he grabbed her arms, she screamed, "Don't you see? I can't stay in this town as long as he's alive!"

"Then don't!" he bellowed and pushed her into the adjacent bus.

She whirled around from the platform inside the bus. The police had moved in, forcing Dele to the pavement. Another officer was beside her father, and Cole was handing him his weapon. The bus driver was standing now, rushing people onto the bus that had been standing in line.

"Move out!" one of the officers directed the driver. "Clear the scene."

Trembling, Dani moved further into the bus to allow the others on, her eyes riveted to the scene. Brandon stared not at Dele and the events unfolding but at Dani, his eyes following her as she made her way down the aisle. She wanted to rush back to him, but he smiled as though to reassure her. He raised one hand and made a motion for her to go.

The officer beside Cole patted him on the back as if to thank him for his quick action. It wasn't over, she knew. It was far from over.

"Dani! Dani!"

She heard the voice as though she was rousing from a distant dream. "Josh!"

Josh half-rose from his bus seat to pull her onto the seat beside him. "Are you okay?"

She nodded. "He won't serve a day," she lamented.

"I don't think your dad plans to defend him."

"He'll find another lawyer willing to take his money."

"I wouldn't bet on it."

She tore her eyes away from Dele as he was pulled back onto his feet and escorted to the back of a patrol car. "What do you mean?"

Josh patted the macramé bag he held in his lap. "Do you even know what you gave us?"

The bus driver climbed aboard. "Everybody, find your seats!" he ordered. "We're pulling out."

The bus began to lurch forward. All eyes were on the scene still unfolding as the driver maneuvered the bus past the patrol cars abandoned on the street. Cole turned away from the officer as his eyes searched the lot for Dani. Finding Brandon, he followed his gaze to the departing bus.

As they passed by Brandon, he put up his hand to wave once more. Dani wanted to run to him; she didn't want to leave him standing there at the edge of the lot by himself with a crooked smile that appeared more like something forced upon his face when he really wanted to cry.

"Why are you here?" Josh was asking.

"What?" she asked woodenly.

"Why are you here?" he repeated.

They were past Brandon now and past her father, and the flashing lights were behind them as the bus gained momentum on the open road. The passengers were murmuring and staring out the windows, but finding nothing more to see, they were settling in for the long ride.

She stared down the center aisle until her eyes rested on the back of the driver's seat. Above the driver's head was a neon sign announcing their destination.

"I guess," she said, turning back to Josh, "I'm going to New York."

33

One month later

Beneath the bedroom window rested an old, bruised dresser with a fresh doily spread across the surface. Dani paused for a moment to open the mail that she'd set there the night before. Sunlight streamed in through the window.

She was in a rowhouse that had been built more than a century prior. The ornate window casing with its intricately carved pattern was a reminder of a more opulent time, as were the crown molding and baseboards. It was a beautiful room on a shady, tree-lined street. The bed was lumpy and her possessions noticeably few, but she had her own attached bathroom, even if it was outdated.

Dani shared the two-story home with three other roommates. One was attending the university. Another was waitressing at a bagel shop, and the third was working in a secretarial position.

She patted down her uniform, which consisted of black slacks and a white blouse, before glancing at her watch. She was due at the coffee shop at three o'clock, but it was only a short walk from the house. She had time.

A small box sat on the dresser, mail that she hadn't removed from two weeks prior. As soon as she'd found the room rental, she'd notified her parents and the newspaper of her new address. Tom had immediately sent a package, curiously insured by registered mail. Inside, she'd found her college savings. In her haste to grab the macramé bag during the party, she'd forgotten her savings were tucked away inside. Tom had removed it, planning to give it back to her, before giving the files to Josh.

Now she opened a package from Jimmy Bob. Inside was a note from the curmudgeonly newspaperman, uncharacteristically telling her that she was a smart cookie and she would go far. He expected a Pulitzer from her someday, he added. To help her along the way, he sent along a carbon copy of a reference letter he'd sent to the *New York Times*.

Dani smiled. She'd asked him for a reference a week ago when she'd applied for a ten-week paid internship at the prestigious newspaper. Much to her surprise, she'd been offered the position just two days later. It paid minimum wages, and she'd have to keep her coffee shop job, at least on a part-time basis. But it was a foot in the door. Perhaps before the summer was over, she would qualify for a news assistant, an entry-level position that in itself carried possibilities.

The second piece of mail was flat and contained a single piece of paper: her GED certificate. Her class had graduated, and she'd passed her GED exam. Now she could make plans to enroll in a university in the fall. She still wanted to become a journalist, and she knew she would get there.

She was replacing the certificate into the envelope when she realized there was something else in the package Jimmy Bob had sent her. She'd thought he'd just tucked one of his newspapers into the box as packing material, but now she reached for it.

Splashed across the front of the paper were photographs of Dele Mason and three men from St Louis. They'd been charged in a synagogue bombing in the Delta and killing a Black man in northern Mississippi. It turned out, Dele's past defense attorney, none other than Cole Evans, had been keeping a file on crimes he knew his client had committed. The file had mysteriously disappeared the night a cottage on his land had burned to the ground, but he wouldn't forget the details. He was now cooperating with the FBI as they linked Dele Mason and a group from St Louis to a string of hate-filled crimes.

Dani thought back to the night she was attacked. The assault had overwhelmed her memories, but now she began to replay the events prior to returning home. She'd stopped to pick up Mae in the storm and drive her home, and she'd had an uncomfortable feeling about the Klan seeing her. In light of the crimes Dele was linked to, she considered the possibility that it was his headlights she'd seen behind her as she picked up Mae. It was his vehicle that was tucked away as she departed Shelby. Perhaps he'd watched her, and like so many Klansmen before him, attacked her because she'd been civil to a Black person.

Dani stared at the photograph of Dele. It was a grainy black-and-white picture, but it was enough to remind her of his light sandy hair and piercing blue eyes. She thought back to her conversation with Rich in the five-and-dime. It seemed so long ago. Yes, she thought, it turned out that the child might have easily been mistaken for Rich's, had their plans for marriage continued.

She glanced through the rest of the paper; it was all news she'd seen in the *New York Times*. As many as 12,000 anti-war demonstrators were arrested in Washington, DC, as they sought to disrupt the federal government. It came on the heels of massive protests in Washington with as many as 500,000 activists. San Francisco's anti-war movement counted 125,000 protesters. Richard Nixon was digging in his heels, vowing that he would not end the Vietnam War without total victory.

A young Army Lieutenant named William Calley was found guilty of 22 murders in the My Lai massacre in Vietnam and began a life sentence. Charles Manson was on death row awaiting execution for his part in the murders of actress Sharon Tate and several others.

On the bright side, a coffee shop had opened somewhere along the West Coast. Dani couldn't think of any reason why it should make national news other than its otherworldly name: Starbucks.

With the Supreme Court's ruling in *Swann v. Charlotte-Mecklenburg Board of Education*, busing was expected to take place in the Deep South to achieve racial desegregation. A young congressman by the name of John Lewis was part of a voter mobilization tour crisscrossing Mississippi. They expected to register millions of minority voters despite strong opposition from the Ku Klux Klan.

And at the end of May, the Mariner 9 was scheduled to launch toward Mars barely two years after

Neil Armstrong and Buzz Aldrin had walked on the moon, despite a setback with Mariner 8.

Dani placed her hand on her belly. Had she made the right decision? She had to believe that she had. The events of that long-ago night had taken her to the deepest, darkest places she'd never wanted to visit. And it had set her on a path to something she had never imagined. The naïve young schoolgirl planning her idyllic future on Rich's arm felt like someone else now. She had been transformed.

She shook her head as if coming back to the present. Glancing at her watch, she realized she would be late if she didn't leave now. She tossed the paper atop her mail, grabbed her keys, and made her way to the door. It was only a short stroll to the coffee shop, and it was a beautiful day.

Notes from the Author

Writing a book set in 1971 Mississippi is a departure for me. I was born in Washington, DC, and lived my early life in Ohio and New Jersey, as my father, an FBI Special Agent, was transferred. In 1967, we moved from Waldwick, New Jersey, to Greenville, Mississippi. My father became Special Agent in Charge of the largest FBI office outside of Washington, DC, as the country battled white supremacy in the form of the Ku Klux Klan.

I was younger than Dani, the main character in this book, and her story is not autobiographical. I lived in Mississippi from the ages of 9 to 18. I returned to Washington, DC, where I opened two computer companies. I provided services to the U.S. Secret Service, CIA, Department of Defense, Health and Human Services, and others. My specialty became the detection of computer crime, including Medicare fraud.

The February 1971 tornado outbreak under which Dani drives the maid home actually occurred; it was the largest outbreak in the state's history up to that time. It was a two-day event that included at least 19 tornadoes and killed 123 people across three states. Mississippi took the brunt of the toll. I changed the day of the week from Sunday to Friday to fit the story. All of the other facts in the book regarding property damages are true.

Dani is a composite character of many young women I knew that grappled with unwanted pregnancies. The variety of options she explores depicts those available at that time. In 1971, Mississippi was operating under an abortion ban; *Roe v. Wade* would not be decided until 1973. An exception was made in the case of rape only if a judge agreed.

As I was growing up, one neighborhood teenager and her mother left for an extended vacation; when they returned, the mother declared she'd given birth while they were gone. No one questioned the fact that the mother was over sixty years old. Bombings throughout the Deep South were also common during that time. And I knew one teenager that was permanently disfigured due to a botched back-alley abortion. I have wondered over the years what happened to her since.

I recently read that overturning *Roe v. Wade* would not end abortions; it would only end safe abortions. And it is still legal in the United States as of this writing for a man to gain parental rights even if the child was conceived through an act of rape.

The story ends without explicitly disclosing whether Dani is still pregnant. This was intentional, as I want the reader to ponder what they would do under similar circumstances.

I also did not reveal the physical appearance of the assailant until late in the book; I wanted readers to question preconceived ideas of the attacker's identity.

I do believe that "in geography lies one's destiny," as opportunities vary widely in urban versus rural areas and from one state to another. Throughout history, it is why migrations occur either on an individual level or en masse. We are each searching for a place in which our intended destiny can unfold.

About the Author

My full name is Patricia McClelland Terrell, and I have been writing under the pen name p.m.terrell ever since a publisher presented me with my first fiction book cover. The graphic designer had also entered my name in lower-case letters; my editor hated it, and I loved it. It's been p.m.terrell ever since.

I began writing when I was nine years old, inspired by a schoolteacher and elementary school principal. Scott-Foresman published my first book, a computer instructional for universities, in 1984. Scott Foresman, Dow-Jones (Richard D. Irwin branch), Palari Publishing, Paralee Press, and Drake Valley Press have published 24 books. *Dani's Decision* is my 25th publication, and Drake Valley Press will release my 26th in 2022.

Before my writing career, I opened McClelland Enterprises, Inc in the Washington, DC area in 1984, specializing in computer instruction for employees in the workplace. I was proudest of my "Train the Trainer" series of classes, which helped launch a new generation of computer instructors in the Secret Service and Department of Defense.

I opened another business, Continental Software Development Corporation, in 1994, which focused on application development, programming, website design and development, and computer crime. I held two Top Secret security clearances with the United States Secret Service and the CIA. My favorite assignment was detecting Medicare fraud and abuse for Health & Human Services, helping to recover millions of dollars.

I was honored to be the first female President of the Chesterfield County/Colonial Heights Crime Solvers. I also served as the Treasurer for the Virginia Crime Stoppers Association. Since moving to North Carolina, I have served on the Robeson County Friends of the Library and Robeson County Arts Council. I launched The Book 'Em Foundation with Waynesboro, Virginia Police Officer Mark Kearney, and assisted in Virginia, New Hampshire, and South Carolina annual events. I launched the Annual Book 'Em North Carolina Writers Conference and Book Fair, chairing it for several years before turning it over to Robeson Community College in Lumberton, NC.

Other Books

A Struggle for Independence
April in the Back of Beyond
The Adventures of Blade and Rye
Checkmate: Clans and Castles
A Thin Slice of Heaven
The Banker's Greed
Ricochet
The China Conspiracy
Kickback

Black Swamp Mystery Series (in order):
Exit 22
Vicki's Key
Secrets of a Dangerous Woman
Dylan's Song
The Pendulum Files
Cloak and Mirrors

Ryan O'Clery Mysteries (in order):
The Tempest Murders
The White Devil of Dublin

Mary Neely Historical (in order):
River Passage
Songbirds are Free

Other Books (Continued)

Non-Fiction:
Take the Mystery Out of Promoting Your Book
The Dynamics of Reflex
The Dynamics of WordPerfect
Memento WordPerfect, Progiciel
de traitement de texte
Creating the Perfect Database